I0617608

BLOOD
RED
SQUARE

Pat Mullan

Pat Mullan

BLOOD RED SQUARE
By Pat Mullan

An ATHRY HOUSE book

Copyright © 2014 Pat Mullan

ISBN-13: 978-0615453200
ISBN-10: 0615453201

This book is a work of fiction. Any reference to historical events, real people, or real locales is used fictitiously. Other names, characters, places and incidents are either products of the author's imagination or used fictitiously. Any resemblance to actual events, locales, or persons, living or dead, is entirely coincidental.

All rights reserved. No part of this publication can be reproduced or transmitted in any form or by any means, electronic or mechanical, without permission in writing from the author/copyright owner.

Book cover design by BEAUTeBOOK
Original Photography: jase™ and
Casey Hugelfink @ Flickr and Ludvig14 @ Wikimedia

Praise for PAT MULLAN

"Pat Mullan is a natural born storyteller with a gripping, engaging style. He may just be the next big thing in Irish crime fiction." **Jason Starr, author of LIGHTS OUT.**

"Pat Mullan shocks us into paying attention from word one, page one and does not let us go until he decides to release us! That is how compelling **BLOOD RED SQUARE** reads! *Like a dynamo running ahead of itself."* - ***novelist Robert W. Walker, The Instinct and Edge Series***

"Another misconception is that thrillers are not well written. Pat Mullan knocks that notion right out of the water. That he is a poet is immediately evident and when you think of that other fine poet James Lee Burke, you'll know you are in the same creative territory. The quality of the writing raises the terrific story to new heights. *Here is the future of the thriller and it's called PAT MULLAN. Glory be indeed!"* ***Ken Bruen, 2004 SHAMUS Award winner for best novel for 'The Guards' and 2005 MACAVITY winner for 'The Killing of the Tinkers'***

"Pat Mullan's latest, **LAST DAYS OF THE TIGER**, is a razor blade down the spine. So fast-paced, expect whiplash. This is Irish noir with a hero whom you'll want at your back in any gunfight. Grab a copy and clear your schedule!" **James Rollins, New York Times best-selling author of BLACK ORDER.**

"A high-powered legal thriller chocked full of betrayal, deceit, corruption, and murder. Mullan is Ireland's answer to John Grisham, with a smattering of Ross MacDonald thrown in. **LAST DAYS OF THE TIGER** will make your head spin." **JA Konrath, author of RUSTY NAIL.**

"**LAST DAYS OF THE TIGER** bristles with ingenuity, and a plot to kill for ... this is a thriller of such high caliber that it transcends all genres ... has all the Irish gifts: dizzy narrative, sly humor, and marvelous readability. It rocks! **Ken Bruen, Shamus and Macavity Award winning author of THE GUARDS.**

"**LAST DAYS OF THE TIGER** is a tight, intelligent thriller. Author Pat Mullan blends political intrigue and murder with a unique Irish flavor that goes down smooth. His hero, Ed Burke, is striking — almost an anti-hero in some respects. To unravel the deception and save himself, Burke must test old friendships, and determine who to trust in an Ireland changed by the Celtic Tiger. Mullan writes suspense with an edge reminiscent of Bob Ludlum. An author to watch." **Cerri Ellis, Mostly Mystery Reviews.**

The CIRCLE of SODOM *is an exciting and gripping novel.* The writing is clean, tight, and tense, and the characters, even the walk-ons, are very real and believable. The protagonist is both tough and likeable, and the villains are credible in their motivations and their private agendas. *The climax is stunning."* **an exciting and gripping novel"** - **Ardath Mayhar , author of sixty novels (Doubleday, Athenium, Berkley)**

The CIRCLE of SODOM takes you on a roller coaster ride. Hang on! Or you won't get to the end in one piece. It begins with one of the most intriguing openings I've ever read. Then it takes you from today's headlines, into the shadows behind them. It is a story of the forces that shape our world in the financial, political, and religious spheres, and of the leaders in these areas who battle for our allegiance. And in the end, I suppose, it boils down to the essential—good versus evil. **What a tale! I couldn't put it down. Number One Thriller!** E.M.Schorb, award winning author and poet: winner of The Frankfurt Grand Prize in fiction for his novel, *Paradise Square*; 1973 International Keats Poetry Prize;Verna Emery Poetry Prize for *Murderer's Day,* his fourth collection of poetry (Purdue University Press).

With rapid-fire pacing and well-drawn characters, Mr. Mullan takes the reader on a magic carpet ride all over the United States, England, Belgium, Switzerland and Hong Kong to weave a tale most evil and scary. The plot involves the very presidency, and the group plotting against our democracy is made up of very determined right-wing fanatics.

Pat Mullan is a mature and knowledgeable writer who puts together a thriller with the best of them. **The CIRCLE of SODOM** is an outstanding first effort from an author who can continue to capture his audience as long as he cares to try. *"An excellent read! "* - *Shelley Glodowski,* MIDWEST BOOK REVIEW

Part Tom Clancy, part Michael Crichton, **The CIRCLE of SODOM** by Pat Mullan provides an entertaining and thrilling read of the first order ... the chilling suspense will keep you restless !!! Mullan is ready with another MacDara thriller, **BLOOD RED SQUARE.** I have already booked my copy!! *"Recommended, highly recommended !!!"* - *Narayan Radhakrishnan,* NEW MYSTERY READER

"You know you're reading a good thriller when you start to cast it for the movie before you've even

finished." The plot is as complex as a Grisham novel, with twists and turns that kept me reading all night. The characters are exceptionally well drawn and the dialogue fairly whips along. All the ingredients for a good thriller are here. **The CIRCLE of SODOM** *is pacey and exciting and filmic in its descriptions, and is an impressive first novel. Definitely a gripping read for those long winter evenings* ....**Eithne Hannigan, Book Reviews, CONNEMARA LIFE magazine**

"a rollicking ride.......a great new book in the thriller genre!" Well, this was a rollicking ride. Read **The CIRCLE of SODOM**, and you'll get to follow Owen MacDara on his odyssey from New York to the Atlantic Ocean, from Palm Springs to the backwoods hills of Tennessee, all in the name of love and daring-do. There's a lot of action packed in these 300+ pages, action dealing with terrorism, spying, attempted coups, and religious fanaticism. Good, tight writing, clean prose that just zips along, and characters that are engaging and memorable all contribute to a great new book in the thriller genre. **Peggy Vincent, Oakland, California, February 12, 2004** (Peggy Vincent is the author of *Baby Catcher....film rights have been optioned by Elliot Gould's production studio and the screenplay has been assigned)*

" Pat Mullan writes an exciting and fast-moving tale ... a timely read" Author Pat Mullan writes an

exciting and fast-moving tale. From almost the first page, Owen MacDara finds himself in danger and confronting men who believe that God has called on them to bring about the end times. The use of computer warfare and cyberterrorism to undermine the economy, discussions of antiterrorism tactics, and the modern militia movement all are well researched and seamlessly incorporated into the adventure. Mullan's strong story-telling provides a completely enjoyable reading experience -
Rob   Preece,   Book   Reviews   Editor, BooksForABuck.com

"Pat Mulan's novel is compelling":   this book is an even mix of Crichton and Clancy and written equally as well. It's a classic page-turner and almost comes across as though it had been adapted from a screenplay... **Who I am** . . .*I am an author and teacher, in that order (for now.) My debut novel (which debuted in the midlist) was released by Penguin Putnam in 2004 and my second novel will be   released   later   this   year.* (http://www.girlondemand.blogspot.com/)

This book is for **Ken Bruen**
because he's *simply the best.*

Pat Mullan

Who killed Hammarskjold?

Pat Mullan

Leopoldville,
The Congo
1961

The Russian paced back and forth past the grimy little window, peering out into the dusk and stopping frequently to listen.   The American lit another Chesterfield from the dying butt between his lips. Two men waiting uneasily in a shabby office stuck to the side of the empty hangar.   The airfield had been abandoned months before, its pockmarked runway testimony to the fierce fighting that had taken place. The American heard it first.   He stubbed out his Chesterfield in an overflowing ashtray, pushed the chair out of his way and took two long strides to the window. At this the Russian stopped pacing. Now both stood at the window, side by side, ears straining.
          "Yup! That's it. Listen," said Kearns.
          "Da! Da! Now I hear," answered Zhukov.
The faint rumble grew louder turning into the steady throb of a jeep's engine.   Two dim lights in the distance became brighter until the jeep stopped a hundred yards from the hangar. A figure emerged moving towards them in a loping gait. Zhukov held the door ajar for the late arrival. Light from the naked bulb in the ceiling struck a big man, over six feet, wiry and lean, his waterproof overcoat opened on combat fatigues beneath and the insignia of a

13

Major in the mercenary command of Colonel 'Mad Mike' Hoare.

"How did it go?" asked Kearns.

"Easy as pie, old boy," answered the Major in an accent more Anglo-Irish than English.

"You will be successful, yes?" Zhukov asked.

"Do you doubt me, Comrade?" asked the Major.

"Nyet! Nyet!" said Zhukov, "we are anxious, that's all."

"There's a lot riding on your success, Major," said Kearns.

The Major strode further into the office, removed his overcoat and sat on the edge of the desk. He helped himself to one of the American's Chesterfields. Then he stood up again and took a pen from the pocket of his fatigue jacket. Telescoping it into a pointer, he walked over to the aging map of the Congo that hung from the office wall. Taking a mouthful of smoke deep into his lungs, he began.

"He'll land here, at Kamina. Then he'll travel overland to his meeting with Mobutu. Three hours later he will return by a different route. This one. Precaution. For his safety. The plane will be refueled and prepared for his flight to Ndola to meet Tshombe. But he will never reach Ndola!"

The Major returned the pointer to his pocket, stubbed out the remainder of the Chesterfield, picked up his overcoat, and said, "Gentlemen, I believe you owe me something."

Kearns already had the envelope in his hand.

"Major, a deposit to your account. As agreed. 50% now and 50% when the job is done... I know... You'll just have to trust us on that. Just as we trust you now."

"Thank you, Gentlemen," said the Major. "We

will not see each other again."

Standing together at the window, they watched the Major's loping gait merge with the dark silhouette of the jeep, listened to the engine come alive, and saw the red taillights recede into the dusk of early evening.

Three days later the plane carrying UN Secretary-General Dag Hammarskjold and his entourage crashed, killing all on board.

PART ONE

Owen MacDara

Pat Mullan

One

**Dune Road,
The Hamptons,
New York**

Kate Whiteside woke up at three a.m. with severe abdominal pain and strange imaginings. Fully awake, she sat up and put on the bedside lamp to chase away the dark. *Maybe it's some kind of warning. Maybe Owen is in danger, even worse. That's ridiculous! Owen will be back tomorrow,* she chided herself. *Maybe I'm losing the baby,* she thinks, and then dismisses that imagining. She believes in extra-sensory perception and has had many experiences to prove it to herself. *Besides, that would not have seemed an irrational imagining to my mother even though I never knew her,* she contemplates, *my mother's genes are in me, talking to me, telling me about the Orient, about Korea. A land I've never seen. One day. That's a promise that Owen and I have made to each other. But it's a promise that'll have to wait. The ultrasound at Long Island Jewish said that it's a boy and Owen wants us to call him Henry – after my dad. The only dad I ever knew: Owen Henry MacDara. Henry Whiteside MacDara.*

The intestinal pain subsided and Kate blamed the chicken curry she'd had for dinner. She'd been advised to stay away from spicy foods. But she loved Indian. Now six months pregnant and the morning sickness long gone, she felt great. So she'd been sure that the curry wouldn't bother her. But she'd been wrong. She turned the light off and tried to go back to sleep but she couldn't turn her mind off. She finally gave up and just lay there. Remembering...

...that last terrible year beginning with her father's disappearance at sea, the attempt on her mother's life and, finally, General Zachary Walker dying in her arms. And then later, much later, her mother sitting out on the deck of their home in Gloucester watching the sunset and finally telling her, after all these years, what she had felt in her heart the first time she laid eyes on her...

You were the tiniest, prettiest baby I had ever laid eyes upon. A China doll. Except that you weren't Chinese; three-quarters American and one-quarter Korean. And you were all mine, all ours. All those years that Harry and I tried. I couldn't have loved you more if we had created you ourselves. You were only two weeks old and less than five pounds in weight. A premature baby but perfect in every way. I had brought you home just two hours earlier and I hadn't taken my eyes off you. You were still asleep and I couldn't see you breathing. You were motionless. But you had the longest eyelashes and the most perfect heart-shaped mouth. That's what I remember. And Harry was happy to see me so happy. He doted on you.

Two

**Manhattan,
New York**

Owen MacDara never felt better. He'd slept well. At seven a.m. a glance out his window told him the morning was bright and dry. Ten minutes of stretching exercises readied him for a fast four-mile run in the Park. Just one of the reasons he stayed at the Plaza. To be next door to Central Park.

He sat on the edge of the bed and reached for a pair of thick white sports socks. As he started to pull them on he suddenly doubled over in laughter. He'd caught himself doing something instinctive he never realized he did. That is, not until Kate caught him. Before he put his socks on he always brought both feet together and, with one quick fluid motion, wiped the soles on the bedcover. He had just caught himself doing it again. As he laced up his sneakers, thoughts of Kate fill his mind. Kate and the child she's carrying. His boy. His son. It felt good.

Out of the Plaza, he dodged the light traffic around Columbus Circle and dashed into the Park, jogging slowly at first and then picking up speed after half a mile. *Yes, I've never felt better,* he told himself. His life was finally coming together and Kate had given it a meaning he'd never experienced. His consultant company was growing and profiting. Good projects, exciting challenges. He thrived on that. Into his first mile, with his speed picking up, he felt a sense of well-being. Everything in his life had begun to fit. And Washington didn't need him for anything.

At eleven a.m., Owen MacDara climbed out of a taxi at the corner of 53rd Street and Lexington Avenue, diagonally across from the Citicorp Center building. He crossed the street against the lights, dodged the traffic and invited a few swear words from the New York drivers. It was a clear Friday morning and Manhattan's air seemed deceptively clean. *"TGIF, thank God it's Friday,"* he said, soundlessly, *"I'm outa here tomorrow." Outa here* meant the Hamptons, his place on Dune Road, where Kate waited for him. Kate and his about-to-be baby son.

He smiled as he looked upwards at the bottom of the Citicorp building. Its design never failed to amaze him. Forty stories tall, standing on *stilts,* the first floor sat suspended seven stories above the ground. Now it had become a unique part of the Manhattan skyline. His lean, six-foot frame bounded down the steps to the atrium two at a time. Heading straight for the elevators he suddenly felt a sharp hunger pang. The aroma of hot-dogs and sauerkraut wafted

23

under his nostrils. That's a temptation he could
never resist. The two prim looking business ladies
who shared the elevator with him gave him stares
that could kill as he wolfed down a jumbo dog layered
with sauerkraut and mustard.

MacDara reached the conference room on the 28th
floor, wiping his mouth. Fifteen or twenty people
were huddled in small, seemingly conspiratorial
groups of two or three in the entrance foyer. His
Executive Vice President, Dick Massey, came
forward to meet him.
　　　"Mornin', Dick. Is everyone here?"
　　　"Everyone but Sam Creamer. He said to buzz
him when you arrived."
　　　Almost on cue, Creamer turned the corner
between his office and the conference room. A big
man, he matched MacDara's six feet but the extra
pounds around his waist made him top heavy so that
he seemed to teeter forward on his tiptoes. People,
when they first met him, held their breath waiting
for him to topple over. Sam Creamer was President
and Chief Executive Officer of Lexicorp World
Services, a Lexicorp subsidiary used as a 'catchall' for
businesses that might no longer be a strategic fit.
GMA, Global Management Associates, MacDara's
management consultant company, had been given
the contract to *look under the rocks*.
　　　"Hello, Sam."
　　　"Good morning, Owen," said Sam and then,
looking at the people huddled in the foyer, he
commanded, "Let's get this show on the road."
　　　About fifteen people squeezed around the
oblong conference table, leaving one end vacant for
the presenter. Five or six analysts and junior
managers perched on the two large windowsills

facing east toward the morning sun. Someone reached up and adjusted the venetian blinds, as Dick Massey put the first slides on the overhead viewer to introduce GMA's study results. Preliminaries and background done, Dick turned the presentation over to Owen MacDara to deliver the 'bottom line'.

Three

Long Island Jewish Hospital

Kate was unconscious when the paramedics carried
her into the emergency room in Long Island Jewish.
The terrible pains had returned at five a.m. She had
called her doctor and then collapsed. At the
operating theater the chief resident, Dr. Ira Levin,
was already standing by with an anesthetist and
three nurses. They hooked her up immediately to an
oscilloscope, inserted an IV, started vital sign
monitoring and got a sonogram of the fetus. At
almost seven months it stood an even chance of
survival.   Dr. Levin did a cesarean section and
removed the baby. They placed him in an incubator
immediately. His lungs couldn't support him. Kate
was still unconscious after delivery.   Her uterus had
ruptured and she was bleeding internally. Despite
their superhuman efforts they could neither stem the
hemorrhaging nor stabilize her vital signs. Kate's
regular heart rhythm became erratic, and
degenerated into ventricle fibrillation. In only seven
minutes she was dead. The baby lived another four
hours. It was almost as though he had decided to
join his mother.

There was nothing left for MacDara to do but verify
the identify of the bodies of Kate and his baby son.
No priest or minister waited to comfort him.
Neither he nor Kate belonged to any Church. The
hospital staff was solicitous, caring, and Owen went
through the motions. Dr. Levin explained all that
they had done for Kate and the baby, explained the
rare genetic syndrome that caused her uterus to
rupture, tried to absolve them all from culpability.
Yet Owen could tell that Levin still blamed himself
for failing to save them. Ruth, Kate's mother, waited
for him. She looked finished, not the vital feisty lady
that he had seen survive her husband's
disappearance two years ago. The loss of her only
child was too much to take. They made small talk,
each too wounded to help the other. They discussed
the final arrangements and Owen left all of that in
Ruth's hands. *It will be therapy for her*, he thought.

MacDara's own therapy started at the bar in
Costello's that same afternoon. Jimmy Connolly, the
proprietor and Owen's close friend, tried to comfort
him but only succeeded in getting smashed himself.
At four in the morning he hauled Owen upstairs and
dumped him on the old leather couch in the paper-
strewn hole that he called an office. He crawled into
the big chair and, somehow, dozed off in a drugged
slumber. When he woke at noontime, Owen was
gone.

The week that followed was a blur for MacDara. His
friends would argue and swear that he was seen in
every pub and dive in Manhattan. Unkempt,

unshaven and incoherent, he was finally rescued, at four in the morning, from Desmond's Pub on the upper Westside, by his colleague and close friend, Dick Massey. Dick spent the next day trying to bring Owen back from the abyss. He decided that Manhattan was not the place for Owen and that, if he was to pull out of this, it would only happen in Ireland, at Ardree House.

Four

Shannon, Ireland

The next thing that Owen MacDara remembered with any clarity was a stewardess trying to wake him up.

"Mr. MacDara, all the passengers are off. It's time to go. Do you need any help?"

"Where are we?"

"We're at Shannon, Mr. MacDara. You slept the entire flight. We didn't wake you for meals. Your friend said that you were still convalescing when he helped you on board at Kennedy. I do hope you're feeling better. I can get someone to assist you."

"No, no! Thank you," Owen declined, "I'll be just fine."

Two hours later the taxi that MacDara had hired at Shannon dropped him in the courtyard in front of Ardree House in Connemara. This was MacDara's sanctuary, his retreat from the world. It was country Georgian, standing on over twenty-three acres overlooking the waters of the lough. The house itself stood amid an acre of gardens. Eucalyptus trees fronted a stand of Chilean fire trees and yucca plants dwarfed the Japanese maples that grew close to their base. There were even rhododendrons that blossomed in January. As the taxi's wheels rattled over the cattle grid imbedded in the ground at the main gate, silence returned and Owen knew that his recovery would begin here; here where he and Kate shared their closest, most intimate times; here where he could still feel her presence; here where her perfume still lingered in the bedroom and the bathroom; here where her closet still held her clothes and intimate things.

In the days that followed, Owen MacDara walked alone. On some days he traversed the hills at the base of the Twelve Bens, the mountain range that ringed Ardree House like the defensive ramparts of Toombeola, named after the mythical Celtic giant whose legend still survived. On other days he wandered the beaches, from the horseshoe shaped Dogs Bay to the cockle rich sands of Moyrus. In the evenings he watched the Connemara sunsets, never tiring of seeing the Twelve Bens transformed as the sun set further into the lough and the marbled grays, greens and ochres turned into shades of bronze and gold.

It was on a Friday night, two weeks after he arrived at Ardree House, that Owen went to bed early. He remembered that Kate enjoyed taking a hot water bottle to bed. She always prepared one for him too.

When he was alone he'd never bother. Tonight he decided to fill one and take it up to the master bedroom. He tried to read but his eyes kept fighting him. He left the blinds open in the large bay window that brought the panorama of gardens, trees and sky into the room. The sky was ink black, the stars sparkled like diamonds and the moon hung close to the earth, like a large white luminous ball. Soon his eyes lost the battle and he drifted into a deep sleep.

He knew there was no one in the bedroom when he felt his way in the darkness to the toilet. They say there's a cold feeling in the air when there's another presence in the room but he convinced himself that it was natural to feel a cold chill in January.
She didn't stir on her side of the bed. He always woke up quietly. He always slid his feet out onto the cold floor and eased the rest of his body out without tugging the bedclothes. She never knew that he went to the toilet during the night.

He never flushed the toilet. The filling tank made too much noise. It would surely wake her up. She always left her watch on the glass shelf by the sink. That's the only way he knew the time. But he really didn't want to know the time. He always left his own watch on the side table by his bed, in the dark where he couldn't read it till daybreak.

He groped behind him with his right hand and found the hot water bottle that she had put in his side of the bed. It was tepid now at three in the morning. He slid under the duvet and pulled it up so that his head was covered, just enough to hide him but not enough to suffocate him.

He lay there as he did every night, trying to get back to sleep. Eventually he did return to sleep but never to the dream he was in before he woke up.

She was always awake before him. He would wake up to the feeling of her arm around his waist, her loins warm against the small of his back and her lips brushing the nape of his neck. He always turned over and blessed his good fortune as his arms encircled her body and he kissed her gently on her eyelids, the tip of her nose, and her soft inviting lips.

He always wondered what she would do that morning when he didn't respond. That morning he was certain would come when she would wake up, stretch and turn around to encircle his waist and brush her lips against his cold, cold neck. That morning when he wouldn't turn over to hold her. That last morning of his life. He always wondered about that.

He was still wondering when he realized it was morning and the light was filtering into the bedroom. He turned and looked over. She was still asleep. He felt as though he had been given a gift today. The gift of morning that she always brought to him. He would bring it to her.

He turned over and circled her waist with his arm. He brushed his lips against her cold, cold neck.

It was the cold that woke him. The cold rubber neck of last night's hot water bottle pressed against his lips. That morning Owen MacDara joined the world again. His mourning for the loss of Kate and his baby son began. But his recovery also began. He didn't know it then but he'd have little time for bereavement. In just four months Washington would need him again.

PART TWO

Conor Brady
&
Misha Kedrov

Five

**UN Headquarters,
New York**

Less than four months after Kate's death....

Acting UN Secretary-General Alexander Ridge
praised himself for getting through most of the mail
in his in-box. He wasn't expecting anyone, certainly
not the new Russian Ambassador who had officially
presented himself just three days earlier.

"Anatoly, come in, come in," said Ridge.
"Thank you for seeing me, Mr. Secretary-
General. I promise you that I am not here on a social
visit," said Anatoly Yeremenko as he took the chair
Ridge offered. Oxford educated, suave and
sophisticated, Anatoly Yeremenko was a refreshing
change from his boorish, intemperate predecessor.

35

"President Yeltsin asked me to give this to you right away," continued the Russian Ambassador as he presented a long white envelope to the Secretary-General. "I can assure you that it's authentic," he said, as though reading Alexander Ridge's mind, "President Yeltsin spoke to me directly yesterday and insisted that I bring this letter to you as soon as I received it. It arrived this morning in our diplomatic pouch. He anticipates your contacting him through the usual secure channels."

The meeting ended just as quickly as it had begun. Ambassador Yeremenko thanked the Secretary-General for taking the time to see him and left without ceremony.

Alexander Ridge leant back in his chair and looked out the window at the Manhattan skyline, so alien compared to his native New Zealand. He should be retired, should be back home. But duty called and he had agreed to fill Boutros Gali's shoes for two months – the time necessary to find a permanent replacement. It now looked as though Kofi Annan would get the job. Only another couple of weeks to go and now this. He held Yeltsin's letter in his hands for a considerable time before opening it. Written in Russian, one of the five languages the Secretary-General spoke fluently, only a page and a half long, he read it immediately and re-read it several times in disbelief. He got on the secure phone to Yeltsin immediately...

Nadia Pankin had also been surprised that morning to see an envelope from President Yeltsin addressed to the UN Secretary-General. Nadia acted as Anatoly Yeremenko's administrative assistant. She was also his lover. Now she hid outside the entrance to UN Headquarters. She saw Yeremenko depart, a mere twenty minutes after he had arrived. She waited. She didn't know why. Just a hunch. And it paid off. Less than thirty minutes later, Alexander Ridge rushed from the front entrance, was met by his chauffeur and escorted to his limousine. By the time they emerged onto First Avenue, Nadia was waiting in a yellow taxi. She directed the driver to follow.

Two hours later, Nadia watched as the 1:30 p.m. scheduled Aeroflot flight to Moscow taxied away from the departure gate at Kennedy Airport and prepared for takeoff. Alexander Ridge was aboard.

Six

Sheremeteyvo Airport, Moscow

Alexander Ridge fidgeted as Aeroflot Flight 317 made its descent. He slipped his left hand repeatedly under his seat belt, attempting to relieve the constriction around his ample girth. Unconsciously, he held his right hand over his left breast, covering the letter in his inside pocket – the letter that brought him there. While traveling privately, and unofficially, and risking the chance of being recognized, he felt the risk worth taking and discovery remote. His face was as yet an unfamiliar one.

The bump of the wheels on the runway brought him out of his reverie. Easing his midriff out of the seatbelt, he leaned forward and retrieved his briefcase from beneath the seat in front. It'd been mere hours earlier that he'd received the letter in New York. Once again, he replayed this event in his mind, striving to learn something new, to uncover some word, some nuance that he had missed...

Moscow,
Prospekt Mira

Conor Brady had chewed his fingernails to the quick a long time ago. With nothing now left to chew, he did his best to eat the rag-nails until the blood appeared. A strange affliction, it demonstrated a contradiction in an otherwise extremely cool and imperturbable person under pressure. And Conor was under pressure now. He'd been at his position for an hour and a half and the cold began penetrating deep within his body, his thermal gloves tested to the limit. Even if his feet were frostbitten, his hands must remain warm. His hands and his eyes were his tools, his instruments of precision.

From his vantage point on the roof, he could see the entire length of Prospekt Mira. Near empty, the street saw an occasional vehicle, some cyclists and the odd native or two, well muffled up and scurrying along to get out of the cold. It wasn't an evening for lingering. Not a soul had entered or left the Imperial Hotel since Conor Brady had arrived. The concierge showed himself once in a while, epaulets shining and the collar of his greatcoat pulled up around his ears. The big Russian would step outside once every fifteen or twenty minutes, take a hasty look up and down the street, grab a smoke, then rush back inside again, leaving lingering wisps of his breath and smoke suspended in mid-air.

Conor moved back into the shadows and checked his equipment once again, never failing to keep a wary eye on the street below. The sniper rifle, fixed on its tripod on the parapet wall adjacent to the chimney stack, gave him the optimum position both to execute his task and shelter him from view. Satisfied, he lingered a while, caressing the stock and scope, feeling the passion arise within.

He'd just finished his checkout when the car entered the end of the street. As he watched it approach, he noted it had the size and distinctive profile of a Mercedes saloon. When it slowed down before the Imperial Hotel, Brady felt certain that his target had finally arrived. Positioned behind the scope, he could see the hair growing out of the concierge's nostrils as he emerged to greet the occupant of the Mercedes which had now come to a full stop. The big concierge moved briskly to the car, opened the door, and held it as his guest rose into view and turned to thank him. The face in the scope and the rotund profile proved unmistakable. Conor coordinated his hands in precise unison with his eyes. He had stopped breathing entirely. As if independent of him, Conor's right index finger squeezed the trigger. Gently. Expertly.

Conor didn't bother to confirm the kill. He never did. He never missed. In thirty seconds he'd returned his weapon to the sheath slung inside his greatcoat and left the roof. In a minute he had left the building. In three minutes he had left Prospekt Mira.

The two *businessmen* who greeted guests at Misha Kedrov's *dacha* twenty kilometers outside of Moscow nodded curtly to Conor Brady when he arrived. One of them accompanied him to the front door. His host greeted him there with a rib crushing bear hug followed by repeated kisses on both cheeks, and then led him into the spacious open living area. Cathedral wooden ceilings, ambient lighting and a blazing fire in the huge grate exuded a grand feeling of comfort.

"I've got your special vodka. We'll toast your success. This is time for celebration, not funeral. We'll let the UN have their funeral." Misha poured two glasses and gave one to Conor. They raised them, downed them at the same time. Misha flung his glass into the leaping flames, grabbed Conor, and hugged him again, "Ah, Conor, you never disappoint me! If you were a woman I'd make love to you!"

"Misha! I didn't know you cared!"

"If every person who works for me executed his responsibilities like you, I'd own the world today. Not just half of Moscow!"

"It's been ten years since my first assignment for you. You were only thirty, thirty-five then? And you are still as emotional as the very first time!"

"Yes, I am. Katerina says very same thing when we make love! That's me. That's why I succeed. Everything must be done with passion. You are the same. I know it. Otherwise you'd be adornment for a headstone in some Buenos Aires graveyard today. Isn't that right, Señor Eduardo Kelly Herrera?"

"Eduardo died a long time ago. Please don't remind me."

"I'm sorry. I forgot. I understand. More than you can imagine. Believe me, I do."

"It's OK, Misha. I don't get angry ... not any more."

"Would another quarter of a million dollars deposited to your account in Zurich make amends for my indiscretion?"

"It would make me absolutely forgetful."

"OK, then. Was credited to your account this morning."

"Thank you, Misha."

"No, no, no!!! I owe you. With this one act,

you have, how you say – *set the wheels moving.*
Russia is in *cross-hairs* now. I only have to squeeze
my trigger. You understand that ...right, Conor?"

"Yes, I do."

In an apartment in another part of Moscow on the
following day, Police Detective Leonid Fomin and his
wife were fighting again.

"Do you know what a loaf of bread costs? And
don't even try to buy fresh vegetables! What would
you know! As long as you can buy your vodka!
That's all you care about! And where were you last
night? I heard you stagger in here past three ...
stinking pig! That's what you are! You don't care!"
she ranted at him.

Leonid tried to cut in but gave up. He knew it
was futile.

"You know where I was. On that sniper
killing. The one outside the Imperial Hotel. Do you
want to know who he was? You don't even fucking
care! I couldn't leave. Even Yeltsin himself was
breathing down our necks!"

But neither Leonid nor Yeltsin was a match
for his wife.

"Fool! You're a fool! If you'd spent more time
on your job than you did on your vodka ... God, you'd
be an Inspector today! And I wouldn't be scrimping
to make ends meet. But no! You've ruined our lives!
Look at me! I said, look at me, damn you! I was
beautiful woman once. But I'm worn out. I can't
take it no more! Do you hear, Leonid?"

She was still screaming at him as he put on
his coat and left. She's right, he said to himself. She
was a beautiful woman when I married her twenty
years ago. But I'll make it up to her. She doesn't
know I have a benefactor. One who's paid me well

for the past five years. Better than the great Soviet Union. Better than our brave new Russia. One day soon, he promised himself. One day soon, I'll take her to the West. I'll buy her new clothes, a new car, a new life. I'll make her beautiful again.

The frost had glued a fine layer of snow to the windows of his car so it took a while to clear them. He stowed the scraper away and reached in to the cavity behind the spare wheel for the bag he had left there only yesterday. He opened it and stared into it again, just to reassure himself. Then he slid it beneath the front seat, put the Lada in first gear and joined the crowded mid-morning traffic on the *Sadovoye Koltso*, the Garden Ring. He expected to reach his destination in less than an hour if he didn't run into traffic jams, and if his fifteen-year old Lada developed no problems. These days he could never trust his car. But now things could only get better, he felt. Life would improve significantly after today.

Leonid's trip proved uneventful, and fifty minutes later he sat sipping a large vodka and watching his benefactor open the letter he had *recovered* from Alexander Ridge's body, having gotten to the dead man as planned, well ahead of anyone else.

Misha Kedrov read the letter that Boris Yeltsin had written three days before. It confirmed what he already suspected. Yeltsin had found out about the missing documents from the KGB archives. Now Yeltsin knows that both KGB and CIA operatives were involved in the death of Dag Hammarskjold. *That's why he confided in Alexander Ridge, thought Kedrov. He still doesn't trust Washington. Perhaps the US President, but not those surrounding him. That's to our advantage.*

The letter confirmed something else for Misha. It confirmed that he had been right to dispose of Ridge. Now it was time to plant his *disinformation* and point the finger at Yeltsin's own State Security *apparatchik. Another nail in the lid of the coffin that will bury the Western Alliance!*

Misha put down the letter and raised his glass in a toast to Leonid. "Does anyone suspect you, comrade?"

"No! No one! I'm only another dumb cop to them."

"Good, Leonid. Keep your eyes and ears open. If you learn anything that I need to know, use the regular contacts. You shouldn't come here again."

Misha ushered him to the door making a mental note that Leonid was a *loose end* he'd have to take care of one of these days.

Seven

Washington, DC,
The White House

General Bartley Shields' office sat right in the heart of the west wing. Bart Shields, as National Security council adviser to the President, had long ago become accustomed to receiving telephone calls directly from the President. So he didn't consider it unusual when Sally, his secretary, buzzed him to tell him that President Clinton was on the line.

"Yes, Mr. President... I'll be there right away."

The President had summoned him to the Oval Office. While Bart Shields was mentally prepared for surprises, he realized how unprepared he was on seeing the President's stricken look.

"Bart, sit down. You'll need to. I've just been informed of the death of the UN Secretary-General. He was murdered – assassinated in Moscow."

"Jesus Christ," exploded Shields. " Who did it? Why? When did it happen?"

"Just a few hours ago. What we don't know is *why*. Yeltsin called me personally. He was in shock. Boris assures me he will turn Moscow inside out to find the killers. I believe he means what he says, but I have little faith in any chance of success."

"But the world will want answers, Mr. President."

"You're right. Every damn person with a conspiracy theory will hit primetime!"

"Some may even want revenge, Mr. President. While others may see this as an opportunity to destabilize Russia even further."

"Bart, you hit my own main concerns on the head. We've got to prevent that from happening. We have to find out who killed the Secretary-General and why. I want you to contact Owen MacDara immediately and make this his top priority." He paused for a moment and asked, "Where exactly is Owen?"

"He's on his way to a business meeting in Zurich, and he told me he was going to spend a long weekend in Italy. He didn't tell me where, but I think I know where he might be. He's still struggling to get over Kate's death. I'll do my best to reach him."

"Thanks, Bart. Let's stay on top of this. I'll want updates from you. At any time, night or day. Now I've got to brief our Ambassador to the United Nations. There is certain to be an emergency meeting of the Security Council."

UN Ambassador Madeleine Albright was halfway to Washington when General Bartley Shields stepped from the Oval Office. She had boarded the first shuttle out of New York after the President's phone call. She was still in shock. Alec Ridge had been a good friend of the United States and had shown her every courtesy in the short two months he had held

the office of Secretary-General. She had first met
him when he'd been the driving influence on
S.E.A.T.O., the South East Asia Treaty Organization.
Alec had helped to end the cold war and had
encouraged the current constructive climate between
the West and the countries of the Pacific Rim. In
doing so, he had gained the respect of friend and foe
and was trusted in Moscow and Beijing. Whoever
had killed him intended to kill what he stands for.
That's a certainty, she believed.

It was almost noon when Madeleine Albright bustled
into the Oval Office to greet a somber President
Clinton.

"Madeleine, I've briefed Bart Shields since we
talked this morning, and I've asked him to find out
who is behind this. I've also told the Cabinet, and
the leaders of Congress will be arriving when we've
finished. I want them to hear it directly from me."

"Mr. President, I am very ...I still cannot
believe that Alec Ridge died at the hand of some
loose cannon. *Somebody* in Russia wanted him
dead. *Somebody* wanted to destroy what he stood
for."

"Madeleine, you'll get no argument from me. I
agree. And that's where your challenge will rest in
the days ahead. I'm sure you'll convene an
emergency meeting of the Security Council. Russia
will be on the hot seat on this one and there are
certain members of the council who will use this...
tragedy to promote their own agenda. I want you to
support Russia without making it obvious. How well
do you know this Yeremenko?"

"Only by reputation and first impressions.
He's quite charming, very intelligent and speaks

excellent English. A Russian with expensive Western tastes. He gave me a signed first edition of his latest book, *The New Russian Revolution.* But I know nothing of the man himself."

"Well, get to know him. I want to find out what is really going on *inside* Russia. Our future depends on it. And I want to make sure that Yeltsin is not undermined by all of this. So, you've got your work cut out for you. But I know I can rely on you. I will keep you informed on anything that I feel you need to know."

"Thank you, Mr. President. I will, of course, do my utmost."

Tears came to her eyes. The President hugged her to him.

Como, Italy.
Villa D'Este,
10:00 a.m.

Owen MacDara pushed open the wooden shutters on his bedroom window at the Villa D'Este and looked out at the placid blue water of Lake Como. He had slept like a baby. It was ten a.m. and people were already lounging around the pool. It whetted his appetite for an early morning swim. The Alitalia flight from New York to Milan had been uneventful but pleasant and he had had the impression that time had collapsed when he looked out of the window and saw the Alps below. A testament to the Italian stewardess who had pampered him. It was Friday morning and he wasn't expected in Zurich until noon on Monday. Time to spend in Como at the Villa D'Este, one of his favorite places, followed by a night in Lugano and a drive over the San Gotthard pass into Zurich on Sunday.

But that was not to be. He had barely emerged from his first dip in the pool when he heard his name paged.

"Mr. MacDara?"

"That's right."

"There's an urgent message for you, Sir. From a Mr. Bart Shields. He wants you to call him. Says it's important. He said you'd know where to reach him."

"Thank you."

So much for my morning swim, thought MacDara, as he wrapped a robe around himself and headed back to his room. It was now 11 a.m. That would make it 5 a.m. in Washington. Bart Shields would still be at home. MacDara was right.

"Bart, what's up?"

"Owen, I'm glad I found you. Something's happened. The President wants you to change your plans. This is not a secure line so I've left a specially encrypted message for you on my system. Please read it immediately. And I want daily updates from you for the next week. Sorry to ruin your weekend, Owen."

That was it. Brief and brutal, noted Owen, as he retrieved his laptop and dialed into the General's e-mail system in Washington. When MacDara had first worked for General Shields the man had provided him with a special internal modem and encryption card with the procedures to follow to connect to the general's private electronic mail system. It was a specially designed modem using top-secret encryption and detection technology guaranteed to protect the contents of any messages traveling to or from the general over his private e-mail system.

In mere seconds the general's e-mail message appeared on screen before MacDara's startled eyes. It read:

> *Alexander Ridge, the UN Secretary-General, has been assassinated in Moscow. Sniper bullet. Outside the Imperial Hotel on Prospekt Mira. Nobody knows what he was doing there. Apparently entered the country privately. Couple of hours before he died. We're sure that the UN Security Council will meet right away. The President and Yeltsin have talked. Yeltsin has promised to 'turn Moscow inside out' to find the killers but the President doesn't give him much chance of success. We all fear that whoever is behind this killing is really intent on destabilizing Russia even further. This is where you come in. We know you were scheduled to be in Russia within the week, but the President wants you to rearrange your schedule. He wants you in Moscow right now. He wants you to find out who did this and why. Owen, the President has a lot of faith in you. Good luck. And, please, keep me informed every day. Even if there's no news.*

"I was right. Brutal it is." MacDara was talking to himself. Swearing about his lost weekend. He hadn't known Alexander Ridge, so he couldn't mourn him personally. But he knew Moscow and its people. He had high hopes for them. *The President's right. This is no insane bastard. This is cold and calculating.* He sent an instantaneous reply to Shields, saying, "I'll contact you when I get to Moscow."

As he gathered his clothes from the closet and folded each item into his case, duffel bag style, in the manner he'd been taught in basic training in the US Army, Owen remembered the first time the President had asked for his help. It had been in the oval office and Bart Shields had been there too. At the time, a coup d'etat in America was imminent and President Clinton couldn't trust his *own* government agents. Together they had defeated that evil. And the people of America had never learned of its existence. Since then Owen MacDara had two missions: as President and Chief Executive of his own international management consultancy, GMA, and available to the President of the United States whenever needed.

" I've got to stop talking to myself," MacDara said out loud as he picked up the phone to cancel his appointment in Zurich and to book a flight to Moscow and a reservation at the Imperial Hotel where Alexander Ridge had been brutally assassinated.

**New York,
Broadway**

Nadia Pankin was on her feet clapping enthusiastically and shouting "Bravo" as Michael Gambon and Lia Williams ran on to the stage of the Royale Theater to take their final bows in David

Hare's play Skylight. Anatoly Yeremenko stood beside her clapping vigorously but with more decorum. There was nothing conspicuous about them. The entire audience was on their feet clapping loudly. It was a standing ovation. Anatoly Yeremenko's great passion was the theater. Nadia shared that passion. He had used his considerable influence to get her assigned to the Russian mission to the UN in New York. They had considered canceling tonight's reservations when they got the news of the Secretary-General's assassination. But Anatoly had decided that 'the show must go on'; just as the anticipated show at the UN must go on.

Later at Cafe Un Deux Trois, a large bustling and noisy place, chosen exactly for that reason, Nadia lowered her wine glass and asked: "And the Security Council?"

"Yes, Nadia. It's going to be tough. They may still be in shock but they'll want answers. Answers that I don't have. Some of them don't care. They're going to blame us anyway. The assassination of the Secretary-General in Moscow gives them the perfect excuse."

"But the Council meets in two days, Anatoly!"

"And I'll be ready."

**UN Headquarters,
New York.
1:40 p.m.**

Madeleine Albright thought that Kofi Annan had just the right demeanor to be UN Secretary-General. A genteel man with a mellifluous and soothing voice, the bearing of an African Chief, and his ebony face framed in gray tinged hair, Kofi exuded wisdom.

"Bad timing. Now, don't misread what I'm saying. I'm not being callous. But Alec's death couldn't have come at a worse time," Kofi said.

Madeleine sighed and waited for Kofi Annan to continue.

"I want to get on with the job of reforming the UN. It's long overdue and this has just changed the focus of everybody in the organization. It'll make it more difficult to begin."

"I understand. But we must deal with this here and now," she replied.

"Oh, we'll deal with it alright. The Security Council meets in two days time and I won't allow it to become a witch-hunt against the Russians. Some members would love the opportunity."

"Well, the US is not interested in any witch-hunt, I can assure you! The President has asked me to make certain that this does not undermine BorisYeltsin. But we must learn who killed Alec Ridge! And why? We won't rest until we do!"

"Very good, Ambassador. We agree then. Tell your President that I will support him in this matter in any way I can."

The bright cold windy Manhattan day had the flags of the 185 member states taut on their poles outside United Nations Headquarters on First Avenue as Madeleine Albright crossed the avenue accompanied by her two aides. It was precisely 1:40 p.m. The Security Council convened in twenty minutes.

The Russian Ambassador to the UN, accompanied by Nadia Pankin, had arrived at the Security Council chamber ten minutes earlier. He took his seat and Nadia sat close behind him and a little to his right, positioned to either prompt him or respond to his requests as the session got under way. She had already placed his briefing and reference document on the desk before him. Fifteen minutes had elapsed and the Security Council chamber appeared full. Anatoly Yeremenko returned Madeleine Albright's nod and smile as she entered and took her seat. The Council had fifteen members and Anatoly Yeremenko noted that all five permanent members · · China, France, UK, US and, of course, Russia – and most of the remaining ten elected members were in the chamber. With members taking their seats, his gaze wandered to the mural painted by the Norwegian artist, Per Krogh, that dominated the chamber – the phoenix rising out of the ashes.

At exactly 2:00 p.m. Kofi Annan, the new UN Secretary-General, convened the meeting. Once preliminaries were taken care of, Kofi extended the condolences of all members of the Security Council to the Ambassador from New Zealand and to the family of Alexander Ridge. He then added, "I trust all in the Security Council will agree that we should now hear from the Russian Ambassador."

"Thank you, Mr. Secretary-General. Russia joins with our member states in offering our deepest sympathy to Alexander Ridge's family. This is a double tragedy for the Russian people. We held Alexander Ridge in the highest regard. He has long been a valued counselor. Whoever committed this atrocious act did not have Russia's welfare in mind. President Yeltsin wants me to assure the Security Council that we will leave no stone unturned in our search for his murderer and any conspirators to his killing."

The Security Council proceedings ran predictably enough, the meeting necessary but ineffectual. As expected, some member states with their own hidden agendas used the occasion to attack Russia, to imply complicity on the government's part. But all such attacks proved puny affairs and Madeleine Albright never needed to support Russia.

Eight

**The White House,
Washington, DC**

*"No employee of the United States Government
shall engage in, or conspire to engage in, political
assassination."*

General Bartley Shields paused to let the two people
sitting opposite him reflect on what he had just read.

"Those are the words in Executive Order
11905, signed by President Ford on the 18th of
February, 1976. It took over a year to issue that
presidential directive. In January of 1995 hearings
concluded by the US House of Representatives and
the Senate recommended just such an Executive
Order. Even Ford said at the time that the CIA's
involvement in assassinations, 'would blacken the
name of every President after Harry Truman.'"

CIA Director Richard Smallwood shifted
uncomfortably in his chair even while he remained
impassive. Looking at Bart Shields, he said: "This is
not news, Bart. I can't speak for the past. But I can
tell you this. The CIA does not assassinate political
leaders today!"

"Maybe not, Dick. But I think you take a lot of

liberty with the rest of that Executive Order. If you openly advocate the removal of people like Fidel Castro and Saddam Hussein and give moral support to groups seeking their overthrow, might I not be free to interpret your actions as conspiracy?"

Dick Smallwood showed the first crack in his facade. A nerve began to twitch under his right eye.

Shields quickly followed up with: "Don't answer that! It's the past I want to know about anyway. The Congo. 1961, to be precise."

He turned his attention to the third person in the office. "Leslie, give that file to Director Smallwood and let him read it."

Leslie Scott reached across to the credenza and retrieved a folder. She crossed and uncrossed her long shapely legs as she gave it to Dick Smallwood. A striking blonde in her mid-thirties, she wore stylishly short hair and dark rimmed glasses, both designed to make her image more serious. A career law enforcement professional, she'd started out in her twenties as an Assistant District Attorney in Queens, New York, followed by a rapid climb in the FBI. Assigned to the Washington office, she'd impressed Bart Shields and he'd convinced her to join him, as his assistant, at the National Security Council.

As Director Smallwood read the document, his right eye stopped twitching and he regained his composure. Closing the file, he looked at Shields and Scott, and chose his words with care. "I assure you, Bart, nothing like this has ever come to my attention. I am reluctant to believe that my predecessor at the time was even aware of this action, let alone gave the order to execute it."

Leslie Scott looked at the CIA Director, unconvinced. She said nothing. This was the General's show. Bart lit another macanudo and almost choked on it in his urgency to speak.

"God damn it, Dick. I didn't invite you here so you could defend every CIA Director who preceded you. Allen Dulles ran the CIA back then and you do know that he ordered the assassination of Patrice Lumumba, the Prime Minister of the Congo. That Congressional inquiry, when was it? – back in 75, I think – inferred that Eisenhower had given his approval. The CIA helped Mobutu capture Lumumba in December 1960. They shot him and dissolved his body in hydrochloric acid. No, the CIA can't claim innocence when it comes to the Congo. But killing Lumumba and killing the UN Secretary-General are two entirely different things!"

Shields stood up, put his macanudo in the ashtray, leaned over and grabbed the file from Director Smallwood. He held it in front of Smallwood's face, and said, "You're looking at a copy of the actual documents from the archives of the KGB. The President received them from Yeltsin this morning. There is no question that there was a conspiracy to assassinate Dag Hammarskjold. These documents clearly show that agents of the CIA and the KGB were involved. Don't insult my intelligence by suggesting that these rogue agents acted on their own!"

"Hold on a minute. I didn't say that these documents were fake. But there isn't a single reference to the Director or to the Government. Besides, other agencies might have been involved. Look at the NSC. You don't tell me what you're doing."

"Dick, I believe these agents were taking their orders from higher up. We need to find out who gave those orders. Before somebody else does. Somebody who doesn't have our welfare in mind."

"What do you mean?"

"There's strong evidence that Alexander Ridge's death is linked to these documents! We believe that someone is trying to find out who gave the order to kill Hammarskjold. Can you imagine what information like that would do to our alliance with the European Union? And to the business we're trying to do with countries like the Ukraine and Georgia? Not to mention China. And I hate to think how many guerrilla movements in the Third World would be inspired by it!"

"What can we do?"

"In the field, nothing. I have one man there now. Owen MacDara. You know him. You worked with him before. I'm going to ask Leslie here to join him. No, Dick, what I need from you is information. About 1961. The Congo. What really went down there? Who was even remotely involved with it? In *the company*, in the State Department, even in the White House! *Anywhere!*"

"I'll get what I can, Bart. But the kind of information you're looking for may not exist."

"Dick, I don't think it does exist. On paper or microfilm or anything like that. But it may exist in the minds of some of the key people who were there at the time. If they're still alive. That's what I'm looking for."

"I'll do my best, Bart. Where is Owen MacDara now?"

"Moscow."

Nine

Moscow

The Imperial Hotel was a bit down market for MacDara who usually stayed at the Kempinski when he visited Moscow. But he had a clean, sparsely furnished room. He tried the bed. Hard. Better than soft. No shower and he didn't feel dirty enough to climb into the antique bathtub, so he shaved quickly and went downstairs to hotel reception. The clerk made a determined effort to look preoccupied. Finally he asked MacDara if he could help.

"As a matter of fact, you can," answered Owen in fluent Russian, a language his peripatetic Aunt Mary had encouraged him to learn when he was only ten years old, " I am scheduled to meet Mr. Alexander Ridge here today. Can you tell me what room he is in?"

With a perfunctory look at the register, the clerk said, "I'm afraid there's no one of that name staying here."

"I understand that someone was killed outside your hotel two days ago. What can you tell me about that?" asked MacDara, as the clerk stiffened and looked for help from the manager, a pudgy sort of Peter Ustinov type, who had joined him behind the desk. At the same time, the concierge reached the desk with a new arrival. The clerk looked relieved and moved away to register the new guest. *Peter Ustinov's* face broke into a large smile and he said, "You're right, Mr. MacDara. There was someone killed right outside a couple of days ago. But we know nothing about it. It had nothing to do with us, I can assure you. None of our guests were involved. These things seem to happen everywhere in Moscow now. Gangsters! Mafia! But, let me assure you, you are perfectly safe with us. Innocent people never get killed in these gang hits. Now, about the person you were looking for. What did you say his name was?"

"Alexander Ridge."

Peter Ustinov examined the hotel register and guest list with care. "No Mr. Ridge staying with us, Mr. MacDara. And we have no record of a reservation in that name either. I'm sorry."

"Did any guest cancel or fail to arrive as scheduled during the past week?"

Again, *Peter Ustinov* examined his records. "No, Mr. MacDara, no guest cancelled or failed to arrive. Perhaps your friend made a mistake. I'm sure, if you contact him, you'll find that the answer is as simple as that."

Defeated, MacDara called a taxi. As the concierge held the door open, he leaned close and said to Owen, "If you want to know more about that killing, talk with Leonid Fomin in the Police Department."

MacDara's taxi had barely reached the end of Prospekt Mira when the phone rang on Leonid Fomin's desk at Moscow Central Police

Headquarters, with a call from the clerk at the Imperial Hotel.

"You told me to call you if I noticed anything unusual."

"Da! Da! What is it?"

"There's an American asking questions about the killing. I didn't tell him anything but I thought you should know."

"Who is he? What did he want to know?"

When the call ended Leonid phoned Misha with the information.

Misha Kedrov's administrative assistant interrupted him in the middle of his meeting with an EU Industry & Commerce delegation. He excused himself, left the meeting, and picked up the phone. He listened to Leonid Fomin, finding Fomin's news hard to believe. He knew MacDara as President of GMA, the consultants who were working on the management information system for his Financial Services Group. He was scheduled to meet with MacDara in three days time on that project. MacDara always stayed at the Kempinski, never the Imperial. None of this added up. Misha picked up the phone again and asked the operator to put him through to a number in Washington, DC. It was six a.m. in Washington and the sleepy voice at the other end soon woke up when Misha requested immediate information on MacDara. And that's exactly what he got. Immediate information. *It's remarkable what money can buy,* he reflected three hours later when he received the return call from his source in Washington.

"MacDara is a US agent. He works for the National Security Council and the President. If he's asking questions about Alexander Ridge, then he's wearing both hats on his Moscow visit this time."

"You're sure of your source on this one?"

"You know about that *unpleasantness* in the US last year, don't you?"

"You mean the incident where that Senator, what was his name, Hardy or something, died protecting America from some militant Militia. What has that got to do with MacDara?"

"That's what the US wants you to believe. The Senator was a failure. He died with a bullet behind his ear. MacDara was there and knows that's how he died. But I'm getting ahead of myself. Let me tell you what I found out."

The Source described the events leading up to the *unpleasantness* in the US, as he liked to refer to it.

"They underestimated Owen MacDara. He's resourceful and clever. And he's stubborn!"

"And you're sure of this?"

"Very sure. As sure as the words of Bob Maxwell, the former Chairman of the Ways and Means Committee. He was part of the Hardy plot and was forcibly retired by the President. The good Senator Maxwell has a weakness for young boys and we are there to see that he indulges his weakness. You might say that he is in our debt."

"Well, MacDara must not win this time. The trail must not lead him to me. Certainly not till after the G8 summit."

Misha sat there motionless for a long time. Thinking about his father and mother. Reaffirming his mission. *Revenge!* Reaffirming that his drive for revenge was still strong. Even stronger than his drive for power. But there could be no revenge without the power to deliver it. Eventually he forced himself out of his reverie, got up and walked over to the window. He could see workers sandblasting an old building, uncovering its hidden grandeur. The Mayor's workers, preparing Moscow for the 850th anniversary of the city's founding. *Another mad venture of Yuri Luzhkov. Well, let Luzhkov delude himself. Let him think he runs Moscow. I own it.*

Ten

The street vendor pointed out Leonid Fomin as he emerged from the front door of Police Headquarters. Owen MacDara slipped the promised ten-dollar bill into the vendor's eager hand, crossed the street and got into step directly behind Leonid Fomin. *An ordinary looking man, the kind of faceless person that populates the streets of every major city*, thought Owen. When Leonid reached the street corner and waited for a break in the traffic, Owen moved up beside him. He had the good sense not to approach Fomin on the street. That could lead to a confrontation, one that he was sure he wouldn't win. So he followed close behind until Fomin stopped at a local café and went inside. Owen decided to risk it, went in, saw that there were few people in the place, stood beside Fomin as he waited for his order, and spoke. "*Preevyeht*, Officer Fomin. You don't know me but we need to talk."

"Who are you? What do you want?"

"It doesn't matter who I am. Let's just say I'm here to find out what happened to Alexander Ridge."

"I don't know what you're talking about."

"Oh yes, you do. Alexander Ridge was killed outside the Imperial Hotel four days ago. And you were the police officer at the scene. Isn't that correct?"

"Da! Da! That one! But there are so many killings in Moscow now. Mafia. That's what it is."

"But this wasn't another Mafia killing. You know that. It's not every day that the Secretary-General of the United Nations gets murdered on the streets of Moscow."

"What do I know? I'm just a policeman. I just do my job."

"Was there anything unusual about the body? Was he carrying anything? A package? A letter?"

"Nothing! Nothing! I saw nothing. Just a dead body!"

"I think you're not telling me everything you know. I think you're hiding something."

"I don't have to talk to you. Who are you?"

"If you know something you're not telling me, your life may be in danger. But I think you know that anyway. If you change your mind you can reach me at the Imperial Hotel. I'll be there for the next three days. My name is Owen MacDara and I work for the President of the United States. If you're in trouble I can protect you."

Owen MacDara thought that he could see a flicker of fear in Leonid Fomin's eyes.

That night Leonid Fomin lay in bed trying not to toss and turn. At four a.m. he still couldn't sleep but he didn't want to wake his wife and invite her wrath on his head. His mind went back to Owen MacDara, back to that encounter. He felt fear. But he didn't understand why. He hadn't killed anyone. And he hadn't talked about it to anyone. Nobody knew about the letter. Nobody knew about Misha. He was certain of that. *But how does MacDara know about me? Who told him I was at the Ridge murder?* he wondered. *The police department? Nyet! They wouldn't tell him a thing! So how does he know? And if he knows, who else knows?*

At five a.m. he knew he wouldn't sleep and his shoulder hurt from lying in the same place. So he slid out of bed and took his cigarettes with him to the toilet. With just enough room to close the door, he sat on the toilet seat and lit a cigarette. Five cigarettes later, with the small toilet thick with smoke, he gasped for breath, and felt a deep fear. But he had made a decision. He would go and see Misha.

Eleven

Misha Kedrov escorted Owen from the reception area through an opaque glass door emblazoned with Kedrov Industries to an airy open office space. Four people sat at computer terminals. They did not look up.

"MIS! That's what they do. That's what I live by. Information. As you know most of my business is independently run, almost like franchises. I delegate everything. I only insist on information. Absolute. Accurate. Timely. And correct. But that's the reason you're here, isn't it?" Kedrov shot a knowing glance at Owen.

"Correct! And thanks for choosing GMA."

"I didn't choose GMA. I chose you. You speak my language. You know my country well. You're an entrepreneur. You built GMA from nothing. I can relate to that."

They sat in Misha's office. Unstuffy, modern, functional. Light Scandinavian wood furniture and a couple of tall tropical plants in the corners. Misha's circular tabletop desk put him on the same level with everyone else. Perception. One of Misha's cardinal rules.

Owen took a slim document, bound in soft leather and lettered in gold, from his briefcase, and gave it to Misha. Misha opened it and read the two page executive summary. "Excellent! This will give me the state-of-the art MIS system that I need. Tell me, Owen, you can get US approval to export this technology?"

"GMA has done lots of projects for the US government," replied Owen. "We're well known and well respected. Besides, we will not be violating any laws. There's been a significant reduction in the paranoia about that since the collapse of the Soviet Union. Now we want to make you capitalists, just like us. We want to turn you into free market competitors. So, there'll be no problems getting the technology."

"You're talking my language."

"OK! That's great! When do you want us to start?"

"Yesterday! Right away! And I want the first deliverable in six months. Not in nine. I'd like you to look at that again."

The four key members of the Russian office of GMA sat around the table in the small conference room. Bob Stebbins sat at the end of the table. A bulky six-footer with long nimble fingers now pointing steeple-like, Bob had taken early retirement from the Paris office of Chase Manhattan to avoid being sent back to the States. He had wanted to stay in Europe and an executive headhunter had soon landed him the job with GMA. A young Muscovite, Andrei Petrov, the *best and the brightest* of the new post-Soviet breed, sat next to Bob. Facing them sat Dr. Valentin Cretu, with a dark Transylvanian countenance, a Moldovan with a Stanford Ph.D. in computer language development. The fourth person smiled affectionately at Owen as he entered the room. A flashing dark-eyed, dark-haired Azerbaijanian beauty, Anna Yachmi had joined GMA in New York just as her temporary US work permit expired. An inspired systems analyst with a Masters in operations research, Anna had jumped at the Moscow assignment. Owen had interviewed her at the time and he took a personal interest in her career. At least that's what he told himself. Anna told herself something entirely different. She had fallen in love with Owen that very first day and she knew she would do anything for him. *Maybe now that his Kate is gone*, she thought, as Owen sat directly opposite her.

"OK, Bob, let's go," said Owen.

Bob Stebbins stood up and inserted the first overhead slide in the projector highlighting in large bold letters the name of the project: IAMIS, Integrated Accounting and Management Information System. For the next hour Bob, and then Andrei, and finally Anna, took Owen through the project schedule. When they had finished, Owen said, "Kedrov wants the project done in six months, not nine. Can that be done?"

"There's no way! Look at that critical path. We're already performing a miracle by committing to deliver in nine!" said Bob.

"How about breaking it up? Give him his precious MIS in six months and the accounting piece in nine," suggested Owen.

"If we do that it'll turn into a year's project. The MIS, at six months, will be missing some of the key general ledger numbers and we'll have to redo that after the accounting subsystem is installed. That will mean an extension of at least another three months. But this is all off the top of my head. We'd have to take a hard look at everything again. What do you guys think?" asked Bob.

"You're right. I'm not even sure if it's possible to do that," said Aleksei.

"It depends on what information Kedrov wants in six months. We'll have to go back to him for another requirements analysis," said Anna.

"Good! Do that! And tell me in ten days' time whether you think this is feasible or not," said Owen.

The meeting was over. Owen closed his briefcase and looked around the table. "I hope you have nothing planned for this evening. You've done a great job here and I'd like to show my appreciation. Drinks are on me!"

Everyone accepted, except Dr. Cretu, who said he had a prior engagement.

Twelve

Seamus, the bartender at Rosie O'Grady's, topped up Owen's pint of Guinness. When he was in Moscow Owen always dropped in for a pint and reminiscence about the *old country*. Owen and his team had decided to hang out at the bar instead of taking a table. Andrei Petrov had another commitment and left after one drink. As Andrei left Owen nodded to Seamus and said, "Agus aris, Seamus!" The Irish literally meant, *and again*.

"I'll just have a glass of white wine this time. One Guinness is quite enough for me," said Anna.

"Jaysus! You only had one glass of the good stuff. I'd understand if you'd had a pint," said Seamus.

"It's an acquired taste, Seamus. But then, coming from the bogs of Clare, what would you know about these things?" said Owen.

At that, Seamus made a mock attempt to leap over the bar and throttle Owen while Bob made an equally mock attempt to restrain him. Anna began to laugh uncontrollably and backed into one of two men who had sat silently at the bar since shortly after they arrived. He pushed Anna back against the bar, and yelled, "Bitch! Whore! Get away from me!"

Anna's laughter changed to cries of pain. Owen reached for her, put her behind him and faced her molester. The second man moved into a blocking position near Bob. "Apologize to the lady! And do it now!" demanded Owen.

"Fuck you!" said the molester and began to circle Owen, moving agilely on the balls of his feet. Seamus jumped over the bar and held the second man, pinning his arms behind him, making the contest even. But no contest like this was ever even against Owen MacDara. Holder of a black belt in karate and honed by regular weekly workouts in the gym, Owen's body was its own weapon. The man lunged. Owen sidestepped him, planted one foot firmly on the ground, grabbed him as he passed and used the man's own momentum to propel him headfirst into the bar. Stunned, he turned again, shaking his head like a punch drunk boxer and rushed Owen. Owen's arm, firm as steel, sliced through the air and the edge of his right hand, toughened enough to break wooden blocks, caught the man on his Adam's apple. That ended it. The molester fell to the floor gurgling and gasping for breath. Owen and Bob picked him off the floor and, helped by Seamus, threw them both out into the street.

Anna looked pale and unwell. Her tears smudged her eye mascara, making her look even worse. Owen held her and comforted her. Seamus poured them all large glasses of Bushmills. No one said anything for the longest time. Finally Bob spoke. "I think that's enough excitement for me for one evening. I'm going home. Anna, can I see you home?"

"Thanks, Bob, but I'm too upset to go home right now," said Anna.

"That's OK, Bob. You go on ahead. I'll get her

home safely," said Owen.

Two hours and a bottle of *Matrassa* later, Anna had regained her composure. Owen had insisted on dinner and had chosen well. The Baku restaurant was Azerbaijanian. "There's nothing more comforting than soul food," said Owen, looking at the menu.

Owen MacDara hadn't wanted to be with any woman. Kate's death had scarred that part of his soul. Though he knew he'd be scarred forever, he knew he was healing. As he lay beside Anna watching her easy breathing he felt reluctant to leave but he had a mission. The President was relying on him to find the answers to Alexander Ridge's killing. Without waking Anna, he slid out of bed and quietly dressed, leaving her a brief note of explanation.

At three a.m. Owen MacDara walked along the Raushskaya riverbank looking for a taxi to take him back to Prospekt Mira. A stampede of young people rushed out of a nearby nightclub and almost trampled him. Taken unawares he stumbled into the street and into the headlights of an oncoming car. The car slowed and then accelerated straight towards him. It missed him by inches. As it passed he saw the sneering face of the molester from Rosie O'Grady's behind the wheel. He got up and ran but the car turned around and came after him again. He ran off the road and headed for the riverbank. The car followed. It seemed as though its headlights were trying to drill a hole in the back of his head. He hit the ground and flattened himself out. The molester lost control. The car swerved across the riverbank and ploughed into the same group of young people who, only moments earlier, had rushed laughing and shouting out of the nightclub. It careened on, unstoppable, into the Moskva Reka, leaving a trail of blood and broken bodies behind.

MacDara tried to help the injured and waited until an ambulance arrived. Then he left immediately. Being pulled in for questioning by the police would not be in his best interest.

Thirteen

Back at the Imperial Hotel Owen sank into the large antique bathtub to soothe his shattered body. Once in bed he slept until ten a.m. and woke telling himself that four hours sleep was better than none. He shaved, dressed quickly, and then hooked up his laptop and dialed into General Shield's e-mail system. One message waited for him:

> *Owen:*
>
> *The President received today the enclosed document from Boris Yeltsin. It's from the KGB archives and shows the involvement of agents of the KGB and CIA in the death of Dag Hammarskjold in the Congo in 1961. We believe there's a connection with the killing of Alexander Ridge.*
>
> *Find Zhukov if he is still alive and try and get him to talk.*
> *Bart.*

The attached image of the KGB document read:

BLOOD RED SQUARE

Top Secret
Special Folder

Committee
of State Security of the USSR
March 19, 1968 No. 762-Ch
Moscow

TO THE CENTRAL COMMITTEE of the CPSU

Results of the investigation into the death of
UN Secretary-General Dag Hammarskjold
in the Congo in 1961

Anti-Soviet elements within the Communist Party are engaged
in efforts to undermine the Soviet State and enrich themselves.
They are in collusion with the Russian mafia and international
criminal elements. They are also being used by Capitalist
subversives who want to undermine and overthrow the USSR.
They are engaged in the distribution of anonymous materials
containing terrorist statements against leaders of the CPSU and
the Soviet government. A significant number of incidents of
anonymous material distribution occurred in Ukraine,
Kazakhstan, Latvia, Lithuania, Moscow and Leningrad.

We have uncovered evidence that these same anti-Soviet
elements worked to undermine the efforts of the USSR in Africa,
most especially in the Congo where they were involved with
American capitalist elements to enrich themselves and ensure
that their puppet, Mobutu, became the leader of the Congo. We
believe that the UN Secretary-General had become aware of this
conspiracy and was about to take measures to defeat them. We
have strong evidence that criminal agents of the KGB, the CIA
and MI5 working in collusion planned the death of
Hammarskjold and that mercenaries paid by these people
tampered with the Secretary-General's plane.

The KGB is available to provide materials to the Central
Committee showing clear evidence of our findings.

For your information
Committee Chairman   /s/ V. Kherikov

Strong diagonal lines had been drawn across the document and the order to DESTROY handwritten in bold letters and signed by Georgy Zhukov. "Obviously, someone failed to obey Zhukov's order," MacDara said aloud to himself.

A couple of days search turned up Zhukov. He had been pensioned out of the KGB but it was a search of Moscow's administrative records that did it. Georgy Zhukov had applied to the city in 1992 to take ownership of his Moscow apartment and the records were recent and available.

No one answered at the apartment. MacDara turned to leave as the door to the next apartment opened and a buxom lady emerged. Seeing Owen, she told him that Georgy would not return until September. "He's in Safonikha with his vegetables," she said.

Safonikha is a small village sixty miles northwest of Moscow. MacDara asked an elderly man, the first person he saw, if he knew where Georgy Zhukov lived. "Everybody knows where Zhukov lives," the old man said, and pointed to a house a couple of kilometers away. Zhukov's one-room log house sat in the middle of flat open country, surrounded by some apple trees, and bordered on all sides by orderly green rows of well tended vegetables. He found Georgy Zhukov bent over, hoeing his potatoes. Zhukov was hard of hearing and Owen had to shout his name before he straightened up and looked around. "Georgy Zhukov?"

"Da. What do you want?"

"I want to talk to you. I've come a long way to see you. From Washington."

"Go away. Leave me alone!"

"I can't. You need to help me. I need to know

what happened in the Congo. I need to know about Hammarskjold's death."

Georgy Zhukov straightened his spine beyond the ability of his seventy years, held his hoe like a regal staff and looked long and hard at Owen MacDara. He seemed to be making a judgment, a decision. Owen waited. Finally he asked Owen to follow him and he propped the hoe against the wall before he entered his one-room peasant's home, furnished from strong wood, toughened and scarred from years of use. Owen had brought a gift, a bottle of good single-malt Scotch whisky. He gave it to Zhukov whose face warmed at the sight. He held it up and looked at it. He didn't open it, just reached up and stood it on top of a cupboard. He pointed to a chair, inviting Owen to sit down.

Owen took the chair that was offered and sat down at the table. Georgy Zhukov returned with a plate of sliced cucumber and a large bottle of samogon, homemade vodka, and two glasses. He poured out generous portions and then sat back.

"I could ask you to go away. But there is something in your eyes. Who are you?"

"My name is Owen MacDara. I am working for the President of the United States. Let me tell you what has happened." Owen started with the killing of Alexander Ridge, an event that was news to Georgy Zhukov and ended with a copy of the KGB document that he had received from General Shields. "Now you know why I need to talk with you. Whatever happened in the Congo in '61 is not over. Someone knows. And we think they killed Ridge."

Georgy took a large mouthful of the strong samogon and Owen instinctively followed only to find his throat seared and his face turning firey from the brew. Georgy smiled and gave him time to recover. "I am not a criminal. I was not corrupt. Do you think I would be working like a dog at my age just to stay alive? Just to have some food for the winter. This place has been in my family for generations. But all the old ones are gone. Soon I will be gone too. If I had to live on my KGB pension I would not make it."

Zhukov lifted the glass to his lips and emptied it. It seemed to fill him with a burst of energy and he continued. "The Congo is the heart of Africa. It sits in the middle of that great continent between north and south, east and west. Do you think that *perestroika* and *glasnost* began with Gorbachev? Nyet! That didn't happen overnight. For years many of us wanted change. But we had to work inside the system to do it. So maybe the Soviets were right. We were subversives. Anarchists. But we wanted to stop them from expanding. And we wanted to free our people. Da! Maybe the KGB were right. Maybe we did work with capitalist criminals. But sometimes you have to get in bed with the devil. Sometimes the end justifies the means. Don't you understand?"

"Tell me what happened in the Congo. Did you kill Hammarskjold?"

Zhukov ignored MacDara's question about Hammarskjold and answered in his own fashion. "Do you know what was at stake in the Congo? Uranium! Copper! Minerals! Power! Whoever controlled that controlled Africa. Patrice Lumumba and Moise Tsombe fought over it. Tsombe wanted to control Katanga where all the minerals were. Lumumba wanted Soviet support. The Americans were afraid that Lumumba would win and that the USSR would control the Congo. The heart of Africa would be theirs! Your President – Kennedy – was caught in the middle of all this. He was a liberal, an idealist. He wanted the Africans to shake off their

Colonial masters and run their own affairs. But the real power in Washington didn't care about that. They wanted control of Africa's wealth. That's all. So Kennedy became their enemy."

Zhukov stopped, filled the glass in front of him again, got a second wind and went on. "There were many of us in Russia who wanted our country back too. We are nationalists. The Communist Party are not. So we did not want them to control the Congo. That's why we helped the CIA to kill Lumumba. That's why we got in bed with the devil."

"But why kill Hammarskjold?"

"The UN were up to their eyeballs in the mess. Who do you think captured Tsombe? Da! The UN, that's who!"

"The President needs to know what happened. He needs to know who ordered Hammarskjold's death. He believes whoever killed Ridge wants to know that too. If the world finds out that somebody in Washington ordered the death of Hammarskjold, your Evil Soviet Empire might just be reborn. Do you want to run that risk?"

"Nyet! Nyet! We have come too far to see it all lost." Zhukov picked up the glass he had just filled, put it to his lips, and emptied it in one long gulp. Almost as though it were his last. "I'll tell you. I do not know who were the criminals in Washington. I only know who worked with us. The CIA. His name was Kearns. I never knew his first name."

"And who tampered with the Secretary-General's plane?"

"Ah, yes! I remember him well! A mercenary. Major Lacey. An Irishman, I think. He was businesslike. It was only a job to him. He'd done jobs for us before. Simply for the money. I don't think the Major believed in anything else."

"Where is this Major now?"

"How would I know? I assume he went home after the Congo. That was a long time ago. Is he still alive? We're all getting near the end."

He said that with a sigh, now exhausted after the talk and the painful memories. He finished the last of the bottle, offering none to MacDara, and sat down wearily. He suddenly looked older than his seventy-something years. Owen tried to continue but Georgy Zhukov sat there, staring into the distance, staring at nothing.

MacDara's gut told him that Zhukov wasn't telling him everything but his head told him that he would learn no more. What was Zhukov holding back? And why? Was he protecting someone? Protecting his new Russia? Was he protecting himself? Was he afraid? MacDara looked at the old man again. He just couldn't imagine Zhukov being afraid for himself. Still, old age may have made him more vulnerable. Owen decided that he might never know. At least he had a name: Major Lacey. He'd settle for that. For now.

Misha Kedrov's dacha

"We don't know what Zhukov told MacDara," said Misha.

"Nothing! He didn't know enough," said Conor Brady.

"Maybe. But I can't take a chance on that. Never assume anything. You'll live to regret it. Or, I should say, you'll die to regret it," said Misha.

"Are you asking me to take care of the matter?"

"Yes! If those incompetents hadn't failed, we wouldn't be discussing this. MacDara would be lying in the morgue, just another victim of Moscow criminals."

"When would you like this done?"

"The sooner the better. You pick the time and the place. That's your business."

Fourteen

Khimki Woods,
Moscow

Gathering ferns was an annual spring ritual for Tatiana and Irina. Their mother cooked the fern stems, added spices, and served them as a family delicacy. The forest is central in Russian folklore and is seen as a source of food and protection. In the fall it provided mushrooms, nuts and berries and always ferns in springtime. But the forest could be a malevolent force too. Folktales speak of the evil witch, *Baba Yaga*, and the female hobgoblins, the *kikimoras.* They punished anyone who entered the forest to do bad things.

Tatiana and Irina were so busy gathering ferns that they lost all sense of time and direction. Suddenly Tatiana looked around and couldn't see Irina. She retraced her steps but the sun was setting and its dying rays penetrated the treetops. She panicked and called Irina's name louder and louder but got no answer. She started to run but the forest floor was littered with obstacles. Her foot caught a root and she stumbled. She clung to her precious ferns, afraid of losing them. Pitched forward, her head hit a fallen tree, stunning her. Everything seemed to be getting darker and darker and she thought she'd lose consciousness, but she didn't. She lay there and felt the pain in her head begin to throb. Then she got up slowly and started looking for her sister again. She walked this time, calling Irina's name over and over again. Finally she heard the screams – terrifying screams. Her sister's screams. Ignoring her own safety, she dropped her precious ferns and ran toward the screams.

Minutes later she saw her. Irina stood with her back firmly against a tree, her arms behind her, looking as though she'd been impaled. Her screams had been replaced by loud sobbing. Tatiana ran towards her and tried to take her in her arms, asking her over and over again what was wrong, but Irina wouldn't budge. Tatiana saw the terror in her sister's eyes and turned in the direction she was staring.

She saw the dim outline of a car but nothing else. Letting go of Irina she approached the car slowly. It was an old car, a Lada. She was almost on top of the car before she saw them. Her hands automatically flew to her mouth to stifle her own screams. But she knew she had to remain in control. For her sister's sake. Slowly her mind began to comprehend what her eyes told her.

The woman was lying on her side with her face pressed against the window. Her eye was open and staring, left like that when rigor mortis sat in. The other side of her face was missing. Just a bloody pulp with one eyeball dangling where her cheekbone should be. Bits of flesh and clotted blood had pebbledashed the inside of the windscreen. The man sat upright – too upright – behind the steering wheel, a shotgun braced between his knees, the muzzle in his mouth, and his finger wrapped around the trigger. His brains were sprayed all over the car.

The official news release buried in small print in the Moscow Daily News simply stated that Leonid Fomin and his wife had ended their life in a murder-suicide pact brought on by the husband's gambling debts and their mutual descent into alcoholism and despair.

Fifteen

Moscow

Alexandr Gelman lived alone. He was twenty-two
years old and he lived for two things only, Misha
Kedrov and Kedrov Industries. Abandoned as a child
he had no future until Misha took him off the streets.
That was thirteen years ago. Now he lived and
breathed Kedrov Industries. Inside the company he
was regarded as Misha's protégé. Misha entrusted
him with many special assignments. His current
was the most important he'd ever had. Officially he
was Kedrov Industries' MIS Project Manager,
assigned the responsibility of ensuring that the MIS
System being designed by GMA performed as
specified and, most importantly, was implemented by
the date that Misha had dictated. That date was one
month before the G8 conference in Birmingham,
England. Only Alexandr knew the significance of
that.

Kedrov Industries weekly MIS project review began,
as scheduled, at 9:00 a.m. Alexandr Gelman sat at
the end of the table, flanked on the left by Anna
Yachmi and on the right by Andrei Petrov. Bob
Stebbins stood at the head of the table, adjusting an
overhead chart on the viewer.

"This is the critical path. There's not an hour of fluff in it. That nine-month implementation date is a 'drop dead' date. It's already risky because it depends on us getting everything right on every task leading up to it! And now your boss wants us to deliver in six months instead of nine! That's impossible, Alexandr! You know that."

"Hold it, Bob. Don't get excited. Let me tell you what he wants. He wants the hardware installed and operational. He wants the new operating system fully performance tested. He wants the network, how would you say, *glitch free*. Beyond that, he's willing to accept less application software within the six month deliverable."

"That's still 80 to 90 percent of everything we have on this critical path."

"I don't think so. I want you to take the project apart and look at it again. Take a week."

"A week. You mean a week of twenty-four hour days, don't you?"

"Alexandr, I'd like to meet with your boss to look at the business requirements again," said Anna, "I want to find out what's the least he will accept in his six-month deadline. Can you arrange that?"

"That seems like a reasonable request. I'm sure Mr. Kedrov will make time for you in his busy schedule. After all, this is important to him."

And none of you would even begin to know how important this is to Misha, thought Alexandr, as he looked at the three concerned people.

Sixteen

National Security Council, Washington, DC

Guardian News Service, Moscow:

'President Boris Yeltsin yesterday sacked his defense minister, General Igor Rodionov, and his deputy, in a sudden purge of the military top brass designed to reinforce his control over an underpaid, disaffected and near-mutinous army.   Mr. Yeltsin theatrically turned on General Rodionov (60), a career general with a reputation for honesty and plain speaking, blaming him for the stalled military reform and accusing him of presiding over an army whose generals built themselves oversized dachas while their soldiers had nothing to eat.   "Soldiers grow thinner and generals get fatter," Mr. Yeltsin said before the television cameras. "Generals have built dachas all over Russia. I wonder where this fashion came from!   Generals are not interested in reorganizing the army because they may lose their privileges. They are the main obstacle to implementing army reforms."   Shortly after the outburst, General Rodionov and the chief of General Staff, General Viktor Samsonov, were dismissed. General Igor Sergeyev, the commander of the Strategic

Rocket Forces, was named as acting defense minister, while Colonel-General Viktor Chechevatov, head of the Far East Military District, was strongly rumored to become the army's new chief of staff. General Chechevatov had first come to Mr. Yeltsin's attention for standing as a candidate in last year's presidential election, and then standing down in favor of the President. He recently had to defend himself from newspaper revelations that he had built an enormous dacha outside Moscow, rumored to cost over $500,000, saying he had borrowed the money from a bank.'

Bart Shields lifted his head from the newspaper clippings and reflected that at least he was getting news from Russia, even if it was bad news. During the Cold War he got no news. No news is good news. But, during the Cold War, no news was always bad news! Swinging his chair around, he reached for his laptop and dialed into his e-mail system. One message, from Owen MacDara:

> *Zhukov gave me two names – an Irishman who was a mercenary in the Congo in '61, Major Lacey. And the CIA man in the Congo at that time was called Kearns or Cairns. Try and find him. I'm on my way to Ireland to look for Lacey.*

Shields' intercom buzzed.

"OK, Sally. Send her in."

Leslie Scott usually looked like a breath of fresh air when she visited the general. Not today. Her arms were burdened with documents and her eyes red-rimmed. "You look like you've been up all night! What have you been doing?" asked the general.

"Getting an education – on the Congo."

"Sit down, sit down," said General Shields almost fatherly, then buzzed Sally and asked her to send in a pot of fresh coffee. Leslie spread out the documents on the coffee table and sank into the couch. Sally appeared with the coffee. "Hold any calls," said the general. "I don't want to be interrupted. Unless it's the President!" He turned back to Leslie and asked: "What did you learn about the Congo?"

"God! Where do I begin? Early 1960's, I guess. That's when Hammarskjold died."

She fished among her documents and retrieved a folder filled with loose typewritten pages. Giving two of them to the General, she asked him to take a minute to read them. Tilting his chair back, he started to read:

Sixteen new African nations joined the UN in 1960 and by 1963 there were thirty-two independent African nations. Most of these nations were not prepared to govern themselves. They had no capital, no expertise, and no institutions upon which to build. But Africa was rich in strategic materials. This was especially true of Katanga province in the Congo. The US was afraid that Russia, or even China, would gain control over this mineral wealth so they got deeply involved in the messy civil war in the former Belgian colony. The Congo's Prime Minister, Patrice Lumumba, was supported by the Soviets, whereas Moise Tshombe had taken control of the breakaway province of Katanga. The Belgians were propping him up, hoping to retain control of Katanga's wealth. But the US wanted to control the Congo and prevent the Soviets, the Belgians, and the French from getting control over these strategic minerals. So, in 1961, they directed the CIA to assassinate Lumumba and twisted the arm of the UN to capture Tshombe and reunite the breakaway province of Katanga with the rest of the country. The CIA role in the murder of Lumumba was first disclosed in John Stockwell's book, *In Search of Enemies: A CIA Story.* Stockwell had been the Chief of the CIA's Angola division. Stockwell states that Lumumba was assassinated to keep 'a half billion dollar investment in mineral resources' from falling into Soviet hands. The National Security File holds twelve reels of microfiche covering US involvement in Africa. One third of those reels deal exclusively with the Congo. Richard Helms, who was CIA Director from 1966 to 1973, testified before Congress that he had ordered the destruction of the documents about the Lumumba assassination. Did documents ever exist on the Hammarskjold killing? If they did, were they also destroyed? One person survived that crash. His name was Harold Julien from New York and he maintained that Hammarskjold's plane was rocked by a series of explosions prior to the crash.

General Shields handed the two pages back to Leslie and played with an unlit macanudo as she swallowed two great gulps of coffee before taking a deep breath. "Exploitation! That's the story of the Congo. Katanga was the prize. Everything from uranium to diamonds! They all fought over it. The French, the Belgians, the Russians, the Americans. Even the Cubans were involved!"

"The Cubans?"

"That's right. I'll get to them. But I want to

start with Lumumba. He was the Congo's first President after it gained its independence from Belgium. He was a socialist and he was getting very friendly with the Russians. The Russians were using him, but Lumumba didn't see that. He wanted the Belgian and French mining companies out of Katanga. That angered the French. So they conspired to break up the Congo, set up an independent Katanga state and installed their own puppet, Moise Tshombe, to run it. The US was getting really worried by this time. They didn't trust Lumumba. They were sure he'd bring in the Russians. And they were mad at the French for taking over Katanga. Basically the US wanted Katanga for themselves. So they ordered the CIA to assassinate Lumumba. Then they persuaded the UN to send in 18,000 troops to take Katanga back from the French. This is where the mercenaries come into the picture. People like Black Jack Schramme and Mad Mike Hoare."

Leslie Scott paused to refill her coffee cup and Bart Shields waited till she was ready to continue.

"It was a dirty fight between the Americans and the French. At the time there were rumors that French agents were involved in the plane crash that killed Dag Hammarskjold," said Leslie.

"The French! Hah! I wouldn't trust them. Any country that would send its agents to New Zealand to attack a Greenpeace ship is capable of anything!" said Shields.

"But, sir, now that we've seen the KGB documents pointing the finger at the CIA and the KGB, it seems more likely that the rumors about the French were just that. Rumors! Disinformation! Probably planted by 'elements' on the US side," said Leslie Scott as she continued. "Of course, the US installed Mobutu as President of the new Zaire. But the Russians had spent a fortune trying to control the mineral wealth of Africa. They weren't too happy about the killing of Lumumba or the loss of Katanga to either the French or the Americans."

"And that's where the Cubans come into the picture?" said General Shields.

"On both sides!" said Leslie.

"Both sides?" echoed the General.

"The Russians tried to use Che Guevara and Cuban troops from Angola to overthrow Mobutu. Remember, this was Che's attempt to take his Cuban revolution to the world. Che joined up with Laurent Kabila to fight Mobutu. The very same Kabila who has just ousted Mobutu, taken over Zaire, and renamed it the Congo. Che took 100 Cuban troops to the Congo in 1965 to fight alongside Kabila. But that's all history now. Kabila's in control. Zaire is gone. Long live the Congo!" said Leslie.

"Are we in for another power struggle in the Congo, another fight over who controls its minerals? That's what I'd sure like to know," asked the general, rhetorically, and, as an afterthought, "I'll have to talk to Smallwood."

Leslie answered anyway. "That's what it's always been about. The wealth of the Congo. They've got all the strategic minerals. They have seventy percent of the world's cobalt. Not to mention copper, diamonds, tin, zinc. And, of course, oil! That's what really killed Hammarskjold?" She picked up a large black and white photograph and held it by the edges to give the General a good view. "That's a photo taken at Kamina airfield. B-26 bombers. And the pilots are Cuban. Anti-Castro Cubans. The CIA sent them in to bomb their fellow countrymen! We know that the CIA have been involved in Africa for years," said Leslie.

"What a mess! Good work, Leslie. Thanks for

the briefing. By the way, I just received this from Owen MacDara. Read it," said Bart Shields, handing the e-mail printout to her.

"Who *is* Owen MacDara?" asked Leslie after she had read the e-mail.

"That's a good question, Leslie. Will the real Owen MacDara please stand up?" joked the general.

"I'm serious, sir. You're asking me to work with him and I don't know a thing about him," said Leslie.

"In a way I am serious. There's more than one Owen MacDara. The first one I met in Korea twenty-five years ago. I was a Battalion Colonel and MacDara was a young Irish immigrant draftee. In those days, if you were an immigrant and you were healthy you were classified 1A as soon as you entered the US and you got Uncle Sam's greeting letter about six months later telling you to show up for induction into the army. MacDara was a good paramedic and a good soldier. I tried to convince him to go to Officers Candidate School and make a career out of the service. But he wanted to make it big in America. He wanted to be a millionaire. You know, the Horatio Alger dream. He had stars in his eyes."

The general stopped, twiddled with his macanudo, stuck it between his lips and slowly burned the tip with a long match, watching the smoke spiral up towards the ceiling. Satisfied, he seemed to be mentally searching for where he left off. Leslie prompted him. "Did he make his dream come true?"

"Yes, he did. I never doubted that he would. He runs his own international consulting company, GMA. Gives him the perfect cover when he works for us."

"Why is he working for us?" asked Leslie.

"It began two years ago. A friend from his

army days in Korea was murdered and he looked me up. Asked for help. Thought there was some kind of a conspiracy going on. Neither of us knew at the time that his friend was murdered to protect the Chairman of the Joint Chiefs and hide a right-wing conspiracy to take over the country. You know the rest. It's history now. Our government survived. In many ways we owe MacDara for that. The President would trust Owen with his life."

"So you asked him to help on the Ridge assassination," said Leslie.

"I didn't. The President did. GMA has important clients in Moscow and Owen goes there regularly. So it was a good fit. With one exception."

"Exception, Sir?" said Leslie.

General Shields stopped talking and stared off into the middle distance before speaking again. "Owen has just suffered a great loss. His partner, Kate, died giving birth to their son. The baby died, too."

Leslie suddenly felt very tired. This news, on top of her lack of sleep, seemed to act like a knockout punch. She slumped deep into the chair. The general stared into the distance again. Finally, he spoke: "The President thinks Owen needs to be busy. Very busy. Help him to cope with his loss. Better than drinking himself to death!"

PART THREE
Murder

Pat Mullan

Seventeen

**Buenos Aires,
Argentina**

1929

"Next year in Birobidzhan!" The first secretary of the Russian Embassy raised his glass in a toast as the thirty people assembled in the large anteroom of the synagogue smiled and nodded approvingly to each other.

Isaac Davidoff grabbed his wife, hugged her fiercely, and shouted loudly over the low murmur of voices, "Da! Our own land! At last!" Olga didn't show the same enthusiasm. She had become fluent in Spanish, had made new friends in Buenos Aires, and had begun to feel at home. But not Isaac. Never. He couldn't settle. He'd been homesick for Russia ever since they'd arrived in Argentina sixteen years ago.

Later they walked the three miles from the synagogue to their home. They walked in silence for a while until Isaac could stand it no longer.

"What's the matter? Why are you not happy?"

Olga didn't answer so Isaac continued. "You think you are happy here? You're not. So what if you can speak their language. They'll never accept you. You're still a Jew. Don't you understand that?"

Olga couldn't take any more.

"Isaac, are you going to run for the rest of your like? Is that what you want? And what about our son? What about Roberto?"

"What about our son? It was your idea to call him Roberto. Give him a name just like a native. Well, I'll tell you something. He'll never be a native. Never! That Kelly boy is the only friend he has. Even he is mostly Irish. If it wasn't for his money he wouldn't be accepted either."

"Isaac, that's not true. The Kelly Herreras are well respected in Buenos Aires. Señora Clemencia has been good to us. We owe them much."

"Money! That's what buys them respect. And, of course, the Señora is good to you. You're her slave. You clean up after them in that big house of theirs. Money, Olga, that's what it's all about here."

"And what money do you think you are going to get from Stalin?"

"We're getting something better than money. Land! Land of our own. A homeland. We've never had that. We won't have to run again. We can build a home for Roberto and our grandchildren. We will be with our own people. Running our affairs. Stalin has promised that to the Jewish people. Didn't you see the new railroad station they are building in Birobidzhan? And the sign above it in Yiddish. Not Russian –Yiddish!"

"But Roberto will soon be fourteen. This is his home. How are you going to make him understand your promised homeland?"

Isaac didn't answer. He knew what Olga said was true. But he had his mind set. Roberto would get over it. He'd make new friends. See a new world. Be with his own people. Yes, he'll hate me now but that will pass. They spoke no more about it and walked the rest of the way home in silence.

At sixteen, Carlos Kelly Herrera was almost two years older than Roberto Davidoff but they were the same size and build. They sit and talk on the wall outside Carlos's home. There's no joy in their voices. They know that this is probably the last time they'll see each other.

"I'll miss you." There was a lump in Carlos' throat. Roberto heard him choke on the words.

"I'll write to you. I'll send you photos," blurted Roberto, defensively.

Carlos said nothing. They sat there, not looking at each other, both absorbed in their own thoughts. There hadn't been a death in either family so neither had experienced the loss of a loved one. Nothing had prepared them for the loss of each other. Finally Carlos spoke. "I'll write too. I'll write every week. I'll tell you everything," he said, trying hard to be brave.

They looked off into the distance again – each knowing that they were uttering words to hide their pain, each knowing that they'd write once or twice, each knowing that they'd never see each other. But each knew that they'd remember their friendship. Forever.

Pat Mullan

Eighteen

Birobidzhan,
Siberia

1930

"You see, Olga, I told you," said Isaac, pointing to the signs above the railroad station, written in both Yiddish and Russian, as they disembarked at Birobidzhan. Olga said nothing but had to admit to herself that someone had gone to a lot of expense. The platform led to a magnificent newly built hall. It seemed to Olga that it had been built for them. *Maybe Isaac's right*, she thought, *maybe this is our new homeland.* She looked back to see Roberto struggling with the baggage and said a secret prayer in her heart for him.

Their new home was spartan, a simple log cabin on Sholem Aleichem street. Very soon they discovered that the photos they'd been shown of happy young men on their tractors harvesting their crops had only been propaganda to lure them here. The land around Birobidzhan was wild and unsettled. Most new arrivals suffered from a homesickness that seemed incurable. They were far from the social milieu of European Russia and they had no infrastructure to compensate. Isaac Davidoff started to blame himself for bringing them there – a blame that would prove fatal.

Five years after their arrival in Birobidzhan Roberto fell in love. He was only twenty. Her name was Zina and she had arrived with a group from the Ukraine. Two years later Birobidzhan had the biggest Jewish wedding that's ever been seen. Everyone said that Roberto and Zina were so beautiful. You could hear a pin drop in the synagogue just before Roberto crushed the glass in the linen napkin at his feet. The wedding celebration lasted well into the night, the wine flowed, and the dancing never ceased, with encore after encore requested of the bride and groom.

That would be the last joyous occasion for the Davidoff family in Birobidzhan. Two years later, Isaac Davidoff died from a massive heart attack. A broken-hearted Olga wailed over and over again as they sat *shiva*. Roberto was now head of the family. Within five years of his father's death, he led the Davidoff exodus out of Birobidzhan. It was the end of 1944 and the war in Europe was over. They went back to their roots, their beginnings, back to Leningrad, the city his parents had left those many years before when they emigrated to Argentina. The young men of Leningrad were no longer being conscripted and sent to the front. Roberto Davidoff was twenty-nine years old.

Nineteen

Leningrad,
The winter of 1959

Roberto Davidoff was a rarity: a capitalist in a communist state.   He'd prospered since leaving Birobidzhan and he had become one of the most powerful businessmen in Russia. His mother Olga, now in her seventy-fifth year, doted on him. He made sure that she was well taken care of.   A private nurse attended her daily, the best doctors were always available, and even her trips to her favorite ballet were provided regularly and in comfort.   Roberto's business took him away for long periods but Zina had found her fulfillment in motherhood. Mikhail had arrived in 1947 and Nadia in 1952. They were the center of her life.

But all was not what it seemed to be. Roberto Davidoff lived a double life. In his other secret life, he was an agent of the fledgling Israeli state. Only ten years old, Israel's founders had pledged, "never again" – the same pledge Roberto had made to himself the night his father died and he became head of the family. It was then that he vowed that his people would stop fleeing like unwanted nomads from land to land. When their ancestral home of Israel was reborn, he pledged that that would forever be their Promised Land. And he would ensure that by all means at his disposal. This was the age of the Cold War, the age where nations believed that peace could only be maintained if the consequences of war were unthinkable. So, to further the aims of peace, nations were building ever more destructive weapons of war, nuclear weapons. Israel's survival, in the middle of a threatening Arab world, could only be guaranteed if it also possessed such deterrents. Roberto Davidoff had become a spy, a traitor to Russia, and a patriot to Israel, a procurer and purveyor of Russian nuclear secrets.

Twenty

Moscow,
May 1961

Colonel Nikolai Stankevich bounded across the street and through the front door of the Lubyanka. He took off his gloves and presented his credentials to the guard on duty. The guard recognized him but still asked to see his identification.

General Konstantin Horbatuk got up to greet him when he entered. "You brought the evidence?"

"Yes, comrade general," said Colonel Stankevich as he opened his briefcase and took out a reel of film. The general had procured a projector in anticipation. The colonel threaded the film and turned on the projector. He stood back and watched the general's reaction as the film rolled. It had been taken over the course of a month of elapsed time and condensed into twenty minutes of film. The colonel provided the narration.

"That's him. David Gershman. One of the three top Israeli industrial spies. We've wanted him for a long time."

The camera followed Gershman into and out of trains, buses and taxis, from hotels to restaurants, from morning to night for four days. A monotonous, dreary viewing. Gershman saw no one, met no one, and never smiled. Nothing happened. That is, not until the fourth day when he boarded a train for Bataysk.

"There he is. Getting off the train. He's taking a taxi to his hotel. The entrance to the hotel. Next morning. Look, that's him. He's leaving the hotel. Walking. It's now an hour later and he's still walking. Now, look at this. He's reached a small park just across the street from the Bataysk Industrial Complex. He sits there on that bench for two hours. People pass by but no one approaches him. Now, watch this closely. You see this man walking towards us. He sits down beside Gershman. They don't acknowledge each other. The man reads his newspaper. Now he's getting up and leaving again. Now Gershman finally gets up and walks away. Look closely! He's carrying a newspaper! He didn't have one when he sat down!"

"Got him!" said the general.

"Exactly! We arrested him immediately. There was an envelope inside that newspaper. It contained microfiched pages of the latest test results from our nuclear program!"

"But you lost him last night, didn't you?"

"Yes! That is unfortunate. Gershman was tough. He resisted our best interrogators. He wouldn't talk. Last night his heart just stopped."

"He told you nothing!"

"Nothing! Nothing!" affirmed the colonel, but rushed to add, "But all is not lost. We've found the traitor. Let me show you."

He turned off the film, went back to his briefcase, and returned with a number of black and white photo enlargements. He gave them to the general and watched the recognition and shock spread across the general's face.

"But it can't be! That's Roberto Davidoff! I know him personally. He's a member of the party. This is a mistake!"

"Nyet, comrade general! No mistake! Davidoff had access to our Atomic Research Center. He supplied much of the electrical circuitry and components for the control center and he was always welcome there. That's where he filmed the test results."

"But do you have proof? You're charging a very important citizen with treason!"

"We have proof! And we'll get more! When we do, we'll bring it to you."

One hour after the colonel left, the general left his office too. His official car whisked him across Red Square and into the heart of the Kremlin. The two others were already waiting for him when he reached his destination. The general bypassed the usual courtesies and went straight to the heart of the matter that had brought them together at such short notice.

"These are the photos taken when Davidoff passed the microfiche to the Israeli. There is no mistake about it!"

Sergei Karakulov was a diminutive, mousy man. An anonymous man to most Russians but the brains behind The Fifth Directorate, formed to infiltrate and persecute all dissident groups but eager for any and all 'dirty' work that the state required. He took the photos from the general and shared them with the third man in the room. Igor Sokolov was the ruthless head of Russia's counterespionage force and a law unto himself.

It was Sokolov who broke the silence. "Why don't we arrest him right away?"

"We could. But think of the consequences. He's too powerful to simply eliminate or put in an asylum," said General Horbatuk.

"So we put him on trial! And then we execute him!" said Sokolov.

"No, Igor! It would turn into a show trial. This man has powerful friends. In Israel. In America. In Argentina...remember, he was born there," said Sergei Karakulov.

"Sergei's right, Igor," said the general.

"But he's a traitor! We can't just ignore that. He must be stopped. And he must be punished," said Sokolov.

"May I make a suggestion?" said Karakulov.

"Yes! Please!" said the general.

"We must stop him. And I don't know how you feel but I'd like to see him suffer for his treachery."

For the next hour the three of them debated Sergei Karakulov's *suggestion*, accepting that it offered them a solution and then planning the most difficult aspect of it all. *The execution*.

Twenty-one

Leningrad,
June 1961

Roberto and Zina Davidoff were carefree and happy. They were preparing to take the first family holiday together since Nadia was born. Misha and Nadia were very excited. They'd spent all of the previous evening looking at maps of their intended route. Roberto and Zina were intrepid spirits and they wanted to see places that they had only read about. But to Misha and Nadia it was an adventure – a full four weeks of adventure.

"When we reach Mongolia, can we sleep in one of their tents?" Misha asked excitedly.

"Absolutely!" responded his father. "That's what this is all about and we want to see how people live."

"Oh, Mamma, I'll keep a diary. I'll write in it every day!" said Nadia.

That night Misha and Nadia packed and unpacked again, finding it impossible to take everything they wanted and finding it equally impossible to leave many of their precious things behind. Roberto and Zina relished everything, realizing that this was a time with their children that they'd look back on with great nostalgia.

They didn't know that evening that they would never live to look back. They would never reach Mongolia. The end would come suddenly and violently, a few days later. And it would come in the uniform of Russia.   Just to let Roberto Davidoff know that he was 'suffering for his treachery.'

It was midnight. They awoke to the prodding of guns in their ribs and the leering faces of soldiers in Russian uniforms. The one that seemed to be the leader called Roberto Davidoff a traitor and said that the state didn't intend to waste its money trying such scum. Roberto pleaded with him to leave his family alone, pleaded that their problem was with him and him alone. But he received the butt of a gun for an answer and heard the leader tell his men to do what they had come to do...

Misha remembers:
...remembers the five or six sneering soldiers, remembers his father pushing him behind him, remembers the sound of the gunfire, remembers his father falling, remembers all that blood, remembers his mother bent over a wooden trestle with her dress pulled up and the soldiers raping her and raping her, remembers them cutting her throat when they were done with her, remembers being knocked unconscious as he pummeled the soldier that was molesting his nine year old sister, remembers, and

remembers, and remembers...he has never stopped remembering.

They did not kill Misha and Nadia.   They were under orders.   The Karakulov solution did not extend to the children.   So they were taken from that place of slaughter and removed to Moscow. There they were put in an orphanage.

Nadia remembers:
...There was no love in the orphanage.   Only discipline. Get up. Go to bed. Eat. Don't eat. Sleep. Wake up. Stand still. Speak only when spoken to. Obey. Obey. Obey. And there was no hope in the orphanage...no hope until Madame Kedrov arrived...

Madame Kedrov visited the orphanage once a week. She only stayed one hour.   She was permitted to bring just a few essentials, a new pair of socks for someone, a hair ornament for another, a child's book for someone else.   Nadia met her on her very first visit and immediately began to hope.   Madame Kedrov was lonely.   She had no children.   Nadia began to call her Mamma.   Madame Kedrov responded.   And so it was that after six months, Madame Kedrov applied for permission to adopt Nadia and Misha. She didn't want Misha but Nadia would not go without her brother.

PART FOUR
The Terrorist

Twenty-two

Buenos Aires,
Argentina

1974

Eduardo Kelly Herrera's family was prominent in the small influential Irish-Argentinean community. Spanish and Italian on his mother's side, Eduardo was full-blooded Irish on his father's. Professional and social achievement in three generations of Kellys had not eradicated the family remembrance of oppression in Ireland. The Argentina of Eduardo's youth was run by a succession of dictators. His family led a privileged life. His father was one of Buenos Aires' most prominent bankers. But it was the stories of his family's rebellious past, preserved by his uncle Patricio, that enthralled the young Eduardo. His hero was Dr. Ernesto Guevara Lynch, another Irish-Argentinean, destined to be known to the world as 'Che.' The Kelly Herreras and the Guevara Lynchs shared the privileged life of the elite of their class. Their social and fraternal obligations brought them together. Often the Kelly Herreras spent summer holidays at *San Patricio*, the great *estancia* outside Buenos Aires founded by Che's ancestor, Patricio Jose Lynch, who had built an international shipping company and became one of the richest men in Latin America. But Eduardo was too young to meet Che. He was only three years old when Che marched into Havana with Fidel Castro in 1959. But Che's fame and pure revolutionary zeal impressed the young Eduardo. He had been disconsolate for weeks when he learned that Che had died in Bolivia. But that was five years ago and time and his studies had dulled the rebellious fires that burned inside him. Despite the tales of his uncle Patricio, Eduardo's life should have been predictable. The family expected him to follow his father and his grandfather into either banking or the law. But an event in his last year at University changed all that forever.

It was the summer of 1974. Eduardo arrived home from school, two days early. It was mid-afternoon and he hadn't expected his mother or father to be at home. So the voices and laughter coming from the second floor surprised him. *They must be home after all*, he thought as he bounded the flight of stairs to the landing outside his parents' bedroom. The door was ajar and he can clearly see the uniform jacket of a military officer lying on the floor inside the door. His mother's laughter was strong and rich, with that loud gurgling sound she made, deep down in her throat. Drawn to the open door, Eduardo was stunned by the sight before him. His mother was naked, with her legs wrapped tightly around the waist of a man thrusting up and down in the throes of passion.

The scene seared itself into Eduardo's brain, his eyes burned and his suddenly parched throat struggled with the howls that began deep inside it. They both saw him at the same time. His mother grabbed the sheet and draped it around her nakedness. The man jumped off the bed and dived toward his uniform on the floor. He turned with a pistol in his hand just as Eduardo jumped him. The shot reverberated around the bedroom and the man fell to his knees clutching his chest. Blood seeped through his fingers, spreading a stain on the carpet beneath him.

Eduardo's mother screamed hysterically. The officer's driver had been waiting, heard the shot, and ran into the house. Eduardo had no time to consider anything. He only had time to run. As the driver raced up the main staircase, Eduardo left by the back stairway, through the garden, and disappeared into the adjoining streets.

General Antonio DeSalvo was a member of the most powerful political family in Argentina. There would be no scandal. The cover-up was airtight. The official announcement of the general's passing stated that he had died of a massive heart attack. The nation was in mourning. The funeral mass was concelebrated by the cardinal and five archbishops. There were only two requirements that the family insisted on: silence and revenge. The general's driver died when the brakes failed and his car left the roadway, crashing in flames down a hillside. The small news item describing that event attributed it to a combination of mechanical failure and speed. The family was reassured by the fact that the knowledge the driver possessed died with him. So that left the matter of revenge. Indeed, revenge was a matter of honor for the DeSalvo family, inseparable from their Sicilian heritage. The Kelly Herreras were also powerful and important. A war between the families would be bad for business, bad for everyone. The DeSalvos did not want that. But they wanted a full measure of revenge. They decided. They would settle for the boy, Eduardo. He would pay with his life. They informed the Kelly Herreras that this was their price and there would be no negotiation.

For three days after his flight, Eduardo lived rough, hiding out by day and traveling by night. He knew where he was going. There was only one place to go at a time like this. To his Uncle Patricio. *Patricio Kelly. Named for his father: Patrick Joseph Kelly. How often had Uncle Patricio told me about my grandfather? How, at only twenty, he'd been a leader in the Young Irelander revolution in Ireland in 1848. Captured and sentenced to death, the sentence was commuted to life imprisonment in Van Dieman's land, Australia. No doubt I'll hear about grandfather again! Uncle Patricio never tires talking of him.*
      Patricio Kelly was expecting his nephew. His brother, Carlos, had called him. Eduardo was 'on the run' and he was certain that he would seek refuge with his Uncle Patricio. Carlos reckoned that he'd be safe there for at least a week. The families still had great respect for their old ones. Uncle Patricio was in his eighty-fifth year.
      It was nearly midnight when Eduardo reached Uncle Patricio's house. But the old man was waiting. Awake and alert, he reached for Eduardo and crushed him in a bear hug. A Kelly 'on the run' was a family legacy. His father had often been 'on the run' during the troubles in Ireland. Eduardo hid out at his uncle's house for ten days, each day

seeming longer and riskier than the previous one. The evenings were shortened by his uncle's story telling. As Eduardo had expected, Uncle Patricio's favorite topic was his father. "You know, my father was sixty-five years old when I was born. My mother was his third wife. And the last one...Clemencia, his second wife, was your grandmother. But the three of us – your father, your Aunt Caitlin, and myself – we were brought up as one family. Your grandfather wouldn't have it any other way. Used to always call your father Charlie. He had an uncle Charlie, on his mother's side, back in Ireland."

"He died almost forty years before I was born. But it's as though I knew him, Uncle Patricio," said Eduardo.

"He was a good age when he died. Ninety-two. Exactly seventy years, seven decades, in this country. He was only twenty-two when he reached here, you know," said Uncle Patricio, just getting into his stride. Eduardo had heard the story many times before. He knew he was going to hear it again.

"He was your age, only twenty, when the English sentenced him to death. They were going to hang him. Like a dog! He taught me that sentence, word for word. I've never forgotten it:

"'The sentence is that you, Patrick Joseph Kelly, be taken from hence to the place from whence you came, and be thence drawn on a hurdle to the place of execution, and be there hanged by the neck until you are dead; and that afterwards your head shall be severed from your body, and your body divided into four quarters, to be disposed of as Her Majesty shall think fit.'"

"But you know the rest. That sentence was commuted to transportation for life to the penal colony in Australia, known as Van Diemen's Land. His friends were shipped out too. I remember the names. He often spoke of them. D'Arcy McGee and Thomas Francis Meagher."

Uncle Patricio's eyes sparkled and the blood surged to his cheeks, giving a glow to his entire countenance. Eduardo listened, entranced.

"But your grandfather escaped from that penal colony. Stowed away on board a merchant ship heading for these shores. They discovered him when they were three days at sea. So they put him to work. Let him earn his passage. Besides, they had no great love for the English. Within five years McGee and Meagher had also escaped. They went to North America. D'Arcy McGee became one of the founding fathers of the Canadian Confederation. Meagher became a General in the US and fought for the Union in the American Civil War. Later he was Governor of Montana. My father never let me forget these things. He hated every tyrant in the world. You could do worse than follow his example."

"What would he tell me to do, Uncle Patricio?"

"He'd tell you to fight! And I think he'd tell you never to get caught. He had a good life here but I think he'd have been a happier man if he'd died in battle fighting the English back in '48."

"But I can't fight the DeSalvos."

"But you can fight their kind, Eduardo! First, you must save yourself."

"But how, Uncle Patricio?"

"Your father will know. He'll be here tomorrow night."

Twenty-three

It was dark when Carlos Kelly Herrera slipped past the man watching his brother's house. He reached the rear courtyard without being seen. Eduardo opened the door for him and they embraced in the hallway. But this wasn't a time to get emotional. This was a time for action and Carlos got down to business immediately.

"Your name is Conor Brady. You were born in County Mayo in Ireland, educated in Mexico, Argentina and the United States. You are an Irish citizen. This is your passport."

Eduardo took the small dark green passport from his father. Emblazoned with an Irish harp it was lettered in gold in Irish and English: *Eire/*Ireland. Opening it his smiling photograph stared back at him and his nationality was asserted in Irish, English and French: *Naisiuntacht/Nationality/Nationalite: Eireannach/Irish/Irlandaise.*

His father spoke again. "I have set up an account for you in Zurich. There's two hundred thousand US dollars in it. No one but you can gain access to it. Here is the number. Commit this to memory now and destroy it. You'll need money right away so here's twenty thousand dollars in American Express traveler's checks. Sign them as Conor Brady. You'll need to get used to your new name."

Eduardo said nothing. He took the traveler's checks and started to memorize the Zurich account number.

His father continued. "I am sending you to my oldest friend, the closest friend I ever had. We grew up together here in Buenos Aires. His parents were Russian. Jews. They went back to some homeland that Stalin promised them. His name is Roberto Davidoff. I haven't heard from him in thirty years. This is the last address I have for him. Find him if he's still alive and give him this letter. He will take care of you. I'd trust him with my own life."

Eduardo thanked his father but Carlos continued, businesslike; a style that protected him from the emotions that he felt inside. "Airline tickets. Take them. Conor Brady is booked on a flight from Montevideo to Paris two days from now. Mendoza is waiting for you. He will take you across the border to Uruguay tonight. You will stay with his cousin till it's time to leave. Don't worry. I've paid them well. Mendoza is almost a member of our family. And he has little love for the DeSalvos. So you're in good hands."

Uncle Patricio took him by the arm and led him into the study. "There's something I want you to have," he said, as he held Eduardo's hand open and then forced it shut on a roll of money, five thousand US dollars, "I know you don't need it. Your father has provided well for you. But I want the first thousand dollars you spend to be mine. In that way I can be with you. Take it. It's really a selfish act of an old man. And take this too. You may need it even more."

He leaned across the ornate carved desk, pulled a drawer open and took out a leather shoulder holster. He opened it and withdrew the gun, released the ammunition clip, checked it and put it back with a firm boost from the heel of his right hand. "Fully loaded. Safety's on. And here's a spare magazine," he said, as he examined the weapon, never giving Eduardo a chance to refuse.

That was it. No tears. No last farewells. Just a massive hug from Uncle Patricio and they were gone. Into the night and past the watcher outside.

They were halfway to the meeting place with Mendoza when two men appeared out of the darkness in front of them. One held a gun directly at them. The other spoke: "Señor Carlos, this matter does not concern you. We do not want you. Only your son."

Carlos immediately jumped in front of his son, yelling, "Eduardo, run! Andale! Andale!"

But Eduardo had already decided. Pushing his father forcefully in the small of his back, he knocked him face down on the ground. The man in front fired and missed. Eduardo's bullet hit him in the left breast, severing his aorta. The second man turned to run but Eduardo's next shot found his leg, crippling him, and he fell to the ground screaming in agony. Carlos regained his feet and urged his son to flee. But Eduardo had made up his mind to finish the job. He walked deliberately to the wounded man and shot him in the head. Carlos looked on in disbelief. *This is not my son. This is not the son I know.*

Mendoza was waiting exactly where he said he'd be. Carlos bade his son an awkward farewell.

Twenty-four

Leningrad, Russia
One month later...

The trip from Montevideo to Paris was uneventful. Eduardo spent a week in Paris, walking the Champs Elysee, visiting the Louvre, spending his evenings in Montparnasse and the Pigalle. But he was anxious so he moved on to Zurich where he withdrew twenty thousand from Conor Brady's Swiss account for living expenses.

A month later, Eduardo reached Leningrad. He arrived late in the evening. It was a 'white night' of summer, light until midnight, and the streets were filled with people out walking or going to watch the raising of the bridges across the Neva. After Paris, the broad avenues and classical facades of Leningrad looked surreal to Eduardo. The buildings somehow seemed out of place in this Northern Russian city.

He drank a coffee in a café on Nevsky Prospekt and decided to ask the two middle-aged men at the next table for directions to the Davidoff address. After a heated discussion, they finally agreed on the best route. Following their advice, he took the metro to Sennaya Ploschad and then walked down Sedovaya Ulitsa till he reached the Kryukova canal. He walked alongside the canal till he reached apartment building number 38, overlooking the Priazhka River. Entering the building, he was confronted by a large mahogany reception desk and a small bald bespectacled person, barely visible behind it. He struggled with his few words of Russian showing the Davidoff name and address on the envelope he'd received from his father. The little man rose out of his chair, raised himself to his full five feet and looked up at Eduardo. Surprisingly he said, in impeccable English: "Do you speak English?"

"Yes, yes," said Eduardo.

"Good. This building was turned into a museum years ago. Anyone still living here at that time was moved somewhere else. I'm sorry. I cannot help you."

In the days that followed Eduardo visited every agency, talked with every bureaucrat, pursued every lead, but found no one who had any record or memory of the Davidoffs. It was as though they had disappeared from the face of the earth.

Twenty-five

Europe

Six years would pass before Eduardo found the Davidoffs. After Leningrad he wandered for more than a year from city to city and place to place. His face was as familiar as the Gucci clad 'Eurotrash' in the best clubs from Milan to Nice. He followed every girl that he became infatuated with. But as soon as he caught his prey, he became disinterested and restless and moved on. Until he met Malrika, an Arab beauty with a Greek grandfather. She always claimed that her ankles were too thick, that she had inherited them from her grandfather. They spent the summer of '75 together and Eduardo did not get bored and did not feel restless. But it was Malrika who set the agenda as autumn approached and the leaves were turning gold outside the window of their apartment on the Ile St. Louis on the Seine.

"I must leave tomorrow, Eduardo."

"Where? I'll come with you."

"No! I must go alone."

"But why? When are you coming back? "

"I'm not coming back."

127

"What do you mean? You're leaving me? But why? What have I done? I thought we were so happy together. I don't understand, Malrika. I love you!"

"Eduardo, I can't tell you. I do love you but I haven't been honest with you. I am a Palestinian. There is nothing for us in my future. I can't explain any more. I've said too much already."

"Malrika, sit down. I have not been honest with you either."

Libya

And so it was that Eduardo joined Malrika in the PLO. It was easy for him to identify with a national liberation struggle. In a Libyan training camp three months later he met two senior members of the Provisional IRA. Their dedication to the struggle for Irish freedom seemed a continuum of his grandfather's struggle in the same cause. Casting his lot with those who risked everything gave Eduardo a new direction in his life. His innate ability to kill, without any remorse or compunction, made him ideally equipped for his new role. It was in that same Libyan camp that Eduardo met a fellow South American, Illich Ramirez Sanchez, known more infamously as Carlos the Jackal. A year later Carlos took the credit for an operation that was actually planned and organized by Eduardo: the kidnapping of eleven OPEC oil ministers attending a meeting of the Organization of Petroleum Exporting Countries in Vienna. Payment of millions in ransom inflated the public image of Carlos and sent a clear message to the secret anti-terrorist organizations of the West; they had a new and deadly foe: Eduardo Kelly Herrera.

Antwerp

But Eduardo would not restrict his activities to national liberation movements. Their dogmatism bored him too easily. His unique expertise brought him to the attention of that international marketplace where contracts meant 'terminations'. This led him to Antwerp, to the European hub of Misha Kedrov's drug empire. Using a complex of import/export businesses centered in Antwerp's well-established Russian community, Misha's Russian mafia, the *vory v'zakone* or 'thieves in law', trafficked in heroin and cocaine with shipments passing through Singapore, Bangkok, Antwerp and New York. Misha also used the same trade network to supply a million dollar a year business in ozone-threatening CFC chemicals to feed the demand in the US for repairing cooling systems in cars and freezers.

It was easy for Eduardo to ply his trade to the *vory v'zakone* and become their 'assassin extraordinaire'. Very soon he came to the attention of Misha Kedrov who ran a background check on him and learned that Eduardo Kelly Herrera was the son of his father's close friend in Argentina. Few of Misha's Russian mafia 'godfathers' and none of his 'operatives' knew that the Chairman of Kedrov Industries was also the Chairman of all the Russian mafia. Misha was reluctant to breach this 'wall', even for the son of his father's old friend in Buenos Aires.

Cairo

Eduardo still joined his former PLO compatriots in an occasional operation. One of those occasional operations ended at the airport runway in Cairo in 1980. Eduardo and five compatriots had hijacked an El Al plane in Paris and had demanded the release of three PLO leaders being held in Israel. Elite Israeli troops and US Delta Force commandos staged an assault on the El Al plane, freeing 158 passengers and killing three of the hostage takers. The remaining terrorists detonated charges they had planted, igniting the fuel and turning the aircraft into an inferno.

Conor Brady mingled with the freed passengers and Eduardo Kelly Herrera died in the inferno.

Moscow

In Eduardo's *death,* Misha Kedrov saw the beginning of new possibilities. And he saw a way to repay the family obligation he felt that the Davidoffs owed the Kelly Herreras. Two days after the hijacking ended in Cairo he invited Conor Brady to Moscow and Eduardo Kelly Herrera finally found Mikhail Davidoff, the son of his father's good friend, Roberto.

It was the middle of the night and the wine had changed to vodka. Conor could hold his own but he knew he'd met his match this time. "So many times my father talked about your father to me," Misha said. "Many times, in the weeks before he died, he would tell me about Buenos Aires."

"My father was different. He never talked about your father. But that didn't matter. He still remembered. These were his last words to me before I left. 'I'm sending you to my oldest friend. The closest friend I ever had. He will take care of you. I'd trust him with my own life.'"

"Conor, if my father were still alive he'd take care of you like a son. So I will take care of you like a brother."

Misha tossed his vodka glass onto the shards of his earlier glasses, reached for Conor and kissed him passionately on both cheeks. That night Conor began his new career as Misha Kedrov's personal assassin extraordinaire.

Twenty-six

Shannon,
Ireland

'THE GREEN IRELAND OF YOUR ANCESTORS'
Dr. Ernesto 'Che' Guevara Lynch de la Serna

Aeroflot Flight 697 landed at 2:30 p.m., just fifteen
minutes later than scheduled. Conor Brady grabbed
his carryon bag and was one of the first off the plane.
His Irish passport propelled him through and soon he
was turning the keys in his rented car. Conor was no
stranger to Ireland. This was his fourth visit since
he had left Argentina. His trips to Ireland had been
necessary: necessary for his own soul; necessary for
his own identity; necessary for his understanding of
his grandfather; necessary to help him survive under
a false name. It was the 'green Ireland of his
ancestors'. Those words had branded his soul ever
since the day he saw the postcard that Che Guevara
had sent to his father from Dublin in 1964. His
mind's eye still saw the words, *'I am in the green*

Ireland of your ancestors. When the television found out they came to ask me about the genealogy of the Lynches.'

But he wasn't thinking about any of this as he maneuvered the car through Shannon and headed for Ennis and Galway. He was thinking instead about Owen MacDara. His mission troubled him this time. Usually he never gave these assignments a second thought. Always the target was nothing more than a target. A cardboard cutout. Maybe it was MacDara's Irishness that bothered him. No, he thought about that for a minute. He had no compunction about taking out an Argentinean. Why should it be any different with an Irishman? Maybe it was curiosity? Maybe it was the need to know the victim? Whatever it was, something inside him made him want to meet MacDara, made him want to see what made MacDara tick. Maybe it was the need to find a victim worthy of his skills. Maybe he wanted to risk himself this time. Maybe it was boredom. He had briefed himself well on Owen MacDara: born in Ireland, paramedic in the US Army in Korea, black belt in Karate, founder of his own consulting company, self-made millionaire, special agent for the President of the United States, lost his partner in childbirth only a year ago, and now the biggest obstacle for Misha. Yes, he had to meet MacDara.

Conor was still trying to come to grips with this behavior of his when he realized that the city of Galway was behind him and he was squeezing his car through the crowded narrow streets of Oughterard, the village beside Lough Corrib. He pulled the car over and ran in to Keogh's, the little village supermarket, to satisfy his addiction for a Coke, his non-alcoholic beverage of choice. As he paid for it the mounted photo of Bob Hope taken on his last visit was proudly displayed over the cash register.   To Conor's curious look, the lady at the register said,

"Ah, sure he's just a darlin' man. Comes here all the time. To visit his daughter, you know. She's been livin' here for years."

As Conor slid the coke into the slot beside the ashtray and slipped the car into first gear he thought that the little scene involving Bob Hope's picture defined the Ireland that he'd come to know. A place where everybody knew everybody. Small enough for the famous and the notorious to rub shoulders in the nearest pub with the locals. A place where nobody was unduly impressed by celebrity. A place where people respected your privacy. A good place for a Conor Brady.

A few minutes later the landscape changed dramatically. The green fields were gone, replaced by brown heather dotted with clumps of yellow gorse running down to shimmering water that sparkled like diamonds and bogland reaching the foothills on the horizon with the hazy outline of the Maamturk Mountains tracing craggy lines in the sky. He was now in Connemara. Forty-five minutes later he reached Clifden, the capital of Connemara, a small market town on the Atlantic shore. He was expected at the Abbeyglen Castle Hotel. He had stayed here before. They made a point of remembering.

Owen MacDara lay on his back about a half mile from Ardree House. His elbows dug into a bed of springy sphagnum moss and he watched a large black bird circle overhead. Soon a smaller bird joined it and they climbed higher, two black dots against the blue ceiling. Flying free. That's what Kate and my son are doing now. Their souls are flying free. But I'm not a believer. I don't believe in reincarnation. Still? He pondered deeply as he watched the two birds separate. Now only one remained – the little one. A tiny black speck in that vast expanse of blue. Suddenly, he was twelve years old again, lying out on his father's bog, resting from his morning's turf cutting, watching the lark in the sky above. *I wrote a poem about that. I wonder if I can still remember the words. Let me see...*

The barking dog brought him out of it. He pressed his hands deep into the moss till he felt firmer ground. Then he leveraged himself to his feet and looked across the hillside. A farmer was herding his sheep, his dog rounding up the strays. It was time to go. He'd flown in from Moscow two days before and had spent the time tracking down Major Lacey. It hadn't really been very difficult. That's the advantage of Ireland. Small enough that everyone knows everyone else. Or have a sense that they do. One phone call to a friend, a member of the Military History Society of Ireland and he soon discovered that the Major was in reality Richard de Lacey, the seventh Earl and head of the de Laceys. It was no secret that Lacey had been a mercenary with 'Mad Mike' Hoare in the Congo. Colonel O'Beirne of the Military History Society seemed to take a vicarious pleasure in that when he briefed MacDara. President Mobutu of Zaire employed Hoare in the Congo in the early sixties. Some of the actions of Lacey and his mercenary colleagues, such as rescuing nuns, made heroes of them. But they were totally ruthless. They took no prisoners, especially their Simba rebel captives. O'Beirne was only too glad to relay stories of these events to MacDara. Especially if it included dinner and copious amounts of his favorite South African pinotage. They were on their second bottle.   Actually the Colonel was on their second bottle and MacDara was still on his second glass when the stories started to flow.

"Y'know, Owen," said Colonel O'Beirne, using 'Owen' in that instant intimacy bestowed by alcohol, "this is confidential. Not classified – not secret, mind you – but, still confidential. Right from the horse's mouth. In Jo'burg."

"Jo'burg?" quizzed MacDara.

"Johannesburg. I was attached to the UN in the seventies and eighties. Ireland, neutral nation and all that. Thought we could be honest brokers between the ANC and the Afrikaners. It was O'Brien's influence, y'know. The Cruiser."

"The Cruiser?" Owen repeated, although he already knew the reference.

"Sure. The Cruiser. Conor Cruise O'Brien. Another relic of the Congo. He was the UN Representative in the Congo in 1961. You knew that, didn't you?"

"Yes, yes. Of course," said MacDara, but the Colonel had moved on, not really waiting for an answer.

"Where was I?   Jo'burg?" continued the Colonel, finishing his glass and it. He offered to top up Owen's glass but Owen declined.

"Kruger.   That's who told me. He had been there with Lacey. In the Congo. When Mike Hoare formed '4 Commando'. He was never sure of Lacey's standing in the chain of command. As a Major Lacey was a rank higher than Hoare's rank of Captain."

The Colonel stopped just long enough to gulp down more of the pinotage and then looked intimately at MacDara, "Did you know that about a third of 4 Commando were South Africans?"

"No, I didn't. Why so many?" asked Owen.

"That's easy! South Africa was up to its ears in the Congo."

Major Lacey was still alive and living only a few miles away. Owen had called that morning and made an appointment. The Major was expecting him at three. He glanced at his watch. Just past noontime.

Conor Brady had also heard the dog barking. He adjusted the right eyepiece of his Nikons and watched the skill of the sheepdog for thirty seconds. For the past hour he'd lain on a rocky, heathery knoll that commanded a view of Ardree House and the surrounding countryside and watched Owen MacDara lying on his back staring at the sky. If only binoculars had the ability to read minds. He'd have given a lot to know what was going through MacDara's head as he lay there staring at the sky, occasionally flicking a hand across his face. A perfect target. I could easily fulfill my contract right here. Getting away couldn't be easier. There isn't a soul around except for that farmer and his sheepdog. But I'm in no hurry. MacDara has a flight booked to New York three days from now. New York will do fine. He swung the binoculars back in time to see MacDara rise to his feet and walk back towards Ardree House, picking his way through the hidden minefield of bogland swamp. He was beginning to enjoy his cat and mouse game with MacDara. Usually these contracts of Misha's were boring and predictable. Not this time. He was in no hurry to take out MacDara. He put the binoculars back in their case, slung them over his shoulder and began his trek back down to the main road.

MacDara was only six miles from Ardree House on a road that he had travelled numerous times. And yet he couldn't find the major's house. He turned back for the third time, traversing the same stretch of roadway. This time he saw it. The opening was barely visible between overgrown hedgerows and whin bushes. It had to be the entrance, he decided as the bushes brushed the side windows of his car. Once inside he could see that he was on a solid lane, much wider than he expected. It was covered with tufts of grass and weeds, testimony to its lack of use. A jungle of trees lined each side, blocking any vision of what lay beyond. So it was a surprise when he turned a corner to find himself in front of a house that had once been an elegant mansion. The architecture was mixed, part French chateau with Palladian style wings, but it had been allowed to deteriorate. An ornate fountain, now dry and surrounded by ferns and nettles, formed a centerpiece in the middle ground that used to be a circular driveway. As MacDara left his car and walked toward the front door he could imagine other days, days of dinner parties and carriages arriving with ladies and gentlemen in their finery.

MacDara was expected but not at the front door. A door in the right wing was ajar and Major Richard de Lacey, a tall thin, Patrician looking man in his early seventies, extended a bony hand with a remarkably firm grip.

"Mr. MacDara?"

"Please just call me Owen. And thank you for taking the time to see me."

"Do call me Richard. All the 'blow-ins' call me Major but the locals always refer to me as 'His Lordship' although I have never used that ridiculous title. And, Owen, don't thank me. Time is all I have these days. Now, just follow me. Mind your step here. The floor is a bit irregular at this corner."

They negotiated a narrow, dimly-lit corridor whose walls were covered with ancestral paintings, dark in pigment, many of them almost floor to ceiling, until they emerged into a flagstoned entrance hall squared between two enormous fireplaces. MacDara had a glimpse of pistols on the mantelpiece and crossed sabres on the wall as the Major's loping gait seemed to gather speed crossing the hall. Almost in a tour guide voice, without stopping or turning around, the Major said, over his shoulder: "We haven't used this entrance in years. Not since our grandmother passed away."

Crossing into another corridor extending beyond the central entrance hall they soon reached a large dark green oak door. The Major opened it and ushered MacDara inside. The contrast was stark. Comfortable chairs, booklined walls, collectibles and art, all warmed by a blazing fire in the hearth made the room personal, lived-in, human.

"Please make yourself comfortable," said the Major, directing Owen to a chair by the fire as he crossed the room to an array of drinks displayed on a corner table.

"Cognac, Irish, Scotch?"

"A Paddy please, if you have it."

"Indeed I do. I like it myself. Smooth. I'll join you."

The Major returned with two large Waterford tumblers generously filled with the amber glow of Irish whiskey. They toasted in the Gaelic.

"Slainte!"

The Major didn't sit down. Instead he wandered over to the bookshelves. He looked as though he intended to reach for a volume, then changed his mind and turned to face MacDara. "The original De Lacey came to Ireland in the twelfth century with Strongbow. The Norman Invasion! And you know that Strongbow was Richard de Clare, the Earl of Pembroke, a Norman himself. So when the Irish say that the English invaded Ireland, it was really the Normans, my ancestors. A century or two later we'd become 'more Irish than the Irish themselves.' But you know all that, don't you, Owen?"

"Yes, Richard," said Owen, and quickly tried to keep the Major from wandering, "the reason I came to see you..."

"I know the reason you came to see me," said the Major, and then proceeded as though that was unimportant. "How many of us own our ancestral lands today?" It was a rhetorical question. He didn't wait for an answer. "Very few. But *we* still do. It hasn't been easy. How much do you think it would cost to heat this whole place? The Colonial Service of the Crown. That's how we did it. That's how we kept our lands. We practiced the Art of War and the spoils of those foreign wars paid our servants and our debts. But the Empire ended and we weren't needed."

"And the Congo...?" MacDara tried again.

"What skills did I have? Only those of the warrior. It was either that or lose our lands. Can you see me in some one-roomed cottage? Of course you can't. So I fought for the person who paid me the most. Colonel Mike Hoare was a fellow Irishman. He and I had served together in the British army. So when he asked me to join him I couldn't refuse."

"But the CIA and MI5...and the KGB?" asked MacDara.

"Oh, don't be so naïve, Owen. I worked for all of them. Numerous times. War is a dirty business!"

"But why the Secretary-General of the UN?"

MacDara's tone got louder.

"The UN! Hah! They were not peacekeepers. They were up to their eyeballs in that mess in the Congo. The Secretary-General was one of their Field Commanders. He was fair game and we weren't playing by the Marquis of Queensbury rules. Besides Colonel Mike could never have paid me what the Yanks and the Russians did. You see, Owen, I would have done anything to save our lands. I did not want to be remembered as the de Lacey who lost the ancestral home and sold off the family titles to some vulgar Texas oil millionaire."

He gulped down his whiskey, refilled his glass and offered Owen another. But Owen declined and went straight to the heart of the matter, his reason for being there.

"Richard, we know from the KGB documents that Zhukov was the Russian who contracted you for the Congo assignment but they didn't give the American's name. That's why I am here."

"You know, old boy, you really can't prove any of this and I've got little time left so it doesn't matter to me any more. Prostate cancer. Six months at best," said the Major matter-of-factly, as he finally conceded that his strength had ebbed and sank into the armchair opposite MacDara. Owen waited, sensing that he would get what he came for.

"I never liked the American. A bully, I'd say. It doesn't matter to me if you know his name or not. It was Kearns. Yes, that was it. I don't believe I ever knew his first name. We weren't really on a first name basis. But I don't see what good it will do you. It was obvious to me that they were just somebody's messenger boys. And you may not want to find out who that somebody was. For your own health, I mean."

The Major was enjoying the company and

141

would have been quite happy to entertain MacDara all evening. But Owen had got what he came for and, as graciously as he could, made his exit. As he turned at the green oak door to say goodbye, the Major spoke again, his voice tinged with just the right sense of curiosity and bemusement.

"Owen, I do think you people should talk with each other. I told all of this to that young Russian lady from the UN who came to see me a couple of days ago. What was her name? Nadia? Something like that."

Twenty-seven

Galway Airport

Owen MacDara walked out of the terminal building toward the waiting Fokker 50 turbo-jet. It looked new. He remembered the small propeller driven plane that he'd taken on his last trip from here. A very noisy plane that bounced around at the slightest turbulence in the air. He felt better about this flight.

He was first on board. A trickle of people followed and it looked like there were only going to be ten or twelve passengers. The last passenger climbed aboard just seconds before the stairs were pulled back. MacDara was surprised when the man chose to sit beside him seeing that there were plenty of empty seats in the plane.

"Hope you don't mind? I prefer company when I fly. But if I'm bothering you I'll be glad to move. Just say so."

"No, no, I don't mind. It's a short flight anyway," said Owen MacDara.

"Name's Conor Brady."

"Owen MacDara."

"Vacation over?"

"You could say that. But I keep a home here too. What brings you to Ireland?"

"Roots, I suppose. I was born here. County

143

Mayo. But my family moved to Argentina when I was only five."

"I'm a Derryman. But I've spent most of my life in the States. I'm sure that's pretty obvious."

"Oh, I don't know. There's still a bit of Ulster in your voice. Where's your home?"

"Connemara. I try to get back as often as I can. To recharge the old batteries, you know."

"Connemara! That's a coincidence. I spent the last few days there. In Clifden. Did a bit of golfing, bit of fishing, a lot of drinking!"

"That's Clifden! Lives by its own rules."

The plane taxied out on to the runway and everyone lapsed into the usual silence that descends at takeoffs and landings. The acceleration was smooth and they were in the air before they realized it. Conor Brady exchanged some pleasantries with the flight attendant and turned to talk with Owen MacDara again just as a loud noise, almost like an explosion, rocked the plane. The plane dipped suddenly to the right and the cups slid off the tray tables spewing hot coffee and tea over everything. Then the plane seemed to commence a slow fall almost as though it was coming in for a fast landing. MacDara's fists clenched tightly on the handrests and he knew the plane was going down. A middle-aged lady diagonally across from him had taken out her rosary beads and started praying in a loud voice. "Holy Mary, Mother of God, pray for us sinners now and at the hour of our death."

Conor Brady looked across, his dark complexion a shade grayer. "It must be comforting to believe all that stuff," he said.

Just then the Captain's voice came over the public address system. He sounded steady, controlled, but his words were not reassuring. He explained that an engine had failed and there had been damage to the controls. They were losing altitude and they would not be able to make the airport. He advised everyone to prepare for an emergency landing and said that he'd come back on the air just before landing. He then asked the flight attendant to prepare the passengers for an emergency landing. Owen looked around and saw the fear in people's eyes just before he crossed his arms, grabbed the back of the seat in front of him and rested his forehead on the back of his hands. He had no time to think about living or dying except for one crazy thought: *if I still believed like that lady I could look forward to seeing Kate again.* The last thing he heard before they crash landed was the Lord's Prayer from the woman with the rosary. The next sensation he experienced was the smell of jet fuel and somebody struggling to free him from the seat belt. He regained consciousness in the middle of a grassy green field and looked up at the face of Conor Brady as the plane exploded and flames and black smoke spiraled skyward.

MacDara was admitted to the hospital and held over night for observation. The pilot and five of the passengers never made it. Their bodies had been cremated in the fiery inferno. Owen knew that he owed his life to Conor Brady but, despite his attempts to find him, he had disappeared without a trace.

Twenty-eight

New York

Two days later Conor Brady stepped off an Aer Lingus flight at JFK in New York. He had already been checked through US customs and immigration at their desk at Shannon airport. Within minutes he emerged into the waiting stares of people in the visitor's lounge. He saw her immediately. Nadia Pankin rushed to greet him. They hugged like lovers and headed for the taxi stand.

Half an hour later they were in a midtown hotel and Nadia Pankin watched Conor Brady slip out of his clothes and saw the muscles tense in his lean body as he moved towards her on the bed. She and Conor had only one thing in common. Lust!

When she woke later he was sitting up smoking a cigarette and watching some B movie. She untangled her hair from under his thigh and struggled onto one elbow.

"Conor, we have to stop meeting like this."

"That line is right out of this movie!"

"Seriously, Conor!"

"Oh, Christ! Didn't you enjoy it? Hell, we

seldom do this! When was the last time? Two years ago! Paris. Wasn't that it?"

"Exactly two years ago. That's why we have to stop it. I can't stand the withdrawal symptoms!"

"Hah! Then we'll just have to see each other more often!"

Nadia threw the covers off and ran her fingers around the tips of his nipples and gently through the strands of curly black hair that covered his chest. She circled his navel and watched him getting aroused again. He hit the remote and the television went black, killing the only light in the room.

Twenty-nine

National Security Council, Washington, DC

General Shields was expecting MacDara. He had called from Dublin before his flight departed. They met in the General's NSC office in the west wing of the White House.

"Not a scratch on you! You must have nine lives!" said the general.

"No, just lucky. I owe my life to Conor Brady. He pulled me from the plane before it blew up. But I couldn't find him to thank him. Were you able to find out anything?"

"Well, my old friend, the Irish Ambassador, has promised to do all he can. If anyone can find your Conor Brady, he can!" said Bart Shields, and then changing the subject: "Owen, I've asked someone to join us for your briefing." He noted the quizzical look on Owen's face as he spoke.

Almost on cue, the door opened as the general finished speaking, and Leslie Scott entered. Tanned and wearing a light blue Armani business suit, she crossed the room briskly as MacDara came to his feet.

"Owen, I'd like you to meet Leslie Scott. Leslie is my Special Assistant at the National Security Council," explained Shields.

"I've heard so much about you from General Shields, Mr. MacDara," said Leslie Scott.

"Not all bad, I hope," jested Owen, "And the name is Owen."

They stood appraising each other, both liking what they saw.

"Owen, I asked Leslie to join us to hear your briefing on your visit with the Major. She already knows everything else," said Bart Shields.

Owen described his visit with Major Richard de Lacey. The general always loved a good story and he reclined in his chair with his foot propped up on an open desk drawer, blowing smoke rings from a freshly lit macanudo. Leslie sat upright and attentive, intrigued by the de Lacey family history and Owen's colorful description of the Major's home. Owen brought Bart Shields quickly out of his relaxed slouch when he reached the major's departing words.

"Is there a Nadia with the Russian mission to the UN?" asked Owen, not expecting anyone to give him an answer. But Bart Shields was already on the phone.

"Madeleine, it's Bart Shields. Thanks for taking my call. Do you know anyone at the Russian mission called Nadia? It could be very important."

"You do! Yes! That might be her, OK. What do you know about her? Very little. That's OK. No, no. We'll find out and let you know." The general hung up the phone. "Nadia Pankin is with the Russian Mission to the UN. She and the Russian Ambassador, Anatoly Yeremenko, are connected at

149

the hip like Siamese twins I've just been told."

"But why would she be interested in Richard de Lacey?" wondered Owen.

"That's the $64,000 question and we need the answer. Now!" said Shields, as he got up from his chair and walked around to stand in front of Owen and Leslie.

"Owen, I've asked Leslie to work with you on this. Find out everything you can about this Nadia Pankin."

Three days later Owen MacDara was back in General Bart Shields' office.

"We found Kearns. Retired. Living in Nyack. Recluse, keeps to himself, sees no one. Wife, one daughter, Sarah, an aspiring actress. Studying at the American Academy of Dramatic Art. But mostly she waits on tables. That's all we know. Go see him. Another thing – remember I asked my old friend, the Irish Ambassador to the US, to help locate Conor Brady for you."

"Did he find him?"

"Well, he did and he didn't. I think you're in for a surprise."

Shields seemed to be savoring the moment. He let MacDara stew in anticipation while he methodically circumcised a new macanudo and then proceeded to burn the end in perfect symmetry before he took a satisfying pull of smoke into his mouth.

"Conor Brady's Irish passport was issued in the Irish Embassy in Argentina. That would seem fine if he and his parents had emigrated there. Except for one thing – the birth certificate he used – it's Conor Brady's all right, but Conor Brady never went to Argentina. He never went anywhere. Conor

Brady died from tuberculosis when he was only three years old. He's buried in a little graveyard in Westport in County Mayo."

MacDara shook his head in disbelief and asked the obvious question: "Well, who is Conor Brady?"

"We know that too! The Irish Ambassador wasn't too happy when he found out that someone had been traveling on a false Irish passport. Apparently there have been a couple of times in the past when minor officials in Irish Embassies and Consulates tried to enrich themselves by selling Irish passports. There was a big scandal at the Irish Embassy in London back in the eighties. But there had been some allegations at the same embassy back in the late sixties. Nothing was proven at the time and the consulate official involved transferred to another embassy. I'll give you three guesses which one. Right first time! Buenos Aires!"

Owen just listened as Shields paused to knock the ash off the end of his macanudo. "I'll cut a long story short. They found this official and he has admitted issuing the false passport in the name of Conor Brady. But he maintained that it was his patriotic duty, that he was doing it to help the grandson of one of the leaders of the Young Ireland movement. They led the fight against the English in Ireland in 1848!"

"Incredible! Is any of this true?" asked Owen.

"It's all true! That's what's incredible!" continued Shields, " Conor Brady's real name is Eduardo Kelly Herrera. That name may not mean anything to you. But it does to me. He's an assassin. A will-o-the-wisp character. In the seventies and eighties it was claimed that he was everywhere: in the Congo; in the Middle East with the PLO; working with Carlos the Jackal; involved with the IRA; mixed up with the Russian *maffiya*. How much of this is true and how much is the romanticism of the press we don't know. But we do know that he's a very dangerous man... and that he's supposed to be dead!"

"What do you mean?"

"Do you remember that plane hijacking in '87? Or was it '88? Anyway it was around that time. Went on for days and days. The plane went from airport to airport in the Middle East while the hijackers demanded that Israel release over one hundred Palestinian prisoners. Of course Israel would never do any such thing. The US tried to negotiate but failed. The plane finally ran out of fuel on the runway at Amman, Jordan, and five passengers were 'executed' by the hijackers. A combined US/Israeli force stormed the plane. They freed most of the passengers before the terrorists set off explosives that ignited the remaining fuel and turned the plane into a funeral pyre. They cremated themselves and twelve unfortunate passengers as well."

"And Conor Brady? I mean Eduardo?"

"A number of the passengers identified him as one of the leaders. It was assumed that he had died in that plane. But it's now apparent that he was one of the rescued passengers. If we check the records I'm sure we'll find that one of the people rescued that day in Amman was Conor Brady!"

"But what was he doing on my flight from Galway? And why did he save my life?" asked Owen, rhetorically.

"That's a mystery. But I don't believe it's a coincidence. Conor Brady was not on that flight by chance. We're now checking all flights that left Ireland for the US in the week following your plane crash. I fully expect to find him on one of them. I'm sure he's here. I have asked FBI Director Tom

Redington to assign some of his best agents. Tom'll be at their New York office tomorrow. Go see him."

As MacDara left the office Shields called after him: "Stay alert! You haven't seen the last of Mr. Conor Brady!"

Thirty

Kedrov Industries,
Moscow

Misha Kedrov's open plan office at Kedrov Industries disarmed Anna immediately. She had no preconceived ideas but somewhere in the back of her mind she had expected a more formal, rigid setting. The man himself disarmed her too. He was small, compact and charismatic. His every movement seemed only a surface ripple on the well of energy deep within.

"Anna, it's my pleasure to make this time for you. Alexandr has spoken well of you. Please sit here," said Misha, as Alexandr moved uncomfortably from one foot to the other at the reference to himself.

"Thank you, Mr. Kedrov," said Anna, as she took the seat offered at the round table that served as Misha's desk.

"Now, how can I help you?" asked Misha Kedrov, pulling up a chair and sitting directly facing her across the table.

"Mr. Kedrov, I'd like to make absolutely certain that we know what functionality you must have in the system in six months time. I think that that is crucial," said Anna, as she reached into her briefcase and retrieved a small Sony tape recorder, "Do you mind if I record this? It usually helps to eliminate any misunderstandings."

"No, absolutely not! Please do. I can give you forty minutes from now," said Misha, checking the time on his wristwatch.

"Mr. Kedrov," said Anna, as she switched on the tape recorder, "please tell me exactly what you need in the system in six months. Tell me what you must have and tell me what you'd like to have."

"That's easy, Ms. Yachmi. My absolute must drop dead requirement is the operating system and the communications network. The guts of the system. Anything else would be icing on the cake. Is that how you'd put it?" said Misha.

"Precisely, Mr. Kedrov!" said Anna, "Tell me more about the kind of network you need."

"You already have the technical specs on that, don't you?" said Misha and, not needing an answer to that, continued. "Let me tell you what I really need, from a user's point of view. Sometimes we lose sight of that in the midst of all these bits and bytes."

Misha Kedrov got up and walked over to the window, looked out in contemplation for a while, and then returned, his mind sharply focused as usual, and began. "Ms. Yachmi, I run a business enterprise that is highly diversified and geographically dispersed. The more decentralized and autonomous the pieces of my world the more I need centralized information. The timeliness and accuracy of that information can often make the difference between success and failure. So, as you can see, timely and accurate information is a priority. But it's not the only one. Communication, clear and unambiguous, is an equal if not greater priority. I need to tell my people what I expect at all times. And I need to do it accurately and efficiently. Likewise I have an open door policy. I insist that any of my key people can communicate with me at any time, day or night. But that doesn't give anyone the right to clutter up my phone or e-mail! If anyone needs to get to me they have that right. But they have an equal responsibility not to waste my time. I want to provide them with a communication system that will enable them to keep me informed at all times on every salient bit of information that I need to know."

He paused, looked intently, almost passionately, at Anna and then said, "Six months? That's what you are waiting to ask me, isn't it? Why six months? That's simple. I have an appointment in six months time. A very public, very professional appointment. I will be chairing an important international forum and your system will be central to my effort. I need the communication network and the top-level management information subsystem. The success of that forum depends on it. It might not be an understatement, or even melodramatic, to say that my destiny is in your hands, Anna Yachmi."

Misha Kedrov stopped talking and looked at his watch. Anna knew that the meeting was over. But she also knew that she had got what she wanted. Well, almost. She switched off the Sony, replaced it in her briefcase, thanked Misha Kedrov and left. Misha beckoned Alexandr to remain behind.

After Anna left, Misha Kedrov turned to Alexandr Gelman and said:
"This doesn't feel right."
"What do you mean?" asked Alexandr.
"I don't know exactly. It's a gut feeling. I

think Anna Yachmi wants to know more than my business requirements for the system. Maybe I'm wrong. But I don't think so," said Misha.

"I'm sure it's OK. She asked for this meeting at our last project review. It made sense. She's very conscientious. That's why I set it up with you. You must be mistaken. I just think she wants to get it right," argued Alexandr.

"I don't know. Maybe she knows more than you think. Maybe she's a spy too. Just like MacDara," said Misha.

Alexandr thought that over for a minute before responding. "You know I ran a security check on all the GMA people on the project. That included Anna. She was born in Azerbaijan. Her family is respectable. Hard working. Shopkeepers. Father is dead now. Mother still alive. She has one brother, unmarried. He lives to work. Runs the family shop from dawn till dusk. Anna went to America to study. At Columbia University in New York. She was hungry to succeed. Just like many young people who go to New York to make it. It's the American way and Anna is indoctrinated. It's some kind of neurosis. That's why immigrants like Anna often outshine native-born Americans. It's the hunger. Her whole life has been hard work and study. She earned her way through graduate school at Columbia by waiting on tables. She's never belonged to any political organization. And she's not particularly religious either. Her career is her life. She's good at what she does and she knows it. And GMA has given her the chance to shine. To be a star. No, with Anna, I believe that what you see is what you get," said Alexandr and as an afterthought, "There's only one weakness that I could find – and it may not be true. There're rumors that she's infatuated with Owen MacDara. Even that she's been sleeping with him."

"That's it!" said Misha, "Don't you see? She'd do anything for him. Maybe he's using her."

"Well, there's one way to find out," said Alexandr, "Get her into a situation where she will expose her hand. Set her up and flush her out. If she's innocent, as I believe, we'll soon know."

As it turned out Alexandr Gelman didn't have to contrive any situation to entrap Anna Yachmi. She engineered the situation herself. She was spending long days, late nights and every waking hour on the GMA project for Kedrov Industries. GMA had committed to deliver a working system in six months. Owen MacDara had committed – and Anna Yachmi had committed. The time was tight – too tight. There was no room for error. They were now in unit testing, that phase of the project where individual programs and subsystems were thoroughly tested on a 'stand-alone' basis. Integration testing, where all the programs and subsystems were 'linked', would follow. Once these performance hurdles were achieved, full systems testing would begin. When the system was proven to be 'bug free' and performing exactly to specification, it would be installed for use. The testing phases were the most stressful and demanding phases of the project.

But Anna Yachmi wasn't happy. She was working late again. It was ten o'clock on a Friday night and she'd stayed behind in the project-testing lab when the other programmers had left two hours ago. Her programs had been 'bombing out' all day and she couldn't find the problem. Her testing depended on linking to a network program and now she had discovered that there were two versions of that very same program. She had linked to the wrong version. But there shouldn't have been two versions. Someone had screwed up. She was livid. There was no leeway for any screw-ups. She wanted to find out who was responsible and 'kill them'. So she obtained the source code for both versions of the network program and was now comparing them line-by-line. That's when she found it – his signature. *His private digital signature!*

Most digital signatures use what is known as public key technology. That means that a person has two signature keys, a public and a private one. The public one permits identification but the private key is the mark of authenticity. No one but the key's owner can author a message or program in his or her name. It's just like a fingerprint. A fingerprint is unique, only the person who owns it can create it – that's the private key. But anyone can verify it by comparing it to an authentic copy of the fingerprint – that's the public key.

But Anna knew his public key. She knew it because he had sent it to her one time. He was so proud of his work that he signed everything he created using a special algorithm created from prime numbers. He was also besotted with Anna but he had never made an overt move.

Anna now retrieved the Insect's public key from her private disk and waited for verification...yes, there was no mistake. *She had found the signature of The Insect!*

Thirty-one

FBI Offices,
Manhattan, New York

Big Tom Redington was a burly New York Irishman
who'd worked his way up from being a beat cop to
heading the police departments of New York,
Chicago and Boston before being offered the FBI
Director's job. Owen MacDara had worked with him
before. He liked him.

"Owen, great to see you again," said Big Tom,
as he grasped MacDara's right hand and held his
elbow with his left, "Bart tells me you're in trouble
again. Why can't you lead a quiet life like me?"

"Tom, I'd like nothing better. Just let me run
GMA. That's enough excitement for me."

"Ah, who're you kidding, Owen. You'd miss
all of this. You're addicted!"

"Tom, you're wrong! Dead wrong! I'd much
rather be back in Connemara. Sipping a pint of
Guinness in O'Dowd's pub in Roundstone. Watching
an artist out on the pier painting the Twelve Bens.

Listening to the water lap against the boats in the harbor."

"Ah, you're a poet as well! All you Irish are the same!"

"Now, Tom, you didn't call me here for this, did you?"

"No, Owen. I'll be serious. Bart briefed me on this terrorist fellow. This Brady. I want to give you something to protect yourself." He picked up the phone. "You can send Pete in now."

Special Agent Peter Wolfe was a couple of months away from retirement but only his white hair suggested that.

"Owen, I'd like you to meet Pete Wolfe. Pete is my expert on weapons and ballistic materials. He's got some stuff for you. Go with him."

Owen MacDara and Peter Wolfe shook hands and then Owen followed him. They took the elevator four floors down to the sub-basement level. Pete entered his security code, inserted his pass card, and they went through a set of double doors into a wide hallway. Doors led off each side. There were no pictures on the wall to alleviate the feeling of being underground, of being in a bunker.

"This way, Owen," said Pete, as he opened the third door on the right and led Owen into a large room filled with floor-to-ceiling metal racks and steel cabinets.

"Take your shirt and jacket off. Put this on." He handed Owen a white colored lightweight vest. As Owen put it on, Pete continued. "That's stood up to a .357 Magnum, an Uzi, and even a 12 gauge shotgun. It's ten times stronger than steel."

"What the hell is it, Pete?"

"It's the best we have in bulletproof vests. Feel it. Thin, lightweight high-performance ballistic material. There're two layers of fibers in there that cross each other at zero and 90 degree angles. That'll stop anything!"

"Can I take a shower in it?" joked Owen.

"Funny man! Well, as a matter of fact, you can! Moisture doesn't bother it one bit. No, don't take it off! Wear it! Get used to it. It may save your life."

Owen didn't protest. He put his shirt and jacket on over the vest and turned around to find Pete Wolfe holding a pistol towards him. "Take it!"

Owen grabbed the pistol almost in mid-air. Pete could see the surprise on his face. "Light! Feels good. Handles well."

"It should. That's the new 9mm Walther P99. I think it's the best on the market. Only weighs about 21 ounces. Ten round magazine. It's yours. You may need it."

Thirty-two

New York

Owen MacDara liked to stay at the Plaza. He
admitted to himself that he was a creature of habit.
There was something 'Old Worldly' about the Plaza,
its facade, inner foyer and courtyard. Especially the
Oak Room, he thought, as he sat at the bar and
ordered a draught Coors while he waited for Leslie
Scott to join him.

MacDara was as much a creature of that Old
World as he was of this New World. As he sipped
his beer and waited he felt 'those old stirrings again'.
Dormant until Anna Yachmi had reawakened them.
He told himself that it was too soon after Kate's
death. But Kate would disagree. She'd say that the
best tribute to their love was to love again. *Oh hell,
that sounds like a line from a cheap romance novel. I
have to work with this woman, not bed her! But first
I want to see what makes her tick.* Owen had these
thoughts as he pushed his empty glass across the bar
and rose to meet Leslie Scott. He immediately
approved. She had removed the glasses, probably
exchanged them for contact lenses, and the Armani

suit had been replaced by sleek black leather pants and a red three-quarter-length jacket.

"Leslie, I'm taking you somewhere special. Let me surprise you," said Owen, as he steered her towards the main lobby. The concierge hailed a taxi and ten minutes later they were dropped between First and Second Avenues, directly at curbside in front of Costelloes. The entrance was carved out of an old brownstone, the awning was faded and the two steps down to the door were not well lighted. Owen guided Leslie lightly by the arm.

"It's not Le Cirque, it's not Lutece, it's not even The Leopard. But it's home to me," said Owen, as he pushed open the door directly into the bar.

They were early for the drinking crowd. Just a few regulars at the bar. Most of them nodded approvingly to Owen as he pushed through ahead of Leslie to the rear dining room. Jim Connolly stood guard at the entrance, able to keep an eye on the bar and greet his friends and customers personally.

"Your own table is ready any time, Owen," said Jim, looking appraisingly at Leslie.

"Thanks, Jim," said Owen and, standing aside, brought Leslie face-to-face with Jim Connolly, "I'd like you to meet Leslie Scott," and, turning to Leslie, "Leslie, this is Jim Connolly, the boss of this fine establishment. He's also my very good friend."

"It's a pleasure to meet you, Jim," said Leslie.

"No, Leslie! The pleasure is mine. I hope you'll become a member of our little club. I'll let Owen propose you for membership any day! Isn't that right, Owen?" quipped Jim, as he escorted them to the round table in the corner, the best table in Costelloes.

"I'll send John over later to take your order," said Jim, as he placed two menus in front of them, "now, what will you have to drink?"

"I'll have a gin and tonic. Tanqueray, with a slice of lime," said Leslie.

"Sounds good! Make that two, Jim. Thank you," said Owen.

Big Jim Connolly headed towards the bar. Owen looked around the small restaurant with the familiar photographs on the wall, the famous and the nobodies. They all mixed with ease at Costelloes. It had been months since he'd last been here. With Kate. Big Jim was discreet. He never mentioned that. Leslie broke the silence. It was as though she were reading his mind.

"Tell me about Kate, Owen."

"What can I tell you? I loved her. It's as simple as that."

"You still love her, don't you?" probed Leslie.

"I still remember my love for her, if that's what you mean. That will never die."

"But I sense she's not just a memory, Owen," persisted Leslie.

"Tonight she isn't. I thought I could bring you here, but I was wrong. This place was very special to us. I can feel her here. Does that make sense to you?" admitted Owen.

"Yes, it does. That's why I asked about Kate. You need to talk about her," said Leslie.

Just then little John arrived with their gin and tonics. Owen placed his usual order. The baked clams, followed by the junior sizzler, medium rare, and a bottle of Mondavi cabernet sauvignon. Leslie deferred to Owen's judgement and let him order the same for her. Owen raised his glass and offered a toast. "To memories. And, to Kate!"

"To Kate! And to you, Owen!" toasted Leslie.

The steak was perfect, the Mondavi was a good year, and their table seemed an oasis in the now crowded and bustling pub. Over dinner Owen told

Leslie everything she hadn't learned from General Shields. He wasn't much good at talking about himself, about his own accomplishments. But he was a natural raconteur when provoked. By the time their after-dinner drinks had arrived, Leslie knew everything about the past three years, about the plot to overthrow the President, about the disappearance of Kate's father, and about the cult of the *Circle of Sodom*. When he had finished she said, "That was only a year ago. Now we're threatened again. And it's not just the US this time!"

"I won't kid you, Leslie. I've got bad vibes about this whole business. We have no time to waste. Let's hope we get lucky tomorrow," said Owen.

Owen and Leslie decided to divide and conquer. She would take Nadia Pankin. He would take Sarah Kearns.

Thirty-three

Leslie Scott knew she couldn't use the usual sources this time. She couldn't afford to have her interest in Nadia Pankin reported to 'the company'. But there was another way. She decided to call in a debt – a debt owed from her days as an Assistant District Attorney in the city. Climbing out of the subway onto Flatbush Avenue in Brooklyn, the aroma of borscht perfumed the air. Vegetable stands and street vendors decorated the otherwise mean streets. Russian and heavily accented English competed with the noise of babies crying. Somewhere, above her, someone was playing Tchaikovsky.

Out of breath she paused on the fifth floor landing as the dramatic first movement of Tchaikovsky's violin concerto reached a crescendo behind the door to apartment 5a. She had half expected to find the music coming from Old Theodore's. She rang the doorbell over and over again but got no response so she resorted to banging the door with her fist as loudly as she could. Finally she heard a movement at the peephole and then the sound of the iron police security bar being removed. The door opened and Old Theodore stood there. The bushy eyebrows, the sparkling blue eyes with the deep crow's feet and the salt-and-pepper mustache adorned a face illuminated by the biggest grin she'd ever seen. He stepped out into the hallway and kissed her on both cheeks, taking her by the arm and guiding her through the door into his apartment.

"Ah, Leslie, what a pleasure to see you. It's been too long. After you called this morning I was so excited. How long? Five years, maybe six? But you're a busy person. Big important job down there in Washington. Sorry for the mess. Watch your feet there. Let me move these out of your way." He rambled on as he guided her past dozens of icons in various stages of completion.

"Theodore, don't worry about it! Are these all yours? They're marvelous," said Leslie.

"Agh!" The disgust came from deep in the old man's throat. "Fakes! They use a fancy word for them. Reproductions! Nonsense! They're fakes! If I was good enough to imitate the work of Rublev they could call it a reproduction. These! They're fakes! But I have to live. Enough of this! Here, you must sit with me," and he guided Leslie to an overstuffed armchair and turned toward the direction of the music.

"I'll turn it low so we can talk. Did you know he only wrote one violin concerto? Peter Ilich Tchaikovsky. My Peter, our Peter, carries the same name," he said, as he returned, pulled up a chair and sat beside her.

"How is Peter doing?" asked Leslie.

"Second year in medicine. Harvard Medical School. He's going to be a fine doctor. Saving lives, not destroying them. We owe his life to you, Leslie. We never forget that," answered Old Theodore.

"No, no, Theodore. Peter saved himself. I only gave him a chance to do that," said Leslie, as she remembered.

Remembered the young man, addicted to heroin, caught with four other gang members after a string of robberies and break-ins. A young man who had lost his parents in a horrific car accident a year earlier. A young man on the road to self-destruction. But a young man with a grandfather who believed in him. Leslie could have prosecuted him to the limit of the law, but she didn't. Old Theodore had been persuasive.

The old man had got up again. Now he returned with two glasses and a bottle of red wine. Looking at Leslie, he said, "I know you didn't come here to drink wine with an old man. It's a nice thought. But why should I deceive myself! You need my help. I can tell. Maybe I can pay you back a little for Peter. It would make me feel good."

So Leslie took Old Theodore into her confidence. She didn't tell him everything. Just enough to let him understand that his two beloved countries were in trouble. She didn't have to explain why she couldn't use her own sources. Old Theodore understood that implicitly. Years of Soviet repression had left him with complete distrust for organizations like the KGB and the CIA. He had good sources. Good contacts in Moscow. Now that the Communists were no longer in control it was easier to get information, easier to get people to talk. Yes, he would find out everything he could about Nadia Pankin. If there was anything to find out.

Thirty-four

Owen MacDara reckoned that Greeks ran every coffee shop and diner worth eating in. They had taken over the business. He didn't care. He always headed for Nick's Diner if he felt like having a huge breakfast. They had all day breakfast. It was Nick Papanikolau's speciality. That, and friendly waitresses who plied you with hot coffee from the moment you sat down. When he learned that Sarah Kearns worked the morning shift at Nick's, Owen felt that he could kill two birds with one stone. He was in the mood for one of Nick's big breakfasts.

Tucked away in the fifties off Lexington, the neon strip lights over the door announced Nick's Diner to the hungry. Nick was a big, beefy, gregarious man with a walrus moustache. He didn't cook any more. Now he acted as maitre d'; more like a friendly dictator to customers and staff alike. He greeted Owen like a long lost brother, flashing the gold in his two eyeteeth and herding him to a corner table.

"The usual, Owen?" stated Nick.

"That's right, Nick. But, wait a minute, I want to ask you something," said Owen, as Nick prepared to leave.

"Ask me anything," responded Nick.

Owen, in lowering his voice, implied that Nick should do the same. "Do you have a waitress called

Sarah Kearns?"

"Yes, I do. See there. That's her, standing at the counter now."

"I'd like her to serve me, Nick. Can't explain at this time but it's important. Do you mind?" asked Owen.

"Not at all. Anything for a good customer, my friend," said Nick.

In less than a minute, there she was. Hovering at his table with a large pot of coffee. A willowy, slightly built blonde with a friendly face, beautiful greenish eyes and wispy long hair. The nametag on her uniform said 'Sarah.'

"Would you like some coffee, sir?" asked Sarah.

"Yes, please. But call me Owen. Nick always does," answered Owen.

"Sure will. Owen's better," smiled Sarah.

"Haven't seen you here before," said Owen.

"No. I'm new. Started a couple of weeks ago. Mornings only," answered Sarah.

"I know! You're doing a Ph.D. at night," quipped Owen.

"No, no," laughed Sarah, "actually I'm studying acting and I'm an understudy in a play in the Village two nights a week."

"I'm impressed!" said Owen.

Sarah had presented Owen with the menu as they were talking. "Have you decided what you'd like?" she interjected.

"No decision. I always have Nick's Special. Best breakfast in the world. And make it whole-wheat toast, please."

"That'll be about fifteen minutes," said Sarah, as she headed toward the kitchen.

Exactly fifteen minutes later, Sarah reappeared with

a large, hot platter full of Nick's Special: thick sausages, home fries with onions, two eggs over easy, Canadian bacon, fried mushrooms and tomatoes. A stack of whole-wheat toast appeared almost from nowhere.

"One Special, as ordered," announced Sarah.

"Geez, I'd better be hungry," said Owen, as he accepted more coffee.

"Sarah, suppose you get famous. I don't even know your last name," said Owen.

"You mean if I'm discovered and become a big star or something. That's a dream! I just want to be a good actress – that's all. And the name is Kearns. Sarah Kearns," said Sarah.

"Kearns, Kearns, Kearns... You know, that name rings a bell," said Owen.

"Oh, it's a common enough name," said Sarah over her shoulder, as she moved away again to take an order from the couple at the next table.

Owen realized that his subterfuge would get him nowhere. *This girl will see through me right away. I'd better play it straight with her. No matter what happens.* That decided, Owen tucked into the sausages and eggs, sharing a funny memory with himself. *Kate used to say that I got real horny every time I ate sausages.* He was just about finished when Sarah appeared with more coffee.

"Refill?" she asked.

"Thanks, Sarah," said Owen, and before she could turn away, "I need to talk with you for a couple of minutes. Please sit down. I'm not putting the make on you, I swear!"

"But I'm busy, Owen," Sarah protested, "Nick wouldn't like me sitting with a customer."

"Nick understands. Why do you think he sent you over to serve me? I asked him. Please! Just for a minute."

Reluctantly, Sarah sat down opposite him, looking wary about the invitation.

"Sarah, I'll come clean. I knew your name when I came in here. I apologize for leading you on, but please listen. When I explain, you'll understand." Owen gulped down the rest of his coffee and jumped right in. "I came here to get you to talk about your father. But I realized very soon that I couldn't fool you. So I've decided to be up front about it. I need to know how he is and I need to see him right away."

Sarah's face said it all. The openness was gone. Her countenance now carried a look of hostility. "What do you want with my father, Owen? If that's your name!"

"Believe me, Owen's my real name. And believe this too – your father's life may be in danger – an operation he was involved in years ago. I need to see him."

"My father's retired. He sees no one any more. You're wasting your time talking to me."

"Has he ever talked to you or your mother about the Congo?"

"Listen, why should I even listen to you? Maybe you want to harm my father!"

The President had given him identification carrying the Presidential seal of authority. Owen reached for the wallet in his inside pocket and produced it. He seldom used it but, when he did, it was accepted. Sarah was no exception.

"My father never talks about the past. He and Mom left all that behind. My dad has withdrawn from the world. He goes nowhere, sees nobody. Mom and I are his whole world these days."

"But, if I'm right, he could be in danger. I need to see him. Will you do one thing for me? Please talk to him. Ask him to see me."

173

"I'll try. But I still think you're wasting your
time. I'm going home for the weekend. I'll talk to
him. I won't promise you more than that. You can
come to the house but it may still be a wasted trip."

"Thank you, Sarah. I'll take my chances."

It was twelve noon when Owen emerged into the
Manhattan midday sunlight. Trying for a taxi at
that time of day on Third Avenue was total futility.
After ten minutes he gave up and, instead, decided to
walk a few blocks downtown. If he still hadn't found
a taxi in thirty minutes time he reckoned he'd give
the subway a try. It'd been years since he had ridden
the thing. Gave it up at just about the time it
became too dangerous and he could afford to pay
cabfares. He found his mind wandering to his first
days in New York, the walkup tenement apartment
in the Bronx, the crowded IRT subway line in the
morning, filled with voyeurs, gropers and garlic
breaths.

Crossing the street, he walked over to
Lexington Avenue and headed south. The streets
were filled with the lunchtime crowd and the smell of
pizza and hotdogs. The aroma of food wafted out of
every eating place, each competing for their share of
the lunchtime business. MacDara figured that if he
hadn't already stuffed himself at the Greek's place
he'd surely be unable to withstand the onslaught on
his senses. What did Oscar Wilde say? *I can resist
everything but temptation!*

At 53rd Street he decided to take the subway
across town. The escalator was crowded and he
squeezed on between a lady overloaded with
shopping bags and a vacant-eyed teenager chewing
gum. When he reached the platform a train was
pulling out leaving behind some people in groups of

two and three.   MacDara found an open space but not for long. Within five minutes the steady stream of people flowing off the escalator had filled every available space around him.   Two young Hispanic men approached.

"Hey, man, what train do we take to Long Island City?"

MacDara was wary. He felt vulnerable. He was about to say he didn't know when an elderly gentleman standing near answered: "It's only one stop from here but you're on the wrong platform. Go back up again and come down on the other side."

"Hey, Pops! Thanks!" they said in unison, and headed back towards the up escalator just as the cross-town train pulled in.   The surge of people, pushing their way on board, carried MacDara through the open doors. Inside he tried to hang on to an overhead handle but it was futile.   The train lurched forward into the tunnel and the mass of people heaved to and fro. He stretched out his arms and braced himself against the window to prevent himself being dumped into the lap of the person seated directly beneath him. When they reached the 5th Avenue station he decided he'd had enough and pushed and shoved his way towards the doors. When they opened he was thrust on to the platform and almost trampled by the stampede behind him. Struggling to regain his balance he found himself *looking directly into the face of Conor Brady!*

Too late! The gun in Brady's hand exploded against his chest and the impact propelled him back into an upright pillar saving him from plunging to the tracks below. Stunned, he tried to get his breath. He could see Conor Brady merge with the departing throng. He pushed himself to his feet, thanking Pete Wolfe for the bulletproof vest, and walked painfully to the exit signs, one step at a time.   When he reached the street, his breathing had returned but his chest felt as though it had been hit with a sledgehammer. He stood and looked north and south on 5th Avenue, the palm of his hand resting on the Walther P99 inside his jacket.

Thirty-five

Moscow

"Bez bumazhki ty bukashka, a s bumazhkoi chelovek"

"Without papers you are an insect, with papers you are a person"

The *pod'yezd,* the main entrance to the apartment building, was cheerless and drafty. Four or five young men, unsteady on their feet, lurked inside, smoking and sharing a bottle of vodka. They stopped talking and looked hard at Anna Yachmi as she entered. They made no move toward her and she thought that their powerlessness had emasculated them, rendered them harmless, worthless.

The apartment building was a *Krushchovki,* named after Nikita Krushchev, the man who had created them. All *Krushchovki* are pre-fabricated, five story buildings, constructed quickly – and poorly – to meet the housing demand in the fifties. Anna had come here to find Yuri, the Insect. Yuri had no residence papers, and was living illegally in Moscow.

Russians without papers are 'insects', as their proverb states.

Documentation, *dokumenty,* rules Russia. The most important piece of *dokumenty* is the residence registration stamp. There are at least three ways to get residence papers: being born in the place of residence, being married to a resident, or buying an apartment. Without papers a person is illegal and can be fined, expelled or even jailed. But the system was being tested. The new mobility, the opening of the free market, the need to move to find work created a whole subclass of insects.

Yuri had been living illegally in Moscow for as long as anyone could remember. He had earned the sobriquet, 'Insect.' No one knew where he came from. Yuri's talent, his genius, protected him. Employers with power and clout made sure that the militia left him alone. Yuri was a computer programmer. But he was that rarity in the profession, a true creative genius. He was one of just three or four computer network experts in Moscow. He was the best. His latest skill made him the best in Java, the language created by Sun Microsystems in California. The Insect had left Moscow only once since he had moved there. It was in those early months after the collapse of the Soviet Union when the Americans were scrambling all over the place. Their bankers, political gurus and technocrats were everywhere. Even religious zealots, from the Mormons to the Moonies had invaded. The American technocrats had 'discovered' the Insect on one of those early projects and had taken him to Boston for six months on one of their temporary work visas. He had spent that six months at Sun Microsystems Labs Boston Center for Networking where he became a member of the team exploring ideas outside the mainstream and working on projects of high risk and great uncertainty. He had worked on the programming language Java and experimented with Smart Cards and an imaginative new device called a Java Ring. The Java Ring looked exactly like an American high school class ring but it was capable of storing information and holding a 'purse' of digital cash. The Insect was working on ways of transferring such cash or information over a tiny 115bps ring reader to other Java Rings. Truly futuristic stuff! And the Insect loved it!

But it was another experiment that fascinated him even more – the attempt to find a way of delivering huge amounts of video at high speeds over an ordinary copper wire telephone line – the network that already connected most people on the planet. If they could deliver over the telephone line the kind of images that only could be received from satellite or high bandwidth fiber optic cable networks the possibilities behind such a quantum leap in communication were limitless. Sun Microsystems used one of those grand computer terms to name this experiment: 'multicasting technology'. Sun was still working on it but, unknown to them, the Insect had continued to work on it after his return to Moscow and he now had a working prototype that could deliver videos and live television over the telephone lines and, most importantly, over the Internet. He had been fortunate in finding a champion to fund his work. His champion was Mikhail Kedrov.

The door to Yuri's *Krushchovka* apartment was ajar. Anna pushed it open and stepped inside. At first she heard nothing but then the faint sound of Yuri's nervous cough reached her. She went towards it and found him seated with his back to her and his elbows on the windowsill. He was oblivious to his surroundings. Yuri lived in his head. She said his name but he didn't seem to hear. She moved closer until she could see what he was doing. He was bent over and his head almost touched the windowsill. A small round cosmetic mirror lay flat in front of him and he was assiduously picking his nose with the index finger of his left hand. A ream of computer printout paper tumbled askew like a broken accordion near his right hand while he made rapid marks on it with a blue marker gripped tightly in his right fist. Anna spoke his name again, almost shouting it. Yuri stopped, looked around and saw her. He showed no embarrassment, just a big wide grin that transformed the cherubic jowls of his Mongol-like face. His hair was crewcut and spiky. He stood up and his baggy suit and roly-poly figure made him look comical.

"Anna, Anna! I did not hear you!"

"That's all right, Yuri. I brought you something."

She took a box out of her bag and handed it to him. He opened it eagerly and then shrieked with joy. It was a large box of Cadbury's chocolates. Yuri was a chocoholic who could only satisfy his addiction with imported chocolate. Cadbury's was his favorite. He offered one to Anna but she declined and then, his mouth crammed, he squeezed out the words as a dribble of chocolate emerged at the corner of his mouth. "What do you want me to do?"

"Why do you think I want you to do something?"

"Anna, Anna! A gift like this is not for nothing! You know I would do anything for these. Now, tell me, what do you need?"

"You're right, Yuri. I do need you. But first I must explain why."

Yuri pulled over two chairs for himself and Anna. He beckoned her to sit beside him. Anna started to describe the computer system she was building for Kedrov Industries, especially the communications network. Misha Kedrov had specified a system that could hold *public* and *private* talks. Its *public* face could communicate over the Internet and access any other system. Its *private* face would speak only to those who had the right access, the right security clearance to penetrate the impermeable firewalls they were building into the system.

As she spoke, Anna could see Yuri's face become more and more animated until a nervous tic appeared under his right eye. She continued: "We're building that 'private' face. It's almost impossible. A 'drop dead' target date and now we've run into 'bugs'. That's why I'm here, Yuri."

Yuri's nervous tic increased and he looked like he was going to say something but changed his mind and pushed a chocolate into his mouth.

"I found your signature on one of the programs. Somebody linked the wrong program, your program, and I've been 'bombing out' for days! What's going on, Yuri? I need to know."

His chest swelled up and he looked like he was going to burst, looked like he'd been holding something in that he wanted to talk about for a long time. He leaned over and reached for Anna's hand. She reached out and held his hand between both of hers. Yuri started to talk and the more he talked the more excited he became. Often Anna would have to stop him so that she could understand what he was saying. He told her about his experiment, how he had found a way to deliver video at high speed over an ordinary telephone line and how Misha Kedrov had financed it. Now Anna was excited too.

"It's you! You're Kedrov's *public face!* We thought that that was only a dream of Misha Kedrov's. We knew that no one had done it. But you have! Kedrov knew this all the time, didn't he? He only wanted our system as a base, as a launching platform! What is he up to, Yuri? What is he going to use it for?"

Puzzlement crept over Yuri the Insect's face, then concern, then disappointment. He was disappointed that he could not tell Anna what she wanted to know.

"Anna, Oh Anna! I'm sorry. I don't know what it's for. I only know that I had to get it finished before he went to that Yeltsin conference this month."

"You mean G8? The one that Yeltsin's going to in England."

"That's it! G8! Yes, that's it. Alexandr knows. Alexandr knows everything!"

PART FIVE

The Wainwright Confession

Pat Mullan

Thirty-six

Deep River,
Connecticut

General Bartley Shields was at his house in Deep River, Connecticut, when he got the call from CIA Director Richard Smallwood. Smallwood was in New York on company business so it was easy to take the Amtrak train to Essex, a small sleepy town on the Connecticut River, about a twenty-minute drive from Shields' house. As he got down from the train, dragging his bag behind him, he didn't recognize the General standing on the other side of the railroad tracks, wearing jeans that were threadbare at the knees and a misshapen Aran sweater that had seen better days.

Bart Shields took his hands out of his pockets, waved a greeting and waited as Dick Smallwood crossed the tracks. A few minutes later they headed out of Essex in Shields' ten-year-old Mercedes.

The general's house was deceptive. At first glance it appeared to be a single story ranch but that was only the 'tip of the iceberg'. Once inside, the house revealed its secret: three stories clung to the hillside and a second story deck captured the panorama of the Connecticut River and the lush, surrounding countryside. The evening was warm and the sky a clear blue, perfect for the table that awaited them out on the deck. Dick Smallwood was a vegetarian and Millie Shields, renowned among the Washington wives for her skill in the kitchen, had prepared a vegetarian goulash with wild rice followed by her special dessert of pears in red wine sauce. Bart already had a bottle of good Chablis cooling on ice and proceeded to decant a bottle of Cousino Macoul, his favorite Chilean red.

Listening to Dick Smallwood's superlatives about the 'best vegetarian goulash he'd ever had' and watching her husband circumcise a fresh macanudo cigar, Millie knew it was time to make her exit.

Bart Shields reached for the tall black bottle of Otard and poured two generous glasses of cognac. They both sipped and savored in silence, lulled into a feeling of wellbeing by Millie's marvellous meal, the excellent cognac and the peaceful vista that stretched beneath them to the horizon. Shields finally broke the silence.

"Dick, I gather you've got something important to tell me."

"That's right, Bart," replied Smallwood, as he reached into the inner pocket of his jacket and retrieved a small, black, scuffed and dog-eared notebook. Handing it across the table, he said: "Read the first three pages."

Shields opened the notebook and, looking at the small, dense writing, fished his reading glasses from his breast pocket. It seemed obvious that the writer had wanted to cram as much as possible into the notebook. He read the first page:

This is my insurance policy, life insurance to be exact, and I hope that it never needs to be used. On the other hand, maybe this story can be told when I am dead – to set the record straight, to correct the falsehoods of history. I haven't decided that yet. For now, its only purpose is to keep me alive. This notebook will be made public if I meet an untimely end. Everything recorded here is true.
This I swear by Almighty God.

Signed this 5th day of October, 1969, John Casey Wainwright

The next two pages were written in the same dense style so it took Shields' full concentration. His cognac sat untouched and the ashes on his cigar had outgrown the ashtray and toppled onto the table. But he was oblivious to all of that. Snatches of Wainwright's 'insurance policy' seared themselves into his brain:

I was there when Director Dulles ordered the assassination of Patrice Lumumba... we were protecting the billions we had invested in the Congo's mineral resources... Helms has destroyed all the documents... my words written here will be all that survive... it was the decision to take out Dag Hammarskjold that has destroyed me... Washington and Moscow are in collusion...

Shields read the last paragraph at the bottom of page three before closing the notebook and looking across at Dick Smallwood:

> *...on the following pages I have recorded the key events and decisions covering CIA involvement in Africa. The dates and locations of each event are accurate. I have identified the people who participated, including those who made the decisions and gave the orders. Where I was present I have admitted that. Where I was culpable I have said so. I am not using this to exonerate myself.*

"Wainwright! Didn't he disappear from the face of the earth? Just like Judge Crater!" asked Shields, rhetorically.

"Yes! He disappeared. About a year after he wrote this. He left the company and just dropped out of sight. It was news for a couple of weeks until it was pushed off the page," replied Smallwood.

"Rumor had it that he was in the running for Director once upon a time," said Shields, seeking confirmation of his recollection.

" I believe if the timing had been right for the appointment of a Director from within the company, he'd have made it. Jack Wainwright had the inside track," confirmed Smallwood.

"How did you get this notebook? And what happened to him?" asked Shields.

"I'll take your last question first, Bart," said Smallwood, as Shields reached over and refilled his cognac glass, pushing aside a weak protest. "Around the time Wainwright was writing this he was also getting ill. Severe allergic reactions. Heart palpitations. Rashes. Lupus."

"Lupus! I thought that was a woman's disease," interjected Shields.

"That's what I thought too, Bart. So I've educated myself on the subject. Apparently a small percentage of men also suffer from the disease. There are basically two forms of it, systemic and drug induced. Some people have gotten lupus from medication, especially drugs that are used to control heart arrhythmia. Nobody seems to know what causes systemic lupus. There was no agreement in Wainwright's case and he had not been on any heart medicine. Some people believed that his ailments were stress related. Others, less kind, said that it was all in his mind, that it was psychological, self-induced. At any rate, he got worse and worse until he couldn't work any more. This was all kept quiet by the company, of course."

"What happened to him?"

"Well, he was finally diagnosed with something called MCS, although most of the medical profession will not acknowledge that there is such a disease."

"What's MCS?"

"Multiple chemical sensitivities. Wainwright had developed severe allergic and immune system reaction to anything and everything that was remotely chemical. And, in our modern world, that means practically everything."

Smallwood was caught up in the drama of his story and Shields noted that he had barely touched the last cognac he'd given him. Getting up from the table he stretched himself, looked out over the Connecticut River, and then turned towards Shields.

"But we think he may still be alive although no one, not even his family, has heard from him in at least ten years. He quit the agency, left everything and everyone and went in search of a place that was free from the poisons that were killing him. He has one daughter and she last heard from him ten years ago. From Fort Davis, Texas."

"Fort Davis? That's as far west in Texas as you can get?"

"It sure is!" said Smallwood, sitting down again and taking a sip of his cognac.

"Now to answer your first question. I'm afraid we got his notebook by devious means. We discovered that he had instructed his daughter to turn it over to the *Washington Post* after his death. The rest was simple. We faked a death certificate and convinced her that he was dead. Then we waited. About a week later she called the *Washington Post.* She didn't know that we were intercepting her calls. So it was easy to set up a sting operation and pose as the *Washington Post.* She had no reason to suspect anything so she turned over the notebook to us."

There was the suggestion of a smile on Smallwood's face, like the look of satisfaction on the face of a cat that had just swallowed a mouse.

"Jeez, Dick!" Shields exclaimed. "You don't give a shit about the laws of the land, do you?"

Smallwood didn't answer that. Shields picked up Wainwright's notebook again, opened it and said, softly, almost to himself: "There's one thing that I must know. Who ordered the assassination of Dag Hammarskjold?"

He paged through the notebook, almost reluctant to find the answer. When he did he read it without breathing, then he sank deeper into his chair deflating like a large balloon that has just burst. Smallwood looked at him.

"Now you know why I had to see you here.

Away from Washington."

"Who else knows this?" asked Shields.

"Only you and me. And Wainwright. If he's still alive," Smallwood replied.

"Well, if he is alive, he may not stay alive much longer. We'd better find him fast. I suggest we get MacDara on this immediately."

"I agree. Where is he?"

"He and Leslie Scott are in New York. Nyack. They went to talk to Kearns."

Thirty-seven

Key Biscayne,
Florida

Victor Kasparov pulled his Bronco off the road and
into the trees that grew thick around the sheltered
cove on Key Biscayne. It was a calm evening, dark
but moonlit. The few boats in the cove lay at anchor
in the silent black water. Everyone had gone home.
The vista looked more like a large painting than a
scene from real life.   He checked his watch.
Midnight. If everything went according to plan he
reckoned that he would have to wait only forty-five
minutes. He took out his binoculars, infrared for
night vision, and laid them on the dashboard. Then
he yanked a cold can of Budweiser from the plastic
ring holding the six-pack together. Popping the
aluminum ring, he took a gulp and settled back for
the wait.

Everything had indeed gone according to plan.
Fifty minutes later he saw the shape of the Russian

diesel-driven Kilo submarine surface just outside the cove, and watched as two figures climbed into a dinghy and detached themselves from the sub. He waited until they were closer and then flashed the prearranged signal. They didn't return his signal but he knew he had made contact. Watching through the binoculars, he saw them change direction and head directly toward the northern point of the cove, where he had positioned himself. Sweeping the water beyond, he could no longer see the sub.

Twenty minutes later, they had disposed of their wet suits and dinghy and were in the Bronco heading out of Key Biscayne and north on US 1. Victor had given each a Bud from his six-pack.

"Victor, good beer, but I need some Stoli, babe!" laughed the stockier, younger one in an almost too-perfect American twang. The older, cavernous one said nothing.

"Rudi, you're going to my place tonight and you can have anything you want. Stoli! Girls! Whatever! Tonight you party. Tomorrow we go to work."

Thirty minutes later Victor edged his Bronco into his reserved space outside his strip club, Lucky Vic's, under the flyover west of Miami International Airport. A large floodlit helium balloon proclaiming 'Girls, Girls, Girls' on one side and 'Triple XXX Rated' on the other, intended to entice drivers off the highway, hung overhead. Dancers from the former Soviet Union and Latin America stripped to the grinding, erotic beat of the music as sailors, businessmen and victims lured from the highway downed their Stoli and beer. Victor deposited his guests at the runway that connected the center stage with the large horseshoe bar that bordered the interior. He ordered a bottle of Stoli for them and watched as one of the dancers invited Rudi to put a dollar in the luminous string bikini she barely wore. Then he made an exit to his office in the rear of the club.

Easing his large frame into his leather upholstered executive chair, he turned on his PC, moused into his e-mail system and sent a message to Misha in Moscow: *Dolphins arrived safe.* Then he poured himself a double Chivas Regal, noting that he now preferred scotch to vodka, and tilted back in his chair contemplating the next days with some relish. He hadn't been on a 'field' assignment in a long time but he had insisted on leading this one. He supposed that Misha considered him too valuable to risk but had to balance that against the need to succeed this time. This assignment seemed like a piece of cake. His biggest problem might be Rudi and his silent partner but he had to admit they were well qualified. *Nyack.* He let the word roll around on his tongue. He liked the sound of it and he liked the place. Just north of New York, nestling on the hillside overlooking the Hudson right beside the Tappan Zee Bridge. Maybe he'd manage to squeeze in a couple of days in the Big Apple, hit the best restaurants, and hang out in some clubs. The Chivas and the daydreaming were as good as a sedative for Victor Kasparov that night.

Thirty-eight

Nyack,
New York

Joe Kearns reminded himself for the umpteenth time that he would have to fix 'that damn gate.' It clanged loudly every time the wind picked up. Gales were forecast for tonight but he never believed the weathermen. Just a bunch of glib talkers, picked for their ability to perform in front of the camera. Image. That's what it was all about these days. But sometimes they got lucky and got it right. Maybe they'll get lucky tonight. It felt like a storm in his bones. His arthritic hips were acting up again. "Jeez, I'm only sixty-seven. That's not old. Not these days. Still, I should have fixed that damn gate," he told himself, as he eased his car out of the short steep driveway and onto the road that meandered down the hill in front of his home.

Once through Nyack village he checked his watch: 7:15 p.m. If the bus had left the George Washington Bridge station on time, his wife and daughter should be getting off at the bus stop on route 303 in ten minutes. He was in good time. Five minutes later he swung the Ford Taurus into the parking lot outside the diner, adjacent to the bus stop. He hadn't seen his daughter in a couple of months. Sarah had caught the 'acting bug', just like her mother, and was studying at the American Academy of Dramatic Art while she made her living at an endless string of waitress jobs. Nora never made the big time. She'd never been out of work though, always off-Broadway or more often off-off-Broadway. It was Nora who decided they should live in Nyack after he left 'the company'. Just a 'hop and a skip' into Manhattan so they could be near her beloved theater. And, of course, 'Helen Hayes lives in Nyack and so does Richard Kiley's mother.' All these thoughts just tumbled through Joe Kearns' mind as he waited. He didn't have long to wait. About six minutes later the distinctive yellow and red number 10 bus pulled in and four or five people got off. Nora and Sarah were the last two, engaged in animated conversation. Joe hurried to meet them.

At about the time Joe Kearns was picking up his wife and daughter, Victor Kasparov and his two associates were getting off the shuttle bus in the long-term parking lot at Kennedy Airport. It didn't take long to find the Toyota Previa, parked exactly where Victor had been told. Feeling under the rear bumper his hand encountered the small square box anchored by a magnet. The car keys were inside. He opened the door and Rudi and his silent partner jumped in. Victor opened the rear door and found the sports bag hidden beneath a pile of black plastic garbage bags. The weapons they had requested were inside. Satisfied, Victor jumped in the driver's seat, confirmed that he had a full tank of gas, turned the key in the ignition and headed towards the airport exit. Checking his watch he could see that it was 8 p.m. If the traffic was moving they should be in Nyack within the hour, he reckoned.

Thirty-nine

Owen MacDara winced as he and Leslie Scott stepped off the elevator at the Plaza Hotel.

"You're still hurting."

"I'll hurt for a while. But there's no damage, nothing broken. The x-rays proved that."

"And what about this Conor Brady? He's still out there."

"That's right. But I'm not going to let him intimidate me. Redington's men are on his ass. Last report said they believe he's left the city."

"What do you think?"

"I don't know. He's a slippery customer. But we must get to Kearns. We can't let Brady stop us."

Owen noted that it had just passed 9 p.m. as he and Leslie walked down the front steps of the Plaza toward the door of his dark green Jag, held open in anticipation by the eager young valet. MacDara tipped him generously and they moved out into the sparse early evening traffic around Columbus Circle. No gridlock. They should make the east side in five to ten minutes. He was headed for the entrance to the East River Drive. That would take him to the Harlem River Parkway and directly onto the George Washington Bridge. Once across the Hudson it would be a pleasant thirty-minute trip north on the Pallisades Parkway before he reached the Sparkill exit onto Route 303. From there another five minutes or so should see him in Nyack.

"Should be there by 10 o'clock?" asked Leslie, as though reading his mind.

"You're right. Of course there's no guarantees in New York. I remember one night it snowed. Took me six hours to get to the Harlem River Parkway! That's normally a fifteen minute ride."

"What are the odds that Kearns will be at home?"

"I don't know. Better that fifty-fifty? We're certainly not going to tell him to expect us. Besides, it's a nice night for a drive."

Just then the first raindrops began to patter the windshield, as though nature was letting him know precisely who was in charge of the evening.

Victor Kasparov drummed his fingers anxiously on the steering wheel as he watched the ambulance pull away from the crash scene up ahead. The two cop cars were still straddled diagonally across the Tappan Zee Bridge and the flashing lights on the tow truck only acted as an irritant. It was 9:15 p.m. and they'd been stuck for half an hour. He knew they'd spoken too soon when they praised themselves for making good time as they crossed Westchester towards the Hudson River. Now they sat in silence. Even Rudi had stopped humming to himself. A Budweiser would have helped. But Victor had a strict rule: no alcohol on a *field* assignment. Finally the logjam ended. The tow truck moved the second vehicle leaving enough room for a single lane of traffic and the cops started to wave them on. It was a snail's pace but, luckily, they were near the head of the line. At 9:30 p.m. they broke free. Victor put the accelerator to the floor and they sped off the bridge into Nyack.

Forty

The logs blazed in Joe Kearns' large fieldstone
fireplace, throwing a warm glow around the three
people sunk into the big cosy chairs in the living
room. Sarah felt the warmth in her cheeks and the
soft carpet caressing the sensitive skin between her
bare toes. The aftertaste of red wine and her
mother's cheesecake covered her tongue in a silky
balm. The wind had blown up outside, making a
noise through the trees like a storm at sea. The
sound made her feel safe inside, almost womblike, as
she looked over at her mother's eyes gently fighting
to stay awake. Lulled into a dream state, it took her
a while to realize that another, harsher sound was
disturbing her world. That, and the swearing of her
father tensed her again.

"That damn gate! Oh, no, your mother
wanted wrought iron," said Kearns, looking
heavenward. "A good teak gate would have been
fine. I suppose I'd better go and see if I can stop the
damn thing from driving us crazy!"

Zipping up his Goretex, he squeezed himself
outside, opening the screen door with his right hand
as he shut the front door with his left. The light rain
of earlier evening had now started to fall in gale-

swept sheets of water. He turned on the flashlight and started down the driveway.

"Your father's been out there for fifteen minutes. What's keeping him?" said Nora Kearns, more to herself than to her daughter, as she poured the hot water into the teapot. It was time for their bedtime snack: cheese, crackers and tea — a nightly ritual for as long as Sarah remembered.

"Oh, mom, don't worry! Dad's had tougher jobs than fixing a gate. If he's not back in five minutes, I'll go get him. OK?" Her mother said nothing. She busied herself with the cheese and crackers and had just made a steaming pot of tea when the front door opened violently and crashed against the wall. Just as violently, Joe Kearns was propelled into the room, ending up in a heap on the floor. Sarah screamed and her mother dropped the teapot spilling the hot amber liquid in an ugly stain across the carpet. Three men stood in the doorway like an apparition.

The taller, older one closed the door and spoke: "Good evening, ladies. It's a shame we had to disturb your evening but we need a little cooperation from Mr. Kearns. As soon as we get that you can get back to your domestic bliss. Ah, blue cheese? I just love it. You must have been expecting us." Victor Kasparov walked to within a few inches of Nora Kearns, who had turned white as a ghost, grabbed a hunk of the cheese, and shoved it into his mouth. The other two stood at the door but Rudi never took his eyes off Sarah.

Losing some of her fear, she yelled angrily: "What do you want? Who are you? We don't have any money! There's nothing worth stealing here!"

"Leave my wife and daughter alone, you

bastards!" The words emitted in raspy gasps from Joe Kearns as he struggled to his feet, blood dripping from a split lip and his right eye puffy and closing. He rushed towards Kasparov but the silent one moved swiftly and pinned both his arms behind his back holding him firmly in place.

"What do you want with my husband?" Nora Kearns' voice was strained but carried clearly in that room, a voice trained to reach the back rows in the theater.

"Just some answers to our questions. Convince your husband to tell us what we want to know and then we'll leave you in peace. We're really quite civilized you know. I find this all so distasteful. And you," Kasparov turned towards Sarah, " my young friend likes you. He's been starved for female company for a long time. Convince your father to talk and I'll do my best to restrain him."

"But I don't know! I never knew!" screeched Kearns.

"I don't believe you! You were the CIA number 2 in the Congo in '61. You and Zhukov paid to have Hammarskjold assassinated. We want to know who gave you the orders. It's that simple. I know you've been trained to resist. But don't even try. Comrade, take the young lady upstairs," said Kasparov.

"No! No! No!" screeched Kearns as Rudi, leering from ear to ear, grabbed Sarah and pulled her after him up the stairs while Nora, overcome, collapsed into the nearest armchair.

Forty-one

"What did I say? No guarantees in New York?" said Owen MacDara as they slowed to a crawl on the Pallisades Parkway. The mild patter of raindrops that had greeted them as they left the Plaza had turned into a downpour, reducing visibility and slowing the traffic to ten miles per hour at times.

"At this rate we'll be lucky to get there by 10:30 p.m. They'll probably be in bed. That's where all sensible people should be on a night like this, isn't it Leslie?" said Owen.

Leslie, pretending she didn't notice the lascivious tone in his voice, said: "There's nothing we can do about it so we might as well relax and enjoy." She reached over, inserted a Van Morrison cassette, and listened to Van warning that *there'd be days like this.'*

Sarah's screams reverberated through the house.

"For God's sake, Joe, if you know anything, tell them. Stop being a bloody hero!" Nora had mustered all her remaining strength to yell the words at her husband just as Sarah stumbled down the stairs naked and terrified with Rudi in pursuit. He caught her hair at the bottom of the stairs and pulled, knocking her off balance onto her knees in front of him.

"You see, Joe, we didn't need all this unpleasantness. But we still haven't convinced you that we're serious, have we?" said Victor Kasparov looking at the silent one and nodding his assent. It only took a split second. The silent one pulled a pistol from his pocket, stepped toward Nora Kearns and shot her right between the eyes. She stood there suspended for a brief moment, that new black opening in her forehead, a look of surprise on her face, and then collapsed in a heap exactly where she'd been standing.

"I so regret the necessity of violence," said Kasparov, pulling Sarah away from Rudi and holding his pistol to her temple. The silent one had resumed his position holding a defeated and limp Kearns with his arms pinned behind him.

"Talk to Wainwright. He knows who gave the orders," were the last words that Joe Kearns ever spoke. A single nod from Kasparov and the silent one had Kearns neck in an arm lock. One quick twist, a snap, and Kearns neck was broken. Sarah screamed again just as Kasparov wielded the butt of the pistol against her temple like a mallet.

Owen MacDara and Leslie Scott had just reached Kearns front door when they heard the muffled sound of the shot that killed Nora Kearns. Drowned by the gale the noise was still unmistakable to Owen.

"Jesus Christ! I think we're too late!" he said, advising Leslie to stay put as he made a quick reconnoitre of the ground floor to find a way inside. The garage door was unlocked. He slid it up a few feet, squirmed underneath and tested the door leading from the garage into the house. He was lucky. It hadn't been locked.

"We're done here! Rudi, pick her up and get rid of her. We don't need any witnesses," commanded Victor Kasparov just as the silent one backed into the fireplace from the impact of MacDara's bullet in his chest. Rudi dropped Sarah again, took cover behind one of the overstuffed armchairs and fired twice in Owen's direction, causing Owen to take cover. Kasparov had already concluded that this was a zero sum game and bolted out the front door knocking Leslie Scott to the ground with a solid blow. He disappeared into the dark rain drenched night. Inside, Rudi had made a fatal mistake. He left his cover behind the armchair and made a dash to follow Kasparov. Owen's shot picked him off in mid-flight. His brains mingled with the now drying amber tea stain on the carpet.

Forty-two

**Nyack Hospital,
Three days later**

"You can only see her for fifteen minutes. Doctor's orders," said Nurse Torres, gently but firmly. Owen MacDara and Leslie Scott thanked her and entered Sarah Kearns private room. She was out of bed, sitting in her white hospital robe, staring out of the window into the drab grey parking lot below. She barely acknowledged Leslie's vase of flowers but in response to their get-well wishes, said, "Doctor Bloom told me you wanted to see me. I'm afraid I can't help. I don't know anything." Her voice was dead, a dull monotone.

"Sarah, I know this is difficult for you, but we want to catch your parents' killer. We got two of them but learned nothing. There was no identification on the bodies; even their clothing was untraceable. So far fingerprint searches have turned up nothing," said Owen.

"What can you tell us about the man who got away?" asked Leslie.

"A nasty person. He was in charge. He gave all the orders, did all the questioning. Tall, over six feet, maybe two hundred pounds. Long nose, puffy cheeks. His skin was sallow. He was definitely foreign. Maybe Middle-Eastern." said Sarah.

"What about the other two?" probed Owen, as gently as he could.

Sarah didn't answer for the longest time. Then she started sobbing. Leslie knelt down beside her, held her shoulders and tried to comfort her. Finally she composed herself and answered: "One of them said nothing. He's the one who shot my mother and killed my father. The young one..." she stopped, the words stuck in her throat, and then made a superhuman effort to continue..." raped me again and again, smiling all the time."

"Sarah, I know how difficult it must be for you to talk about it," said Owen.

"But it won't bring my mother and father back, will it?" said Sarah.

It was Owen's turn to lapse into silence. He had no answer for that.

Nurse Torres was hovering at the door, intimating that their time was up, as Leslie asked: "Do you remember anything that would help us, anything at all?"

Sarah nodded to Nurse Torres to tell her it was all right and then she told Owen and Leslie about the questioning of her father, about the insinuations about the Congo, about the assassination of Dag Hammarskjold, and finally about the name, Wainwright, that she heard her father speak just before she screamed and was knocked unconscious.

Leslie hugged her for a while and, as they both prepared to leave, Sarah said, almost pleadingly: "My father could never have done what they said, could he?"

"No, Sarah! Never!" lied Owen.

Forty-three

National Security Council, Washington, DC

Owen MacDara and Leslie Scott had just flown in from New York and they were waiting in General Shields' office when Dick Smallwood arrived. They nodded in greeting.

"Thanks for making it on such short notice, Dick," said Bart Shields. "Things are moving fast and we need to make some decisions. You know about the murder of Kearns and his wife. Owen and Leslie will brief us. Owen?"

Owen related the events in Nyack including the visit with Sarah Kearns in Nyack Hospital and the words that her father had spoken before he was killed: *'Talk to Wainwright. He knows who gave the orders.'*

Shields looked at Smallwood. "Dick, I think it's time for you to brief Owen and Leslie on Wainwright."

Dick Smallwood had already decided that for himself. He liked the intrigue of the Wainwright story and he had had little opportunity to tell it. Once again, he started from the beginning, just as he had done at the general's home in Deep River, Connecticut.

"We have to find Wainwright if he's still alive," said Owen when Smallwood had finished. "We have to get to him before they do."

Leslie Scott seconded that opinion. "Owen's right. It's obvious that these people want to know what Wainwright knows. They want the name of the person who gave the orders for Hammarskjold's assassination."

"But why?" said Dick Smallwood, to no one in particular.

"We don't know why! But does it really matter? Information like that could stop the world, as we know it. And that's no exaggeration!" exploded Bart Shields.

"I can provide the last information we have on Wainwright. Fort Davis, Texas. Ten years ago. I can't put the agency on this. You know that, Bart. If Wainwright left because of what he knows then my agency are the last people I want involved in this," said Dick Smallwood.

"I know that, Dick. I'm sending Owen and Leslie to Fort Davis immediately. It's been four days since Nyack. That gives them a four-day head start on us. If you were able to trace Wainwright to Fort Davis I have no doubt that they can as well," said Shields.

"If we find him alive, what then?" asked Owen.

Shields and Smallwood exchanged glances before the general spoke again. "Owen, Wainwright has information that puts our nation at great risk.

These people must never find out who gave the orders to kill the UN Secretary-General. Whatever it takes. Do you understand?"

Forty-four

Fort Davis, Texas

Owen MacDara and Leslie Scott knew there was no time to lose. They had to get to Wainwright. Smallwood had traced him to Fort Davis all right. But that's as far as he had gotten. No one knew exactly where in Fort Davis. Five days had passed since the killings in Nyack. Five days headstart for the man who had killed Kearns. And then there was Conor Brady to contend with. But first things first. MacDara booked adjoining rooms in the Hotel Limpia right on the Square in the middle of town. He reckoned that they might as well start at the center of things.

As Owen MacDara swung their rented jeep onto Main Street he felt as though they had been transported into nineteenth century frontier America. The original Fort Davis, named after Secretary of War Jefferson Davis, was built around 1854 to protect people migrating west along the Overland Trail from the Commanches and the Mescalero Apaches. The pink limestone facade of the Hotel Limpia dominated the Square. An old cowboy was rocking gently back and forth on the mission rocking chair on the hotel's wide porch as they entered. He tipped the brim of his hat in greeting.

Owen had a good Texas steak in the hotel dining room and Leslie claimed that the blackened grouper was the best she'd ever had. Hunger abated, they headed straight for Sutler's Club, the hotel bar. They reckoned that that was as good a place as any to start their search for Jack Wainwright. They were right. Bill, the bartender, was a local, in his late thirties. He'd lived in Fort Davis all his life but he'd never heard of anyone called Wainwright.

"What you folks need is a scout. That Wainwright's probably holed up out there in Indian Territory. Lots o' weird people out there," said the bartender, " and I reckon Ole Festy's just about the darned best scout in these parts. You musta seen him when you came in. He's been rockin' out on that porch of ours all afternoon."

Ole Festy was still there, just where they left him. The bartender sent him out his favorite tipple, a double Jack Daniels on the rocks, courtesy of Owen MacDara. Owen and Leslie followed and introduced themselves to Ole Festy.

"Pull up a couple o' chairs and take a load off," said Festy.

Owen and Leslie did just that. The bartender arrived with more drinks and Ole Festy was in a talkative mood.

"My ole granpappy was the best Indian scout in these here parts. He lived to be a hundred, ye know. Used to say, hard work, good whiskey and wild women kept the blood flowin' in a man's arteries. I was only a whippersnapper when he died. But I shore remember everythin' he tole' me. Yep! I know them hills jest like he did."

Leslie thought that Ole Festy had inherited his granpappy's affinity for good whiskey. And women too! He had maneuvered his chair closer to Leslie as he talked and his long bony hand with the leathery skin threatened to rest on her knee every now and then. He looked just as though he had stepped off the Overland Trail back in 1860. Under a well-soiled cowboy hat, his bronzed face and wispy mustache belied his seventy-two years. A faded red bandanna adorned his neck and a black vest rode high above his leather gun belt. A Colt 45 was strapped low on his right thigh and his cowboy boots, scuffed and worn at the heels seemed out of place against the gleaming silver spurs that he wore.

"Where'd you say you folks were from?"

"We didn't," said Owen, "but we're from Washington."

"Bill said y'all're lookin' for somebody."

"That's right. Leslie hasn't seen her grandfather in years and she's worried about him. Found out that he was living in these parts but we don't know where. Bill thought you might be able to help us," lied Owen.

"What did you say your granpappy's name was again, dear?" asked Festy.

"Wainwright. Jack Wainwright. Do you know him?" said Leslie.

"Oh, I know him awrighty. But I ain't seen him in months. Don't know whether he's alive or dead. Beggin' yore pardon, ma'am."

"But you know where he lives. You could take us there, couldn't you? We'll pay you."

"Oh, I know where he lives, ma'am. But it ain't easy to find and he don't like people snoopin' around. But, if he's yore granpappy I suppose you gotta, right? I'll take you in the mornin'. But not before ten. I never go anywhere 'fore ten anymore."

Ole Festy was staring into his empty glass and it looked as though he wasn't about to go anywhere until he got another one. Owen smiled at Leslie, then got up and headed for the bar.

Forty-five

Miami, Florida

The system installed in Victor Kasparov's million-dollar home in Cocoplum in Miami was truly state of the art, more advanced than any hardware, software, and communications system on the market. The security and encryption software was the brainchild of the Insect.

Kevin Mourra sat at the console in anticipation. Victor had told him to stand by between two and four p.m. for a video downlink from Texas. He had told him not to decode the transmission, to record it to DVD, two copies, and then to delete all of the transmission from the hard drive. There should be no evidence that they had ever received it.

Mourra was excited. A Haitian with a Palestinian father and an Irish mother, Kevin Mourra had two passions in life: computers and revolution, not necessarily in that order. It had taken him three months to test and install the system. The software was the Insect's. He knew that. He'd spent a month in Moscow working with the Insect. But he had connected the knee bone to the thighbone; he had brought the system to life. He and the Insect had also perfected the transmission in the video camera that Victor had used that day, a revolutionary breakthrough in infrared communication. Victor's camera had transmitted its video signals, via infrared rays, to cordless devices that relayed them to a uplink truck in Fort Davis. From there the satellite transponder would downlink to his system. No videotapes to be confiscated. Untouched by human hand. Foolproof. So what if that Insect weirdo had thought it up. It wouldn't have worked if he hadn't put it all together. It was his creation. And now it was about to give birth.

At exactly 3:45 p.m. Miami time, the downlink of *The Wainwright Confession* began. Kevin Mourra's nervous anticipation translated itself into action. He monitored the transmission, successfully saving it to his hard drive. Then he copied it to two DVDs, and compared the recording on each with the original on his hard drive. Satisfied, he deleted the original from the hard drive and labeled each DVD with the innocuous descriptor: Texas *sales data: Miami office, Kedrov Industries.*

An hour later, Kevin Mourra boarded an American Airlines flight to New York from Miami International Airport. Nadia Pankin was waiting for him at Kennedy Airport. She transferred the DVDs to the Russian diplomatic pouch and placed it on board the departing Aeroflot flight to Moscow. Then she boarded too. She would personally deliver *The Wainwright Confession* to Misha.

Forty-six

Fort Davis, Texas

True to his word, Ole Festy was waiting for Owen MacDara and Leslie Scott in the Square at exactly ten a.m. He was dressed just the same as the day before, right down to the spurs. They jangled as he climbed into the passenger side of the jeep. Leslie rode 'shotgun' in the rear, at least that's the image that flashed through her mind.

"Where to, Festy?" asked Owen.

"That away. Up into the hills. I reckon it'll take an hour before we get there. Then we'll have to leave this thing and go the rest of the way on foot," said Festy.

Owen turned the jeep in the direction that Festy was pointing. "How far do we have to walk?" he asked.

"Three or four miles, I reckon. But it's pretty rough territory. You wearin' a good pair o' boots, ma'am?"

"Festy, I sure am," said Leslie.

Festy explained that they were headed for High Lonesome Mountain in the high desert, rimrock country. About four miles north they reached the

219

Davis Mountains where the ponderosa pine gave way to juniper and oak as they climbed higher. Another ten miles took them as far as they could go in the jeep. They had reached base camp on High Lonesome and they decided to have an early lunch before setting out. Sandwiches and bottled water for Owen and Leslie but Ole Festy had brought along a beer.

"Does that work?" Owen asked, pointing to Festy's Colt 45.

Festy didn't reply. Instead he picked up the empty beer bottle, walked about fifty yards ahead and placed it on an outcrop of rocks. Then he walked back, drew the gun from its holster, fished in his vest pocket for a bullet, opened the chamber and inserted it. Then he took a classic firing stance, faced his target and fired. The shot found its mark and the beer bottle disintegrated. Festy holstered his gun and looked at Owen. "You expectin' to run into a Commanche war party?"

"There might be trouble at Wainwright's and I wanted to make sure you could defend yourself."

"When you hired me you didn't tell me about no trouble! Who wants to hurt yore granpappy?" Festy directed his question to Leslie.

"Oh, Festy, he used to work for the government many years ago. And he made enemies. He also knows things that some people want to find out and they don't ask nice questions to get the answers," said Leslie.

"Well, don't you concern yourself about Ole Festy," said Festy as he slapped the flat of his hand against the gun that clung to his thigh. "I've taken care of critters like that afore."

After eating lunch, they set out. At first the incline was not too steep and they made good progress for half an hour, following in single file behind Festy as he led them through long scrubby grass and juniper trees, until they reached a small spring where they rested before commencing the steeper climb. Other creatures had visited the spring too. Tracks of coyotes and mule deer overlapped each other. This time the climbing was tough and they had to stop for a breather every fifteen minutes. Soon they reached a vantage point in the hills and Festy pointed south to a mountain range on the far horizon:

"Mexico! That's the Chisos Mountains. We're only half a mile from yore granpappy's place. Let's go."

They climbed the next ridge and had almost reached the summit when an angry voice stopped them dead in their tracks: "You're trespassing! This is private property! Landmines protect it. Another twenty yards and you'll be blown to smithereens! Go back the way you came! This is your only warning!"

Festy started to swear, mostly to himself. "God damn! I forgot about this shit! He was setting this up the last time I was here. There are no landmines. He's jest tryin' to scare folks. But he's a damn good shot!"

All the time he was talking he was scrounging around until he found a long stick. Taking his red bandanna from around his neck, he fixed it to the top of the stick and held it high in the air above his head. The gable end of a small cabin was visible on the ridge just above them. Festy yelled: "It's me, Festy! Don't shoot, Wainwright! We're comin' up!"

Festy led the way, holding the stick with his bandanna high over his head like a flag of surrender. When they reached the small one-room cabin there wasn't a sound. The old metal chair on the front porch sat there empty and the front door was slightly ajar.

221

"Maybe he's gone somewhere," speculated Owen.

"Nope. Somethin's amiss here," said Festy.

They went inside and Leslie was unable to suppress a gasp. Metal shelves had been ripped from the wall and bottles of vitamins and homeopathic pills were scattered all over the carpetless floor. A chair was upended, broken, in the corner. But it was the blood that drew their attention. Festy knelt down, put one finger in it, and then brought it up close to his face. He said nothing, just knelt there for a minute and then walked around the cabin and out onto the porch. He walked around the cabin and came back inside.

"It don't look good, dear. Somebody's been hurt bad."

He motioned them to follow him. Outside he knelt down again on the ground a few feet from the cabin.

"See these tracks. There are three of them. The one in the middle's bein' drug along. Look at these marks. See where the grass is trampled. Here. And here. The one on the right is bigger, heavier."

"Can you tell how long ago?" asked Owen.

Festy got up, looked around as though he was smelling the wind, taking his time to answer. "An hour ago, maybe. They went thataway."

"OK. We might still catch them. Can you track them, Festy?"

"Yep!"

Owen opened his rucksack, took out his weapon and inserted a full clip. He looked at Leslie. "This could get nasty. Maybe you should wait for us back at the jeep."

"Dammit, Owen! Do you think I was a paper pusher in the FBI? I've been in the field before!"

"Aw, Leslie, don't take it like that! I'm just concerned, that's all! If it's anything like Nyack these people are vicious. You saw that!"

"I'm still coming with you."

"Geez, you're stubborn! OK! Maybe you should contact Redington's people. We might need backup."

"We should do that," said Leslie, taking out her mobile phone and putting through a call to the number they'd been given by FBI Director Tom Redington before they left for Fort Davis.

Festy led the way again, stopping every now and then to examine the trail signs more closely. They moved fast. They were traveling downhill and the adrenaline fuelled them onward.

About a mile from the cabin they saw him. Rounding a clump of juniper trees they came upon a small spring. The man seemed to be lying face down with his head in the water. It looked like he was taking a drink. But there was no movement. They stopped and looked carefully in all directions before approaching.

Owen turned the body over.

"Jesus X. Christ!" yelled Festy. "It's Wainwright! Look what the bastards did to him!" then realizing that Leslie was there, he reached for her, "You shouldn't see your granpappy like this. Come away."

"No, Festy," said Leslie, "I want to remember what they did to him."

Jack Wainwright was an old man, in his early eighties, tall and stringy looking. He had been tortured, beaten to a bloody pulp. And he was quite dead. Fractured skull? Heart gave out? All of the above.

Festy looked around: "They're not far ahead."

Owen turned to Leslie.

223

"Stay with your grandfather, Leslie. Call the Feds. Get a chopper in here and get his body out of here right away. I know you want to come with us but you've got to do this."

Reluctantly Leslie agreed, and she was on her mobile kneeling by Wainwright's body as Owen and Festy set out after the 'bastards'.

Festy was right. There were two of them. A large one and a smaller one. They had stopped to eat. Overconfidence. They must have felt that they'd be long gone before Wainwright's body was discovered. Owen adjusted his binoculars, focusing on the larger of the two. Big man. Well over two hundred pounds. Too far away to see his face but he fitted the description given him by Sarah Kearns of the man who had killed her father. Owen moved closer to Festy and said, "I want to take that big bastard alive. I'd like to torture him the same way he tortured Wainwright."

Festy just grinned. That appealed to his sense of frontier justice.

The tall grass and the juniper trees gave them cover. They had moved to within a few yards of the two men when some birds rose squawking into the air. They hit the ground, well within earshot.

Small One: "I don't like it!"

Big One: "Don't be ridiculous! It's just birds. You city boys are scared of your own shadow out here."

Small One: "How can you be so fuckin' sure? Maybe there's someone out there."

Big One: "There's not a soul within ten miles
of here. That's why that weirdo
Wainwright lived here. Nobody knows we're here. Now, will you shut the fuck up and finish eating!"

Owen MacDara picked just that moment to show himself. He walked into view, his pistol trained on both of them. Festy had circled around and taken cover behind them.

"Stand up! Raise your hands!"

They didn't move. Owen picked a spot close to the small one's crotch and fired. The response was instant. Small One jumped to his feet, hands in the air high above his head, yelling, "Don't shoot! Don't shoot!"

The Big One wasn't easily threatened. But he did get on his feet with his hands hanging loosely at his side. His accent was foreign, Eastern European, thought MacDara, but difficult to place.

"Who the hell are you? What's this all about?"

"You killed Jack Wainwright! That's what it's about! And I'm going to see that you pay for that. Kneel down and put your hands behind your head! Do it! Now!"

The Big man made a move to obey but suddenly dived to the ground and rolled aside, grabbed a gun from the bag near his feet and fired at MacDara. Owen had nowhere to hide and the bullet narrowly missed him. He hurled himself at the ground just as the Small One found both courage and a gun. He aimed directly at Owen but never pulled the trigger. Festy's bullet entered his back between the shoulder blades and severed his aorta. The Big One saw his opportunity, got off the ground and ran towards Owen firing wildly. Owen wanted to take him alive but he was given no choice. He aimed his Walther at the Big One's torso. Owen's bullet caught him in the right chest. His momentum carried him to within inches of Owen before he collapsed. He still held his gun like a drowning man's straw. Owen reached him and ripped open his shirt. The bullet had entered his lung and he was losing air. Instinct and Owen's paramedic training in Korea took charge. He ripped the shirt off the Big One's body, tore a strip off the tail, folded the shirt into a large square and tied it tightly over the wound to form a pressure bandage. He wanted this one alive.

The whirring noise of the helicopter reached their ears before it came into view. Festy stood in a clearing waving his bandanna again. Owen stood beside him waving his arms wildly. Minutes later the chopper landed a few yards from them and Leslie Scott alighted and ran towards them.

"After we picked up Jack Wainwright we decided to sweep the area for you. Are you alright?"

"Yeah, we're OK. God, am I glad to see you," said Owen, "This one's still alive and I want to keep him that way."

"Let's get him on board. You're lucky. They have emergency equipment."

Two Fed agents joined her and helped move the Big One to a litter and place him aboard the chopper. They threw the Small One in a body bag in the back. Ole Festy waved his bandanna at them as they hovered overhead before heading north towards Pecos.

Forty-seven

Sheremeteyvo Airport, Moscow

A limousine awaited Nadia Pankin at Sheremeteyvo Airport. Less than an hour later, she hugged her brother at the door of his dacha and handed *The Wainwright Confession* to him. But it was a bittersweet hug. Her laughter turned to tears as the emotion overcame her.

"It'll soon be over. Don't cry," said Misha.

"I'm afraid, Misha," said Nadia, struggling to regain her composure.

"Don't be! We must be brave. We've waited a long time for this."

"Sometimes, I think – oh, I don't know – sometimes I wonder if it's worth it. If we're right."

"Nadia, you saw them kill mama and papa. You watched it. You remember what they did to you. I saw it all. They must pay. *An eye for an eye and a tooth for a tooth.* We made this promise."

"Yes, yes! I do want them to suffer. It's just that I'm afraid."

"It's alright Nadia. A little fear is not bad. We will do this and we will have our revenge. Revenge! That's what we've lived for. Be brave."

Forty-eight

Pecos, Texas

The Reeves County Hospital in Pecos was well
equipped to deal with trauma. The Big One was
rushed from the Emergency Room to the Operating
Room in record time. Two hours later with
MacDara's bullet removed, his lung and surrounding
tissue repaired, and vital signs stable he was moved
to a private room in the post-operative ward.
MacDara had also forwarded the Big One's prints to
Washington. It didn't take long. General Bart
Shields was on the phone to them within the hour.
Owen and Leslie took the conference call in an empty
examining room just off the outpatient area.

"His name is Victor Kasparov. Runs a strip
club in Miami called Lucky Vic's."

"What the hell's he doing out here?" asked
Owen.

"Hold you horses, Owen! Kasparov is a
Russian. Came to this country in 1983. Legally!
We've been after him for a long time. We know he's
mixed up in drug running from Columbia. Gun
running too! But we've never been able to get the
goods on him. He's a clever bastard! I'd guarantee
that he's tied to the Moscow mafia."

"But this doesn't make sense. If he's so damned clever why did he kill Wainwright?" said Owen.

"I'm not sure but let me take a guess," answered Shields. "Let's say this whole business about the killing of Hammarskjold is bigger than any drug smuggling operation. Whoever is behind this wanted to know what Wainwright knew. That's why Kearns is dead, that's why Wainwright is dead. And that's why Ridge was murdered in Moscow. Whoever is behind this wants to know who ordered Hammarskjold's death! Kasparov knows who that is. Owen, as soon as he's ready I want you to get him to talk. I don't care what methods you use. We need to know who's giving him his orders! I've asked the hospital commander to place a twenty-four hour guard on Kasparov."

"He's not well enough to escape," said Leslie.

"Leslie, I think he needs to be protected. From his own people. He's expendable. Especially if they think he might talk. And, I want you to go to New York. You made a contact there. He says he has very important information for you. About Nadia Pankin. He wouldn't tell me anything. He's very loyal to you. What's his name? Theodore! That's it."

Forty-nine

Manhattan,
New York

Leslie Scott had kept her apartment on West 75th Street when she moved to Washington. It was her umbilical cord to the Big Apple. Whenever Washington got the best of her she'd shuttle to La Guardia, taxi to Manhattan, shower and change in her apartment, and walk out into the Upper West Side. She'd stand there on Broadway, like an alien, sucking up the energy of the place, recharging her batteries again.

She stepped out of the shower, beads of water glistening on her body as she toweled her hair dry. There it was again! Her doorbell! She thought she'd heard it in the shower but convinced herself she'd been imagining things. Grabbing her robe, she crossed the living room and slid the cover on the front door peephole. Old Theodore's face, grinning from ear to ear, loomed in front of her right eye. She opened the door and he floated right past her into the living room.

"I tried to find you. You weren't there. So I called that general's number, the one you gave me. What's his name? Shell? Sheel? I had to see you. I have information from Moscow."

He was gasping for breath and Leslie made

him sit down while she brought him a glass of cold water. He gulped half of it and said: "About Nadia Pankin."

"You found out something?"

"I found out much. That's why it took so long. Nadia Pankin is not her real name. Her name is Nadia all right, Nadia Davidoff. It's a long story. Maybe you'd better put something on."

Leslie suddenly realized that she was only wearing her dressing gown. Tied in front, it had slipped open and her left leg was showing all the way to her groin. She quickly gathered it together, went into the bedroom, and emerged in jeans and a sweatshirt a couple of minutes later. During her absence, Old Theodore had gathered his breath and was anxious to get on with his story.

"Nadia Davidoff. She's a Jew. Her parents were killed when she was ten. She and her brother were put in an orphanage in Moscow. But they were lucky. They only stayed there a couple of years before the Kedrovs adopted them. Rich aristocrats. Madame Kedrov was what do you say, a *do-gooder*, always running around making a fuss over the poor. She had no children of her own, couldn't have any. That's why she hung around the children's orphanages. It seems Nadia found out about this and *adopted* her. Clever girl! Anyway, she had to take both the girl and her brother or she'd get no one. How do you say? *A package deal*."

"Kedrov! That name is a familiar one," said Leslie.

"It should be. Perfumes, vodka, cigarettes. Even the first Russian made personal computer is a Kedrov."

"Not the same Kedrovs!"

"Oh, yes. The very same! Or, maybe I should say the very same Davidoffs!"

Old Theodore let that sink in before he continued. He had gained a second wind and there was no stopping him now. Not that Leslie wanted to. She had no idea where this story was going, but there was a tingle running down her spine as Old Theodore continued.

"The Kedrovs were snobs. Commerce was beneath them. The Kedrov Organization is the creation of Misha Kedrov. Mikhail – Misha – Nadia's brother. Mikhail Davidoff! And he didn't build it on any inheritance from the Kedrovs. The word on the street is Mafia."

"You mean he got the money to start it from the Russian Mafia?"

"No! I mean he *is* the Mafia. Misha Kedrov controls all major crime in Russia. But nobody can prove it. There's not a shred of evidence against him!"

"Are you sure of this? Misha would seem to be just the kind of capitalist that's needed in the New Russia."

"I'm very certain of everything I tell you. Nadia Pankin was married once when she was only twenty. It didn't last long. That's where the name Pankin comes from. Be careful. She is not what she appears to be."

"Why are you so sure of all of this?"

"Because I am! I'd stake my life on it. Besides, Nadia and her brother should not be happy citizens of Mother Russia. The Russians killed their father and mother when she was only ten. Misha would have been about twelve at the time!"

Fifty

**Brooklyn,
New York**

Old Theodore felt satisfied as he turned the key in
his apartment door. He had paid Leslie Scott back
for her kindness to his grandson.

He didn't see the two people standing in the
shadows. They rushed him as he opened the door.
Somebody twisted his arm behind his back and
clamped a hand firmly over his mouth. He couldn't
scream. Once inside, they tied him to one of his
straight-backed kitchen chairs. They didn't gag or
blindfold him. Slowly his eyes regained their focus.
He saw the two people. A man and a woman. He
thought he recognized the woman. He looked hard at
her. No mistake. He'd followed her from the
Russian Embassy just to see what she looked like.
Nadia Pankin. Now he knew why they were here.
The man was speaking. In Russian. Fluently.

"Theodore, we're going to ask you some

questions. And we need the answers."

Old Theodore said nothing. Just looked at them defiantly.

"Now, Theodore, we can do this the easy way or we can do it the hard way. It's your choice."

"You know who I am, don't you?" said Nadia Pankin.

"Da," said Old Theodore, realizing he was no good at keeping up a pretense.

"Why were you trying to find out about me and my brother?"

"I don't know."

"Old man, I said we could do this the hard way too. Is that what you want?" asked Conor Brady.

"But I don't know who asked me to find out about you."

"What do you mean, *I don't know*?"

"It was an émigré organization. They paid me. I never saw them again."

"What's the name of this émigré organization?"

"I don't remember."

"Old man, I suppose you want to do it the hard way after all. Gag him!"

Nadia found a dishtowel and tied it around Old Theodore's mouth. Too tightly. He started to gag, so she eased it enough to let him breathe more through his nose. Brady found the kitchen-chopping knife.

"Sheffield. That'll do nicely, won't it, Theodore?"

He whacked it down on the little finger of the old man's left hand, severing it at the second joint. There was little blood. The finger bounced once on the wooden floor and lay there, disembodied, pointing accusingly at Nadia Pankin. Conor loosened the gag.

"OK, I'll give you another chance. Tell me who asked you to find out about Nadia and her brother!"

Old Theodore just sat there staring at Conor Brady, saliva dripping down the edges of his mouth.

"Tell me if you want to make another icon!"

But the old man said nothing. Brady replaced the gag, grabbed Old Theodore's right hand and wielded the knife again. Just as he was about to strike, Nadia said.

"Hold it, Conor. It won't work. He doesn't care about himself. He's protecting someone. There's another way."

She walked around behind the old man and took off his gag.

"You may not care about yourself, Theodore Glusdov. But I know you care about Peter Glusdov, your grandson. What do you think would happen to him if we held him for a month and fed him heroin every night! He would not grow up to be the fine doctor you want him to be. A year from now he'd probably overdose in some flea-bitten room in some slum. Is that what you want? I assure you that's what you'll get if you don't tell us what we want to know!"

Old Theodore knew he was defeated. He would do anything for his beloved grandson. Even betray a friend. That's how Nadia Pankin and Conor Brady found out about Leslie Scott.

A day later Nadia and Conor sat in an official limousine of the Russian Embassy on their way to La Guardia airport. He'd be away for a about a week, he said. 'Closing a deal' in Texas for Misha. That was all she knew about his trip. But she did know a lot more about Leslie Scott. It hadn't taken much investigation to discover that Leslie Scott had once been a New York Assistant District Attorney who had graduated to the FBI and now held an important position in the National Security Council working directly for General Bartley Shields.

"Why does the National Security Council want to know about me? About Misha?" Nadia's question was rhetorical.

"It fits. Fits like a glove!" Conor slammed his right fist into the palm of his left hand for emphasis.

"What do you mean?"

"When Misha asked you to see Major Lacey in Ireland, he didn't mention someone called Owen MacDara, did he?"

"No. He only told me that Zhukov had named Lacey as the Congo mercenary they'd used to get Hammarskjold. Misha wanted me to find out everything that I could from Lacey about the Congo operation. But he didn't tell me about this MacDara. Does it matter?"

"Yes. MacDara is an agent of the National Security Council. He works on assignment directly for the President of the United States. Zhukov talked to him."

"And you think this is all connected somehow?"

"I know it is. I followed MacDara to Ireland where he met with Major Lacey. Did you give Lacey your name when you saw him?"

"I had to. I had no choice. He wouldn't talk with just anyone. He insisted on seeing my credentials before he would talk with me. I had to show him my UN card. He believed I'd been sent to see him by the United Nations. That's the only reason he talked with me."

"Maybe he gave your name to MacDara. Yes. That must be it. That would explain it. They were looking for background on you and they got two birds with one stone. They found Misha. It won't take much intelligence on their part to put two and two together."

"You mean…"

"I mean that they will make a direct link between Ridge's assassination and Misha. That's exactly what I mean."

"What will we do?"

"Nothing. Absolutely nothing! They can't prove a thing. That little weasel Fomin can't tell them anything. He had the good sense to blow his own head off. And his nosey wife's too! We made sure of that!"

"This MacDara you mentioned. What about him?"

"MacDara. Now that's funny. Perverse! That's what it is. MacDara thinks his secret agent job is secret. Misha is actually a customer of MacDara's. MacDara runs a consulting company. GMA, Global Management Associates. Great cover. GMA is building a computer system for Kedrov Industries. MacDara doesn't know it but he's actually making the rope that will hang him! Perverse!"

"But now MacDara knows who Misha really is…"

"It doesn't matter. It only makes it more interesting. Besides, Owen MacDara is living on borrowed time. He's unfinished business. I thought I had taken care of him. But he survived. The man has nine lives!"

The limo had now slowed as it entered the airport and pulled to a stop outside the departures gates. The driver opened the door for Conor. Nadia stayed. She'd return with the limo to the embassy. Halfway out of the door, Conor looked back. "Leslie Scott knows about you. Wouldn't it be interesting if she knew that you know that she knows? Suppose you make the next move. Just like your favorite game of chess."

Fifty-one

City Morgue,
New York

Dr. Dominick Volpe, the deputy coroner, pulled on a pair of surgical gloves and walked to the foot of the autopsy table. He compared the access number and name on the tag tied to the big toe with the information on the chart he held in his hand. Satisfied, he started his external examination, speaking into the small, attached microphone.

" ...body is that of an elderly Caucasian male, blue eyes, gray hair, going bald; the body weighs 187 pounds and is 71 inches long. Generally seems to be in good physical condition and well nourished. There are no unusual skin lesions, tattoos or moles. There are abrasions on the knuckles of the right hand and on the palms of both hands. Further examination of the hands shows skin discoloration and residue under fingernails, most probably from acrylic paints. There is no visible evidence of blood or skin tissue under the fingernails. Samples will be sent for DNA analysis. The index finger of the right hand has been amputated with almost surgical precision. There are bruise marks, approximately 4 cm wide, encircling both upper arms..."

Moving to the top of the table, Dr. Volpe examined the caked blood covering the injury at the back of the skull. The scalp had been forcibly detached from the skull by the injury. He lifted it up and probed the skull with his fingers, continuing to record the examination:

"...severe head injury with palpation showing depression in the skull. There is hemorrhaging behind the eardrum consistent with a fracture through the base of the skull..."

Leslie Scott arrived at the morgue, her eyes red-rimmed from her tears. An hour earlier she had taken the call from Dr. Volpe and learned that Old Theodore was dead. Now she stood in Dr. Volpe's office.

"Dom, call me Dom, please. Thank you for coming. May I call you Leslie," said Dr. Dominick Volpe, and urged her to take a seat. A small compact man wearing thick bifocals, the deputy coroner exuded an energy and personality that seemed entirely at odds with the morbid side of his profession. "I called you as soon as we found your business card in the victim's pocket. I wanted to talk with you before I wrote my opinion for the case file. I believe we're dealing with a homicide."

"Where did you find him?"

"We didn't. He arrived in emergency as a DOA. That automatically qualified him for an autopsy. As I understand it his body was lying on Prospect Avenue, not far from where he lived. Someone called the cops and that's how he got here."

"Why do you think he was murdered?" asked Leslie.

"Let me tell you about his injuries," said Dr. Volpe, and then summarized the findings of his autopsy, " He has a skull fracture. Obviously from a forceful blow to the back of the head. With a blunt instrument. Or he could even have been clipped from behind by a protrusion from a passing truck. That would also be consistent with his injury. But his body shows evidence of torture. His arms were restrained so severely that he suffered considerable bruising. And the index finger is missing from his right hand. No, it wasn't torn away in an accident or anything like that. It was severed neatly, cleanly. Surgically removed. Chopped off. I'd say by a very sharp knife or a cleaver! What can you tell me about him?"

Leslie decided that Dr. Volpe did not have a need to know so she said, "Well, I can tell you his name and where he lived. But little else. I helped his son one time. That's how we met and that's why he carried my card. He appreciated what I had done and he liked to keep in touch with me, tell me how his son was doing. He was a gentle man. I didn't really know him but I was not prepared for this. I can't imagine who might have done this. I'm sure he had no enemies. He did live in a neighborhood that's become pretty rough, people selling dope on the streets, kids on heroin, muggings. Maybe somebody thought he had money. Maybe that's what happened."

Dr. Volpe thanked Leslie for taking the time to see him. At least he had a name to put on his case file. Now the son could claim his father.

241

Fifty-two

Pecos, Texas

The presence of the Military Police gave the Reeves County Hospital a sense of importance. The medics and the doctors were all conjecturing about the identity of the mysterious patient under guard in the post-op ward. Even the patients waiting in the outpatient area were momentarily distracted from their ailments. Owen MacDara sensed all of this as he walked towards Kasparov's room. The MP standing guard outside the room had been authorized to permit entry to the doctors and nurses and MacDara but no one else. He stepped aside and let Owen enter the room.

Kasparov lay awake. An IV entered his left arm and an oxygen tube snaked its way out of his nostrils. He recognized Owen. "Come to admire your handiwork, have you?"

"You don't look to be in any pain. That's a pity after what you did to Wainwright. And Kearns too!"

"You can't prove any of this. I was up here on a hunting trip. I want to see my lawyer!"

"I know who you are, Kasparov. My name's

Owen MacDara and I work for the President. I don't care about your civil rights. As far as I'm concerned, you don't have any!"

"I'm a citizen of this country. You can't do this to me!"

"Oh, yes we can! There's still a death penalty in Texas. But it's too good for you. You should be skinned alive. I'm here to give you one chance to save yourself. Talk to me. Tell me who you're working for. Tell me who sent you to kill Wainwright and I'll get you moved out of Texas. You'll get life and, if you're lucky, we'll deport your ass back to Moscow!"

"I told you. I want to see my lawyer. You can't prove any of this. I don't know what you're talking about!"

"Kasparov, you're not stupid! You see that guard at the door. That's to protect you – from your friends. You got caught, remember. That's not a smart thing to do. Now I can have that guard removed. Think about that. I'll be back."

Owen MacDara felt frustrated. He was sure that no amount of persuasion or threat would make Kasparov talk. But he was also certain that whomever Kasparov worked for might not feel so sure. If he were right, they'd try to silence Kasparov. *At least I hold the bait,* he thought. He turned all of this over in his mind as he walked through the hospital oblivious to doctors and nurses, patients on gurneys, anxious relatives and the frenetic activity in the Outpatient Clinic and the Emergency Room. It wasn't until his hand reached for the exit door that the image trying to force itself into his conscious mind suddenly broke through.

Jesus Christ! It's him! The face of one of the

young doctors he'd passed. *It's Conor Brady!*

MacDara turned, grabbing the security guard he had posted inside the exit door and ran through the Outpatient Clinic and the big double doors into the main corridor leading to the wards and private rooms. Startled nurses jumped out of his way and others raised their arms in protest. The guard outside Kasparov's door was missing. MacDara feared the worst. He had the Walther in his hand as he opened the door to Kasparov's room. But the door wouldn't budge. MacDara and the Security guard braced their shoulders against it and pushed. It began to give. Enough to let MacDara squeeze through almost tripping over the body of the missing guard. His fears were realized. Kasparov lay motionless, a pillow firmly molded over his head. He'd been smothered. The IV stand lay on the floor. Blood seeped out of Kasparov's arm staining the pure white sheets. Kasparov had put up a fight, a futile one.

Fifty-three

Washington, DC

Owen MacDara had come to tell Bart Shields exactly what had happened in Texas and to advise him that he was on his way to Moscow. They were both concerned about Leslie. Neither had heard from her since she had gone to New York to meet Old Theodore. It was as though Leslie Scott had been reading their minds when the phone rang. "Speak of the devil!" answered Bart Shields, and then followed with, "Just a minute, Leslie. Owen's here. Let me put you on the speakerphone. OK?"

"Hi Owen!" greeted Leslie.

"We were just talking about you," said Owen.

"Did you meet Old Theodore? " asked Shields.

"Old Theodore is dead. Murdered," she said.

"Jesus!" said Shields, "what happened?"

There was a long pause before Leslie spoke again. They could almost feel her composing herself, training herself to breathe normally. She said,

"First, I have to tell you a story." She described how Old Theodore had arrived at her apartment when she returned to New York, what he'd discovered about Nadia Pankin, how she and her brother Misha were orphaned and adopted by the Kedrovs; that her brother is the same Misha Kedrov who controls Kedrov Industries and much of the Russian mafia's crime empire as well.

She stopped in mid sentence. They could almost see her look at them directly through the phone. When she spoke again it almost seemed that she had changed the subject abruptly. "The G8 conference in England. The President will be there, won't he?" said Leslie.

"Yes, he will," answered General Shields.

"Do you have a conference schedule?" asked Leslie.

"As a matter of fact, I do. The President gave us copies at our last cabinet meeting. It's here somewhere," said Shields, as he proceeded to rustle through a stack of papers on his desk. Finally: "Hah! Success!" he said.

"Now, look at the Keynote Speaker on Day 2," said Leslie.

"Jesus X. Christ!" swore Shields, "Mikhail Kedrov, Chairman of Kedrov Industries. I'd never have bothered to look at it. How do you know this?"

"I got curious when I discovered that Nadia Pankin was planning to attend. Carrying UN papers and documents from Yeremenko that Yeltsin and his team need for one of their meetings on third world debt. That's when I found out that her brother was going to be the Keynote Speaker."

Leslie went on to describe how Old Theodore had been tortured before he died. She didn't know who did it but she had to assume that Kedrov had found out that Old Theodore had been snooping

246

around and that he was responsible. And she suggested that Old Theodore might have talked and given them her name. From there, it wouldn't take much to connect the dots; tie her to the National Security Council and to General Shields.

"Leslie, where are you now?" asked Owen.

"I'm at my apartment on West End Avenue but I'll be on the first flight to Washington tomorrow."

"No!" ordered Bart Shields and, turning to Owen MacDara, said: "You're out of here to Moscow in three days time, right? Change your plans. Go to New York tomorrow. Pick up Leslie. Then the two of you fly to London. Leslie, I want you in England. G8 is only four weeks away. Owen will brief you on the trip. Then he'll continue on from London to Moscow. Jeez! This really screws things up. Nobody knows this but the President was planning to take a few days to himself, go up to Scotland and do some golfing at Gleneagles. I've got to get to him right away."

"Is that all, sir?" asked Leslie.

"Yes, Leslie. Good work! Thank you," answered Shields, and turned to MacDara as he hung up the phone."

"Let's talk about this. What is your thinking?"

"It all adds up. This is a case of two and two equals four. We knew Misha Kedrov was involved in Ridge's assassination. We just couldn't prove it, that's all. And I'm certain that that poor jerk, Fomin, worked for him. I'm sure I spooked Fomin when I talked to him. He probably ran right back to Misha. Fomin's death was no suicide."

"Why are we worried about this G8 conference? Maybe he's only there to help Yeltsin get support from the IMF and the international investment community. After all, he is Chairman of Kedrov Industries."

"It's too good. It's too perfect. Why did he put pressure on GMA to bring in his computer system by the end of this month? Just in time for G8. No, he's up to something. Something big! He's got the major world leaders captive in that conference. He's not going to waste that opportunity on a canned speech about the free market in Russia."

Fifty-four

**Central Park,
Manhattan,
New York**

Leslie Scott decided to take the afternoon off and enjoy the sights and sounds of her favorite city. The death of Old Theodore and the pressure of recent days was getting to her and she knew that the real challenges and dangers lay ahead. But she needed to take time out, to be kind to herself, to stop and smell the roses, to recharge her batteries. It was a clear day with bright blue skies and the Manhattan air tasted unusually clean. The cross-town streets were uncrowded and the people seemed to be unhurried. Young couples sauntered along, hand-in-hand, enjoying each other, lending an intimacy to the city.

Older people, alone, browsed shop windows. Others walked their dogs, their body language just as intimate as the young couples. Leslie relaxed. This was her New York. Not the large cavernous skyscraper place of the tourist postcards, just a small friendly town to her. She felt the tension leave her body and she reveled in the ordinary things around her. About twenty minutes later she had crossed Park and Madison and Fifth and soon found herself entering the Park. Central Park, that large expanse of country right in the middle of the city.

She followed the path for a while, her leisurely pace punctuated by the occasional jogger, until she heard voices, theatrical voices. Drawn towards them, she came upon a regular event: Shakespeare in the Park, an outdoor performance of the Bard. One of her favorites: King Lear.

Totally absorbed in the performance, she was unaware of the young woman who arrived a few minutes later and stood to her right – unaware until the play ended and the young woman clapped loudly and enthusiastically. She turned to Leslie and in a distinct, but foreign, accent said: "Magnificent! I love Shakespeare! This is good! This is great! Don't you love it?"

Somewhat taken aback, but magnetized by her enthusiasm and a mutual feeling about the performance, Leslie said: "Yes! I do! Lear is one of my favorite Shakespearean plays. I've seen it many times before. But never in the Park."

"Me too! I mean I've seen King Lear before. Once or twice. Last time in London," and then without pausing for a breath, " I'm going for a coffee. Would you like to join me? Please say yes."

Leslie wanted to be alone but the young

woman's approach was infectious. There was something familiar about her too. She couldn't quite place it. The accent was foreign, European. But not one of the easily recognized ones. Not French or Spanish or German. Eastern European – Slavic maybe. As these thoughts flitted through the back of her mind Leslie found herself saying: "Yes, thank you. OK. I will."

Minutes later they were ensconced in a booth in a nearby coffee shop, the aroma of fresh coffee having pulled them in off the street. The waitress filled two large mugs almost before they had a chance to get properly seated. It was only then that Leslie realized that they hadn't introduced themselves.

"It's as though I know you from somewhere. Should I?" asked Leslie.

"I'm sure you know me. I know you," the answer came back with not a hint of hesitation, catching Leslie unawares with its directness. A directness she now readily associated with the young woman's manner. "I am Russian. With our delegation to the United Nations. My name is Nadia Pankin!"

Leslie's coffee mug stopped halfway to her mouth and she kicked herself, figuratively. Why hadn't she caught on? She'd only seen one photo of Nadia Pankin, one of the official unsmiling kind, and it had not done her justice. Looking at her again, Leslie saw the resemblance and realized that there had been just enough similarity with that photo to make Nadia oddly familiar. That, and the fact that Leslie had switched her mind off this afternoon. She kicked herself again before speaking. "You know me. How?"

"Yes, I know you, Leslie Scott. You are successful in your career. Like me. You were the best young prosecutor when you worked in New York. Now you are in the National Security Council. You are Assistant to your General Bartley Shields. Yes, yes, I would say you are successful, Leslie Scott. Are you surprised? You shouldn't be. Do you think we Russians are stupid? You Americans think you can invade our privacy and that we won't know anything about it! How naïve!"

"What do you mean?"

"Don't be – how would you say? Coy? That's it. Don't be coy, Ms. Scott. Did you think you could ask questions about my brother and me without us knowing about it? Did you really think that?"

Leslie realized that there was no longer any need to maintain the pretense. Nadia knew. But what did she know exactly. And how much did she know?

"OK. I admit it. We were asking about you. You went to see a Major Lacey in Ireland and we wanted to know why. We wanted to know what an important member of the Russian mission to the UN wanted with the man who killed Dag Hammarskjold. And we learned that Misha Kedrov is your brother. That explains a lot, doesn't it Ms.Pankin?"

"And just what do you think it explains?"

"Look, let's just stop the shadow boxing shall we? Your brother asked you to talk with Major Lacey. It's not difficult to figure that out. And it's your brother who would like to see an end to *glasnost* and *perestroika*, isn't it. It's your brother who wants to dig up the past again, isn't it?"

Nadia Pankin sipped her coffee and watched Leslie Scott lose her cool demeanor. She felt a sense of accomplishment. This is exactly what she wanted. She had made the next move on her chessboard as Conor had suggested and she was enjoying the game.

"That's just idle speculation on your part, Ms.

Scott. My brother is Chairman of Kedrov Industries. Why would he want to risk all of that?"

"I don't know. But I could hazard a guess. Revenge – for the murder of your parents. Shall we start with that as a reason?"

Nadia's face changed. Changed subtly. A sadness seemed to settle in the eyes. Leslie knew she had hit her mark.

"Nonsense! Renegade soldiers killed our parents when we were very young. It was a tragedy but we can't blame anyone. We were protected, taken care of, and then we were most fortunate to have found a new home. But you know all that. Why would my brother carry all that anger inside? Revenge! Against who? Nonsense!"

"What about the killing of Alexander Ridge?"

"What about it? What are you trying to imply? That my brother had something to do with that!"

"Have you heard of Leonid Fomin?"

"Who is Leonid Fomin? Why are you speaking in these riddles? This name means nothing to me."

"Leonid Fomin was the police officer on the scene after Alexander Ridge was murdered. We also believe that he was in the employ of your brother."

"I never heard of him. All of that means nothing to me. Many people are in the employ of my brother. He is a very generous man and he knows how difficult it is to live in Russia today. So he helps people. Is that a crime?"

The waitress' timing couldn't be better. Carrying a steaming pot of fresh coffee, she pushed her way between them and refilled their cups. It helped to let the steam out of things. After the preliminaries of sugaring, creaming, and tasting, Leslie was the first to break the silence. "What were you doing in Ireland with Major Lacey?"

"OK. I was there. My brother asked me to see the Major. He's been trying to find the killers of Alexander Ridge. He does not want Russia blamed for this crime. And we, at the United Nations, want to find his killer too. We had information that this man Lacey might know something about it. That's all."

"I don't believe you!"

The smug look returned to Nadia Pankin's face. Whatever advantage Leslie had gained in her last move was now gone.

"That's too bad, Ms. Scott. But I really don't care what you and your conspiracy theory friends in Washington believe. Look in your own backyard. I believe you'll find what you're looking for there. I wouldn't waste too much time on my brother or myself. Now I really must be going. It's nice of you to share a coffee with me. Perhaps we can do it again some time."

Checkmate. Well, not quite. But the game had gone well, Nadia reasoned with herself. Until she heard the parting shot from Leslie Scott.

"You might ask your brother about Leonid Fomin. He and his wife were found dead. Suicide! But we think it was murder!"

Fifty-five

**Dune Road,
The Hamptons**

Owen MacDara went directly from the airport to his house on Dune Road. He had a two- day stopover before the flight to London. He wanted to be alone that night and planned to pick up Leslie at her West Side Manhattan apartment before noon tomorrow. As he sipped a whiskey, caught up in his own reverie, watching the boats gently sway at anchor, the phone rang. Tempted to let it ring, he somehow never managed to do that. On the sixth ring, he picked up.

"Owen, it's Anna. I need to talk to you."

"Where are you? I thought you were still in Moscow!"

"I am in Moscow. What do you mean?"

"Sounds like you're next door. What's up?"

"We have a big problem."

"What's the matter? Still hung up in testing?"

"No, that's not it. I wish it were. I've found out something, Owen. Something very bad. Very dangerous! I'm afraid!"

"You'd better tell me what's going on, Anna."

Anna Yachmi described her discovery of the Insect's digital signature and the Insect's subsequent *confession* about the changes he's making to the system for Misha Kedrov.

"What's it going to be used for?"

"Yuri doesn't know. He only knows what it's capable of doing. And that it must be ready in time for the G8 conference. But he doesn't know what Misha Kedrov plans to use it for."

"Who would know? Besides Kedrov?"

"Only one person. Gelman. Alexandr Gelman. He's Kedrov's protegee. I am sure he knows."

"Can you get to him? Can you find out?"

"I don't know. Gelman is a loner. Keeps to himself. Has no friends."

"Anna, please try. But be careful. I want you in one piece. Do you hear me?"

"Oh, Owen. I miss you. I'm scared."

"Anna, I'll be there next week. Just do your best. If you think you're in danger, pull back."

After the phone call, Owen returned to his scotch and tried to make sense of what he'd just heard. Misha Kedrov's system would contain software not in the specs that had been given to GMA. And he needed it in time for the G8 conference in Birmingham. *Kedrov's plotting something. That's certain. But what?*

Owen couldn't hold the thought. The gentle lapping of the waves against the deck and the scotch were in collusion. He began to feel mellow. He kept remembering Kate, remembering the very first time they had made love here in Dune Road. *It's as though it were yesterday.* When they'd first met at her mother's up in Gloucester. They'd both felt it instantly. Just like magnets. They'd taken the shuttle back to New York together, and when he'd suggested she stay over at Dune Road for a couple of days, she'd accepted without hesitation. He remembered it well. That first night they'd shared a bottle of wine and watched the sunset. The second night they'd shared a bottle of wine, made love and missed the sunset. He walked over to the stereo, selected a CD and turned the volume low. The voice of Roberta Flack filled the room as he returned to the remains of his whiskey. She sang the same song as that first night he and Kate had made love here.

> *the first time ever I saw your face*
> *I thought the sun rose in your eyes*
> ....
> *the first time ever I kissed your mouth*
> *I felt the earth move in my hands*

Fifty-six

Moscow

Anna Yachmi set out to seduce Alexandr Gelman. A cold calculating decision, she told herself, as she toweled her body dry after a quick end-of-day shower. She had never deliberately seduced anyone before. Oh yes, she had occasionally had a man she fancied – like a dessert. A present to herself. Usually someone she'd found irresistible. A rare event. On those occasions she'd been equally driven and calculating. But that was sex. – simply sex. Nothing more. Now she planned seduction for another reason entirely. Was it a base reason or a noble one? She ruminated about that. Base, if it was only for industrial espionage – to acquire secrets about Kedrov Industries that GMA could take advantage of. Noble, if it's truly as Owen had said: *'A matter of life or death. The difference between peace and war.'* She trusted Owen. Even though he refused to tell her what he was involved in. She believed him. If Owen said it was a *'matter of life or death'* then her planned seduction of Alexandr Gelman was in a noble cause. *It has to be,* she told herself again. She'd never seduce Gelman for any other reason. He held no attraction for her, mentally or physically. She recalled her phone conversation that afternoon.

"Alexandr? Yes, yes, it's Anna," she said in a hurry, half expecting him to hang up. As it turned out, she did all of the talking.

"I just wanted to thank you for today."

"I mean, the appointment with Misha Kedrov."

"And the nice things you said about me."

"No, don't say it's nothing. It's really important."

"Yes, I think so. A good meeting. I think I got what I wanted."

"No, you're right. I won't really know until the system is up and running."

"No, Alexandr, please don't hang up! I still want to thank you for today."

"No, I insist. Dinner. Tonight. At your place. I'll do the cooking. Unless you have other plans."

"No. Good. That settles it. About eight. Is that OK?"

Alexandr Gelman stood there, looking sheepish. She could see his eyes taking a full measure of her. He had not acquired the sophistication to hide the obvious. She had dressed for the occasion in a slim, sleeveless black dress, cut low to show off her ample cleavage. A classic. She wore no jewelry. She could see his desire move from his stomach to his loins, before presence of mind took control, barely moving aside, forcing her to brush against his body as she entered.

Three hours, dinner, two bottles of the best Moldovan red and much vodka left Alexandr Gelman in a drunken stupor on top of his bed. Half undressed, fully unconscious, exactly where Anna wanted him.

She found the keys to his small office. Tiny, cluttered with books and files, some sprawling on the floor around a chair that faced a configuration of the system she was building: terminal, keyboard, central processing unit, communication modems, disk drives, printer. Gelman has his own prototype to conduct his own tests. One of the keys unlocked a small fireproof steel cabinet that housed shelves of CDs, floppy disks, and DVDs. She reckoned that there was only one way to do this. The hard way. She booted up the system and began inserting every CD and disk and browsing the contents. It was only when she had cleared one of the shelves that she saw it: a DVD labeled *'top secret – for G8 broadcast testing.'* This could be it, she thought. Suddenly she felt nervous and her fingers trembled as she inserted the DVD in the drive and clicked 'run.' Fifteen minutes later she sat terrified. She had just witnessed the torture of a man called Wainwright and the confession of secrets that would bring the US and Russia into crisis. Exactly what Kedrov must want. She was tempted to take the DVD but knew that would achieve nothing. She had to get this information to Owen immediately. He would know what to do.

Owen MacDara was still at Dune Road when Anna called. But only just. In another hour she would have missed him; he'd have been on his way to Kennedy Airport to join Leslie for their flight to London. Anna's news was the link that tied it all together for him: the Ridge assassination, the Congo, the Kedrovs, the whole sorry mess. He told Anna that she had done the right thing, told her that he'd see her in Moscow in a few days time, asked her to get his special briefcase from Bob Stebbins. Bob would know what he wanted, the case that he had designed to hold his weapons. A necessary evil when doing business in a world still threatened by the Russian mafia. Then he called Shields and briefed him on the *Wainwright confession.* They agreed that they had to beat Misha Kedrov at his own game. They would produce their own DVD, a replacement for the Wainwright one. Shields would start work on it immediately. Leslie Scott would coordinate it all in London and deliver it to Owen in time for G8. It would be a tight schedule. They had less than four weeks.

Pat Mullan

PART SIX

Old Revolutionaries

Pat Mullan

Fifty-seven

London
Heathrow Airport

Leslie Scott had been to London once before. Five years ago she had attended an international conference on criminology and tacked on a full month's vacation when the conference closed. She remembered those four weeks fondly. She had done all the tourist things: drooling in the middle of Harrod's food halls, gazing at the lifelike people in Madame Tussauds, buying exotic foods at Fortnum & Mason, spending rainy afternoons in the National Gallery and the British Museum.

Now she felt excited, expectant, as Owen hailed the black London taxi at Heathrow and the driver loaded their bags into the boot.

"Where to, guv'?" he asked, in his inimical Cockney accent.

"Knightsbridge," said Owen, taking Leslie's elbow and guiding her into the taxi.

As they drove into London on the M4, Owen could hear Leslie and the taxi driver talking and laughing. But he wasn't listening. His mind had slipped into another time, another place, another

London.   The London of his past and of his future.
He remembered...

*Nineteen and leaving Ireland for the first time. The
ferry he had taken to cross the Irish Sea from Belfast
to Heysham had been little better than a cattle
wagon. Overcrowded and uncivil. Families huddled
together to keep warm on the cold decks. Young men
got drunk and, as the night passed, many ended
facedown in a stupor. Inside, in the lounge, cigarette
smoke hung in a haze like a London fog and the
smell of fresh vomit clung to his nostrils.*

    *The train that rattled him later that night
through the black, smoke-stacked heart of England
had been no better. Cold, hard seats and indifferent
stares from his fellow passengers reinforced his
isolation, his sense of desolation. Every part of his
body ached when he disembarked from British Rail
at Euston Station on a steely cold Sunday morning.
Somehow he made his way into the city and sat in
awe in the midst of Trafalgar Square feeling the
imperial weight of the Empire all around him.*

    *Days later, after the first shock of seeing 'no
Irish or coloured' stenciled on the bottom of the three
by four cards that advertised flat and bedsit
vacancies, he found a place to stay. The landlady,
Mrs. West, had felt sorry for him in the same way
she'd have felt sorry for a stray cat. Every night she
served him two pineapple rings for dessert. He'd
never been able to stomach pineapple again. Her ex-
British Army husband sat every evening, square and
solid, in front of his TV, occasionally interrupting his
viewing to lecture Owen on the savages in Africa and
why they should be grateful for the civilizing
influence of England. Owen felt he was using Africa
as a metaphor for Ireland.*

Then years later, back again, back as an American, only traces of the Ulster accent remaining. Back as a senior executive to a mews house in Belgravia, shirts bought at Turnbull & Asser on Jermyn Street and laundered at Jeeves where he stood in the queue with old school ties and listened to tweedy, moustache-waxed ex-Brigadiers hold forth on their shooting holidays in northern parts, meaning Scotland...

And then that last lost romantic weekend with Kate. Long, languid breakfasts, hand in hand in the park, window shopping on Oxford Street, using every excuse to touch each other, theatre evenings in the West End, endless afternoons at the National Gallery and the Tate. Oh, how Kate loved art. And, God, how they loved each other. It flooded back until he felt his heart and mind sear with the memories...

"Owen, Owen!" Leslie's voice finally penetrated the past, just as the taxi pulled into Knightsbridge.

"Where exactly, guv'?" asked the driver.

Owen directed him to a house in the middle of a street near the Royal Albert Hall, waited till the driver held the door open for them and unloaded their bags, then paid him and tipped generously.

Owen turned the key in the front door and ushered Leslie inside. "I bought this place ten years ago. GMA had a lot of clients here and London was our European headquarters. I don't like living in hotels. This seemed just right, near the Royal Albert Hall, a stone's throw from Knightsbridge and Chelsea and five minutes from the West End. I use it a few times a year and I sometimes let good friends stay here. The same lady that I hired when I bought it still comes in twice a week and keeps it spotless for me. I'll give you the nickel tour."

Leslie was impressed. She was looking at three floors that reflected the tastes of a very special man. On the first floor, a stainless steel high-tech kitchen, balanced by butcher block counters, was separated from a library that also functioned as a living room, by a pine paneled walk-in wine bar that must have at least two hundred bottles in a floor-to-ceiling rack. The master bedroom, with its own Jacuzzi bathtub, dominated the second floor. But the third floor was the real prize. It was MacDara's own private art gallery, housing both paintings and sculptures. Some fine soapstone carvings sat on display stands at strategic points but it was the paintings that dominated, all abstract or post-modern. She recognized a Miro and a Calder.

"That's a Scully. Sean Scully," says Owen, pointing to a large painting of just horizontal stripes, yet the texture of the paint and the choice of colors made their own statement. "I got that when you could buy a Scully for a few pounds. Now he's in New York and belongs to the masters of the art. I couldn't touch that for less than six figures today."

"Shouldn't you have all of this in a vault somewhere?"

"What? And not be able to see it. I bought it to enjoy. Besides, I have the best alarm system that money can buy, the police keep an eye on the place for me, and, if all else fails, everything is fully insured and appraised once a year."

It was 9 a.m. in London but still only 4 a.m. by Leslie's internal clock. Unlike MacDara, she hadn't been able to catnap on the flight and now felt jetlagged. Owen insisted that she get some sleep, explaining that he had already committed himself to lunch with an important GMA client. "Business is business," he explained. Leslie was too jetlagged to protest.

Ten minutes later, the taxi dropped Owen outside The Irish Club in Eaton Square in the heart of Belgravia.   A   discrete,   often   polished,   brass nameplate announced its presence on the wall beside the entrance. Once inside, Owen adjusted his eyes to the dark interior, ordered a pint of Guinness, and watched the bartender pour it halfway, let the head settle and then fill the glass. The lunch club regulars hadn't arrived yet and the bar was empty, except for one solitary patron sipping his pint. Owen thanked the bartender and took his Guinness to a corner table thinking that, had things been different, he might just be one of the regulars for lunch today. Engrossed in that thought, he didn't see the big man come in.

"Hello, Owen. It's been a while, hasn't it?" The Belfast accent was unmistakable. Even after thirty years in England it hadn't changed a bit.

"Too long, Charlie. It's good of you to come," said Owen, standing to his full six feet, yet finding himself still looking up at Big Charlie Magee.

Magee Construction Ltd. was one of the biggest   builders   in   England,   only   outdone   by McAlpine.   Charlie started on the building sites himself when he came over to London in his late teens. Soon he started subcontracting, with three or four other Irish kids just off the boat. Construction was still his core business but he had diversified in recent times. Always a gambler and a good poker player, he now owned a chain of bookmaker shops, places where the 'house' always came in the winner. *'I'm a Turf Accountant,"* Charlie protested, when anyone referred to him as a 'bookie.'

But Charlie was also another person; one that most people didn't know. He was the senior Irish Republican in England. Owen MacDara knew. And MI5 knew too, but they could never get anything on Charlie. He was too careful and he was too powerful. His generous contributions to the British Labour Party gave him unwritten protection.

"Good Guinness. It doesn't always travel well," said Charlie, as he savored the pint that Owen bought, "but you didn't ask me here to share a Guinness with me, Owen, did you now?"

"No, Charlie, I didn't," said Owen. "I need a favor. I want you to keep an eye on a young lady for me for the next couple of weeks. Till just after the G8 conference in Birmingham."

"What about the Yard? Why not ask them? What's this all about, Owen?"

Owen was already prepared for this question. He knew that he would have to tell Big Charlie why he needed the *organization's* help. And whatever he said would have to be the truth. Big Charlie could spot a fake a mile away.

"I'll tell you as much as I can, Charlie," said Owen, "but I'll have to start a long time ago. Over thirteen years ago. In the Congo."

Big Charlie stopped the Guinness halfway to his lips and Owen knew he had his full attention. Charlie listened. Owen talked.

"I don't see what we gain from this, Owen. Besides, if we help you, we'll be risking the *organization*. Our enemies don't know who we are, how we're organized, where we live. Our own volunteers don't even know their commanders. That's our strength. If we help you, we'll have to activate some of our units. That'll expose us. MI5 have been waiting for years for an opportunity like this. Owen, you're asking us to take a very big risk.

And for what? What do we care if the West pays for its own dirty work? The West has never given a damn about Irish freedom!"

"Charlie, that's not true any more and you know it. Certainly not in America's case!" Owen downed the last of his pint and looked squarely at Big Charlie. "Charlie, the President himself gave me a message for you. He said to tell you that you owe him one."

"Aw, come on, Owen. You're kidding!"

"Charlie, I'm dead serious. The President knows I'm asking for your help. He means it when he says you owe him one."

"OK, Owen. Why do we *owe him one?*"

"Adams! It's that simple! He gave Gerry Adams a visa. He believes you wouldn't have had any agreement on Northern Ireland if he hadn't done that. You owe him, Charlie."

Big Charlie thought about that for a while, conceded that he did indeed owe the President, and then asked Owen what he wanted him to do.

Fifty-eight

London

8 a.m.   Billy Clancy knew the routine by this time. He'd been watching Leslie Scott for three days. She emerged, in a teal sweatsuit, exactly on cue, and started out, walking briskly.   Soon she picked up speed, a gentle canter at first, quickly moving to her regular jogging pace. Billy wore navy blue sweats for the occasion. Jogging wasn't his thing. It seemed as pointless to him as golf.   But he had no choice.   He stayed well back until they reached Knightsbridge and entered Hyde Park.   There he blended into the regular morning assembly of joggers, walkers, pony riders and health enthusiasts.

9 a.m.   One hour later.   Still on schedule, Leslie Scott was back at Alexandra Place.   Billy watched her enter the house and then he went around the corner to his car, changed out of his sweats, picked up a couple of packs of cigarettes and stationed himself at his observation post at the end of the street.

9:45 a.m.   Sure enough. Right on schedule. Leslie Scott emerged again, dressed in black designer jeans and a red top.

11 a.m.   Billy Clancy stood in a doorway in Knightsbridge as Leslie Scott walked past. The sun was shining. Summer was in the air. Foreign and English accents mingled on the crowded pavement. The casually dressed outnumbered the business-attired by ten to one. It was tourist season.

Billy stubbed out his cigarette and followed her, keeping a discrete distance between them. He didn't want her to spot him, but he wasn't too concerned. The throngs of people gave him plenty of cover. She seemed to be in no hurry, not driven to get anywhere. He watched her enter the LA Café, buy a cup of coffee and take it to a counter-facing the window. He held back, out of her sight, where he could keep an eye on the exit and lit a cigarette. As he sucked the smoke deep into his lungs, he contemplated his assignment: watch her, keep an eye on her, protect her, he'd been told. Make sure she's OK. Three days. Then Seamus will take over. *Well, in another nine or ten hours I'll hand her over to him,* thought Billy. But he wished he could stay. He was getting to like this Leslie Scott. Good looking, great body, sexy, confident. *Yeah, that's it. That confidence. I suppose it's an American thing.* He had to admit to himself – this was the best assignment he'd ever had from the organization. Not that he'd had any lately. With the cease-fire and the new agreement, he hoped it was the beginning of the end. He just couldn't figure where she fit in.   *What does she have to do with the cause?   She must be important. Otherwise we wouldn't be keeping an eye out for her.   Jaysus!* He yelled silently to himself. He'd been so preoccupied that he hadn't noticed the cigarette burn down into his fingers.   He quickly tossed it on the ground just as Leslie Scott emerged. She crossed the street only inches away from him; so close he could smell her perfume. He followed at a safe distance.

Fifty-nine

London,
The Prospect of Whitby

James Metcalfe walked into the Prospect of Whitby at one o'clock on Wednesday afternoon. The oldest pub in London, it sits on the banks of the Thames in the gentrified East End of London. Looking just like any other City businessman dropping in for a quick lunch and a favorite brew, Metcalfe avoided the bar crowd and climbed the stairs to reach the second-floor balcony that overlooked the Thames. The morning's fog had not lifted and the river was shrouded in a haze. Two people were already there, an anxious overfed man constantly looking at his watch and a big man standing alone nursing a pint of Guinness. Metcalfe walked over and looked out at the murky shadows moving up and down the river. Soon a young lady, breathless, appeared and embraced the anxious fat man. They left holding

275

hands. The big man closed the distance between himself and Metcalfe, saying, in a strong Belfast accent: "Can't see too much out there today"

"Poor visibility indeed. But then I'm expecting you to clear things up for me."

"James, I may make things even cloudier. We don't have much time so I'll get right to it. Tell me about the G8 conference."

"Nothing to tell. The Prime Minister wants to do it his way and Birmingham will get some extra business. We'll get no sleep till they leave but that's our job. No one will praise us for ensuring that the conference goes without incident. And everyone will blame us if anything goes wrong. You know that. Why do you ask?"

"Something is going down. Do you know Leslie Scott, an American?"

"I'm afraid I haven't had the pleasure. Who is he?"

"It's a she, not a he. And she works for the National Security Council. Assistant to General Bartley Shields, the head of NSC."

"You're talking in riddles. What is this all about? Will you get to the point."

"I will! I will! First, I wanted to see if you knew something. Leslie Scott's in London. And we're providing protection."

"By 'we' I presume you mean your friends in the Provos. What possible relationship could there be between a group of terrorists and the American National Security Council?"

"Now, James, I wouldn't be so quick to use that word 'terrorist'. You know that 'one man's terrorist is another man's patriot.' And the Americans still remember their 'terror' campaign against the British. Even if it did happen two hundred years ago!"

"You Irish will rationalize anything, won't you?"

"Now, James, I didn't ask you here to engage in this repartee. We have made a lot of progress working together over the years. You have convinced your government of our seriousness. In return I have helped you to avert some of the biggest 'terror' campaigns on the mainland. This time it has nothing to do with Ireland. This time it's larger than any dispute between our two countries. We have been asked to look after Leslie Scott by the Americans because they don't trust any government agency, not even their own. They don't trust the CIA and that means MI5 and MI6 are suspect too."

"Maybe you'd better tell me what this is all about."

Just then a noisy group of four young business types disturbed their privacy. Well into their second or third beer it was doubtful if any work would be accomplished in their offices that afternoon. They didn't stay long. The fog and the looks of disdain from the two men on the balcony dampened their enthusiasm. They left almost as soon as they arrived.

"I'll have to start with a story about the Congo," the big man said, to the bewilderment of James Metcalfe.

Exactly twenty minutes later James Metcalfe knew everything that Big Charlie Magee knew and by seven o'clock that evening the Prime Minister knew everything that James Metcalfe knew.

Owen had set the wheels in motion in London. He had a final conference call with Leslie Scott and Bart

Shields to discuss the production of the DVD. They planned to expose Misha Kedrov and his evil empire to the world, to destroy him before he could make his move. A risky strategy. If it backfired at the last minute they would lose all. But if they succeeded they would not only stop him but they would bury the past and assure the future. Leslie assumed responsibility. She would see that it was executed. General Shields would 'enlist' all the best people to get the job done. There was nothing more that Owen could do. He booked his flight to Moscow.

PART SEVEN

The Revenge

Pat Mullan

Sixty

Moscow

If Conor Brady had been in Moscow, Misha would have insisted that he complete his assignment. MacDara was unfinished business of Conor's. But Misha had other *contractors* that he used regularly. In his *maffiya* world, success often depended on eliminating the opposition. Negotiation was usually seen as a sign of weakness. He used terminations to gain market share and to take over emerging businesses. True hostile takeovers. One of these *'other contractors'* stood out above the rest. One who never failed. One that he now awaited at a table in the rear of a restaurant in the heart of Moscow's Chechen ghetto. The Chechens controlled their own criminal world, distinct from Russia's *maffiya*. Until Misha gained control of Russia's *maffiya* there had been no collaboration with the Chechens. In fact the relationship had been marked by bloody battles over territory and frequent *quid pro quo* killings. The Chechens were the more ruthless and they hated the Russians. But soon after Misha gained control of the Russian *maffiya* he formed a truce with the Chechens. It was an uneasy truce.

The conversation in the restaurant had suddenly

ceased. Misha looked up in time to see Sasha enter. She looked stunning. Tall, statuesque, with a perfect body, she was dressed for action: black leather hip-hugging pants topped with a three-quarter length dark maroon jacket. She caressed the sleek, black leather bag that hung gently against her right hip, its bandoleer-like strap crossing the valley between her breasts that even her jacket was incapable of hiding. Misha stood. They kissed, wordlessly, a momento to a time when they had once met only to ravage each other.

"Mine?" gestured Sasha, as she picked up the waiting glass of vodka and downed it at one gulp.

"It's good to see you again, Sasha. How long has it been? Six months?" asked Misha.

"You know exactly, Misha. If I had to live on my income from you, I'd be in trouble. Luckily there's a growing demand for my services in our brave new Russia," said Sasha.

"You look different. Darker. More tanned," said Misha.

"I've been away. In the sun," said Sasha, offering no further explanation.

"Well, this job can be done at home. Your fee in advance as usual. But I'll double it this time. That's how important this contract is to me," said Misha, as he pushed a brown manila envelope across the table.

Sasha took it and inserted it, unopened, into her black bag. She stood and embraced Misha. They kissed again, platonically. She turned and strode purposefully out of the restaurant. Misha Kedrov left five minutes later.

Sixty-one

Owen MacDara didn't enter Moscow by subterfuge. He arrived openly and officially as President of GMA Associates – a normal visit to his Moscow clients. He knew his life was in danger, knew that Conor Brady had tried to kill him. It didn't take a great leap of the imagination to put two and two together and arrive at the conclusion that Misha Kedrov had given Brady that assignment. But Owen rationalized that it was better to hide right out in the open. The audaciousness of it appealed to him. That and an unfailing belief in his own ability to survive. But he did take precautions. Bob Stebbins met him with his special briefcase at Sheremeteyvo Airport. He had a gun in that special briefcase. Stebbins also had a limousine waiting to take him directly to the Baltschug Kempinski Hotel.

Anna Yachmi met Owen at the Kempinski. She ran towards him, her face excited, eyes teary with pleasure, and kissed him long and passionately. When he finished registering, she clung to him on the way to his room.

"Are you hungry?" she asked and, not waiting for an answer, said: "I've ordered some food. It should be in the room..."

"...and I've got a bottle chilling on ice," she added, mischievously slipping her hand under his jacket and beneath his belt, her fingers teasing that erotic place at the base of his spine...

It was a different Sasha who walked into the Kempinski an hour before midnight. This Sasha was dressed for a different kind of action entirely. A tight fitting, red micro mini skirt adorned a pair of magnificent legs, displayed on ultra high-heeled red shoes. A black bolera jacket, open at the front, framed a sheer white blouse, at least one size too small, challenging her ample breasts to pop the buttons. She wore gaudy cosmetic jewelry, too much lipstick, and advertised her wares as she walked straight towards the youngish assistant manager.

Ten minutes later, richer from a very generous tip and convinced that Mr. MacDara was into a bizarre menage-a-trois, the youngish assistant manager directed her to Owen MacDara's room.

"Kate, Kate!" Anna was wide-awake, had been ever since Owen started calling for Kate in his sleep. Now Owen was awake too. And he realized in those first moments of consciousness that he'd been calling out loud for Kate. He looked over at Anna and saw her awake.

"I'm sorry. Did I wake you?"

"No, Owen. I never went to sleep. You've been tossing and turning. And calling for Kate."

"Oh, God, Anna! I'm sorry."

"Don't say that, Owen. Do you want to talk about it?"

"No. I mean, I don't know. I had a terrible

dream. I don't remember it. Just bits here and there."

"Oh, Owen. My poor, dear Owen," said Anna, as she moved close to him and held his head to her breast, "I love you. I love you. Don't you know that?"

"I know, Anna. I know."

Tears rolled down Owen's cheeks and low sobs swept through his body. Anna didn't say anything, just held him close, caressed his head and wiped the tears from his face with her fingertips. It seemed that they'd lain that way for ages, but only a few minutes had passed when they heard the sound. Owen heard it first – a scraping sound. A familiar scraping sound. The sound of the hall table scraping against the wall. The table was too awkward for the space just inside the door. He and Anna had each brushed against it when they first entered the room, squeezing it against the wall and causing that same sound.

Owen gripped Anna's hand tightly and then put his finger over her lips. He slid silently out of the bed and reached for the gun he'd left on the floor nearby. The next sound was unmistakable, the 'pfhtt pfhtt' of a silencer and the impact of a bullet into the pillow that Owen had just left. Anna jumped out of the bed and landed in a bundle on the floor but didn't stay there. Frightened, she rose and tried to run but the next bullet found its mark. Anna's scream died in the gurgle of the blood pumping out of her severed aorta. Owen fired back, missed, and crawled until he felt the base of the nearest floor lamp. Standing quickly, he switched on the light and caught Sasha, framed in the bathroom doorway. The sight startled him. A woman. Sasha was equally startled. She fired and missed. Owen hesitated. But only for a second. His first bullet left a red scorched path across her skull, setting her brain on fire. She stumbled. Owen's second bullet caught her in the midriff. She fell back onto the bathroom floor, her weapon clattering across the tiles, colliding with the bathtub. Owen rushed to Anna. But it was too late. She was choking on her own blood, bubbles forming around her nostrils. She gasped her last death rattle as Owen cradled her in his arms.

Sixty-two

"Jump in!" shouted Bob Stebbins, holding the door open for Owen while keeping the car in motion. Owen broke cover and threw himself into the passenger seat, banging the door behind him. As Bob drove off he looked behind but saw no one following. *Maybe Kedrov doesn't know yet,* he thought, *otherwise his people would be at every street corner within a five-mile radius of the Kempinski.*

"What in hell happened?" asked Bob.

"A hit! Anna's dead! Somebody wants me dead, too – in a very bad way!"

"Did you see who tried to kill you?"

"I did better than that. She's dead!"

"She?"

"Yes! A woman! A damned good lookin' one too!"

"Jesus!" Bob Stebbins let that news sink in for a minute. He still hadn't come to terms with the night's events. "Who wants you dead? And why?"

"I don't know," lied Owen. In his mind Bob did not 'have a need to know.'

"Maybe it's a case of mistaken identity."

"I can't make that assumption. I've got to get

---

out of Moscow. Out of Russia. But I can't just drive to the airport and board the next flight. They'll be looking for me everywhere. Especially there."

"OK. You'll have to lie low for a couple of days. I know a place. If anybody is looking for you they'll never find you. I'll work on a way to get you out of the country."

"Bill, please take Anna home. To Azerbaijan. And do what you can for the family. No matter what it costs. Understand?"

"I understand, Owen. I can't believe she's gone. We'll miss her on the team. It just won't be the same. We all loved her! Goddammit! The bastards!"

Sixty-three

Owen knew it was risky. They'd be looking for him everywhere. But he had to see the Insect. Bob Stebbins tried to stop him but failed. So he compromised, hid Owen in the back of his car, and drove him to the Insect's.

The Insect was waiting for MacDara. Anna had arranged it before she died. The Insect still couldn't believe it. Anna dead. His beautiful Anna. In his own way he loved her. Always had. Even before he'd shared that first Cadburys with her. She understood him. Very few people did. The Insect knew that. He knew he was different. Even when he was a little boy he had come to understand that. He used to cry about it then. Cry when none of the other boys wanted to be his friend. He used to tell his mother that he wished he was like all the other boys. But he'd gotten over that. He'd learned not to expect others to be his friends. His mind had helped him through – and his computers. He loved his computers. Then there was Anna. She was different. She didn't shy away from him. Tears were trickling down his cheeks when he answered the knock at his apartment door. Owen MacDara could see that the Insect had been crying. It didn't take

289

much to tell him why.

"Was she a good friend?" asked Owen, in words that seemed superfluous but were intended to get the Insect to talk about it.

"I loved Anna," blurted the Insect, unable to suppress his feelings.

"I did too. Everyone who knew Anna loved her," said Owen, "she was a very special lady."

"Why did she die like that? She didn't deserve to die like that. Who did it? Why? Why would anyone want to hurt Anna?" asked the Insect.

"Someone who thought she knew too much. That's who killed her. And I think you know who that is," said Owen.

The Insect thought hard about that and didn't say anything for a while. He wiped the tears from his eyes and the drip from his nose with the sleeve of his jacket. Owen continued. "Anna found out about the system you were building for Misha Kedrov. And she found out what he planned to use it for. She didn't live to tell you that. She thought she'd be here today."

"Yes, yes! She was so worried. That's why I agreed to meet you. I wanted to know."

"Well, I think you should know what you've gotten yourself into. And I believe you can get yourself out of it. And avenge Anna too."

Owen MacDara talked. The Insect listened. MacDara held nothing back. The Insect was the key to block Misha Kedrov. Owen knew that he needed the Insect fully committed. If Anna were here she could have persuaded him. Owen could only rely on the strength of the Insect's desire for revenge. And the evil that killed Anna called for revenge. And that evil was Misha Kedrov. Owen kept the Insect focused on that.

"Kedrov is flying to Birmingham in six days.

My company completed acceptance testing his system three weeks ago. You were involved in that. Kedrov's team shipped and installed the hardware for the G8 conference a week ago. So what's left? What's he taking with him?"

"His presentation. His speech to the conference. And my telecommunications software. That'll be installed when he gets there. He didn't want to ship it with the system," said the Insect.

"How is he taking it? What's it on?" asked Owen.

"It's all on three DVDs. His presentation is on one of them. The other two are my telecom software," said the Insect.

"What exactly does your software do? Anna told me a little but I'd like to hear it from you," said Owen.

The Insect's eyes lit up from the fire in his brain. This was his passion. His creation. He started talking. Nonstop. Never considering for a minute that his listener might not understand. But Owen got enough. Between long technical torrents and almost mystical meanderings, Owen gleaned what the Insect had accomplished. A telecommunications breakthrough far ahead of the current state of the art. A system that could 'hit the moon.' The Insect's system would commandeer every terrestrial and satellite communications channel on the planet. It would intercept all broadcasts: national and international news; commuters listening on their car radios. It would broadcast simultaneously in all major languages. No one in the world would escape the message.

"That's what Anna tried to explain to me. That's what scared me. If Kedrov broadcasts his revelations to the world it'll set us back into the days of the Cold War again. And I'm not so sure it'll be a

291

cold one this time. Who knows where Russia's nuclear arsenal really is today? Or who controls it for that matter? Kedrov and his *maffiya* probably have nuclear weapons. That's what we've got to stop. And that's why I'm here.

"I want to replace Kedrov's DVD. We will get it to you when you reach England for the conference. Can you do it?"

"What is on it?" asked the Insect.

"It's the weapon to avenge Anna. If Kedrov broadcasts our DVD it will destroy him. That's what you want, isn't it? Can you do it?" asked Owen.

"Yes! I can do it. Yes! I will do it!" The fire in the Insect's brain ignited again. His eyes burned brightly. His body jerked in spasms. Before Owen could move, the Insect grabbed him and kissed him furiously on each cheek.

Sixty-four

Zhukov was unkempt, unshaven, dirty and drunk. Vodka spilled out of a half empty bottle clutched tightly in his right fist. He lurched across the road, ranting and raving. Still raving unintelligibly, he waded knee-high into a rain-swollen river. The water swirled around him but he waded even deeper. Now the water was up to his chest and his right arm flourished the vodka bottle over his head. It seemed both a symbol of defiance and a cry for help. His shouting became even louder. Now he was up to his neck in the water and his eyes were bulging out of his head. Suddenly he was out of the river, dripping wet, vodka bottle still in hand, now standing motionless like a statue in the middle of the road. Cars seemed to appear out of nowhere, traveling in both directions, missing him by mere inches. Still he stood there like a rock as though daring them to hit him.

MacDara sensed the rapid noisy beating of his heart; next he sensed fear. Sweat poured off his body and the single sheet that covered him felt damp and

clammily cold around his neck. He sat up, turned on
the light and reached for his watch: four a.m. He
swung his feet onto the floor and into the crumpled
pile of his clothes, dropped there when he had fallen
drunkenly into bed two hours earlier. He went out to
the bathroom and splashed cold water on his face.
His heart raced. Alcohol and adrenaline. The deadly
combination. Last night he'd really set out to get
drunk. Oh yes, he'd known what he was doing. He
had wanted it all to go away. Kate's death. Anna's
murder. All the deaths. All the killing. He made his
way back to the bed, climbed in and sat upright,
thinking.

This dream, this nightmare, seemed so real.
His rational mind told him that the drink caused it.
But another deeper sense told him not to be so sure
about that. His Celtic sense of life's mysteries
insisted that life existed on many levels. Maybe it's
an omen. A prophecy. A warning. Some form of
ESP brought to life by his night of boozing. Oh yes,
he knew he'd pay for it. His body was out of practice.
But last night he hadn't given a damn.

It had all started here, at this 'safe house',
where Bob Stebbins had brought him after he fled
from the killings in the Kempinski. The safe house
was Dr. Valentin Cretu's – his Moldovan consultant
– a man with no particular love for the Russians.
Valentin had produced the vodka as soon as he had
arrived back from seeing the Insect. Medicine for
trauma and shock. But it had soon become obvious
as that first bottle emptied that he had wanted more
than a painkiller. He had wanted oblivion. He felt
his eyes closing again, lay back down and
immediately fell into a deep sleep.

Six hours later he woke up with a violent headache.

He was slumped upright in an awkward position. The light was still on. He moved and then winced from the pain in his neck muscles. He felt nauseous and stumbled out to the toilet. His attempts at vomiting only succeeded in dry retching. He wished he were dead – out of his misery. Then he swore he'd never do this again. The price was too great. He sat on the floor beside the toilet holding on to the rim of the bowl for support. The cool feel of the ceramic bowl earthed him, brought his mind back in focus. He remembered his dream, his nightmare. He closed his eyes and concentrated. The entire dream came back to him. He saw the drunken Zhukov up to his neck in the river, then standing statue-like in the road as the traffic whizzed past him. The dream was too vivid to dismiss. He determined to see Zhukov. Even if Misha Kedrov was scouring Moscow for him. He had to risk it. He needed to see Zhukov anyway. He had always felt that Zhukov had not told him everything. Now he thought he knew what Zhukov was holding back. He needed confirmation of that.

Sixty-five

Mariinsk, Siberia

The flight from Moscow to Kemerovo, the regional capital of the Kuzbass region of Russia took a little over four hours. Owen MacDara sat silently beside Dr. Valentin Cretu, staring ahead, blankly, and stupidly. Perfectly in character with his papers which identified him as Dr. Cretu's retarded cousin. To Owen it wasn't too difficult. Unshaven and eyes red rimmed, he still hadn't recovered from his drinking of three nights ago. The morning after that drunken night, Bob Stebbins and Valentin Cretu, at MacDara's insistence, had attempted to find Zhukov. He wasn't at his apartment. He wasn't at his house in Safonikha. No one had seen him lately. A little bribery and couple of cases of vodka soon produced results. It seemed that Zhukov had been arrested for stealing sausages and vodka. He had protested his innocence, but to no avail. He was now in detention, awaiting trial. That could take from eighteen months to two years. There was no bail. Zhukov had already been in prison for three months. Russia's prison system was overcrowded and underfunded. Moscow's overflow is sent to the Kuzbass region in Siberia, the place where the Soviets and the Tsars sent their dissidents, their political foes, and their poets, artists and writers who failed to conform. Many died there from disease, harsh treatment and starvation. Ten thousand people work in the jails of Kuzbass, jails packed with over thirty thousand inmates. Many prisoners spend up to 23 hours a day in their cells. They are undernourished and unhealthy. TB is the biggest scourge of all. Prison hospital colonies are filled with tubercular inmates. That was the destiny of Georgy Zhukov. Dr. Valentin Cretu had learned from his sources, lubricated with sufficient vodka, that Zhukov had caught TB soon after his detention. He was in Hospital Colony No. 27 in Mariinsk. Dr. Cretu posed as his nephew and requested permission to visit his uncle. Permission was granted. The bureaucracy had become lax and non-existent since the collapse of the Soviet Union.

At Kemerovo a car was waiting for them, arranged and paid for by Bob Stebbins. A three hour drive through forest and farmland and they were in Mariinsk. Dr. Ivan Malenkov ushered them into his office.

"You may find that your uncle does not know you, Dr. Cretu," said Dr. Malenkov. "He is old and very sick and his mind wanders. Sometimes he doesn't know who he is or where he is."

"I don't understand," said Dr. Cretu. "Six months ago, he was strong and healthy. What happened?"

"Oh, in a way, he did it to himself. He

wouldn't eat when he came to Kemerovo. Claimed he was innocent. They all do, you know. Claimed it was a conspiracy. To silence him. Another familiar claim," said Dr. Malenkov, eyeing Owen with some interest, as Owen stared blankly into space, fidgeting with the buttons on his coat, "but, of course, those days are gone. We don't have any political prisoners any more."

"When was he sent here?" asked Valentin.

"About a month ago. When he wouldn't eat he just got weaker. Then he caught TB. We're treating him now. But he needs to take all of his drugs. Every day. Even then it may take up to a year to cure him. But only if he eats and only if he takes all his drugs. He's eating a bit, but not enough. We can't be sure if he's taking all of his drugs. There's been very little improvement in him since he came here. As I said, you're welcome to see him. But he may not know you," said Dr. Malenkov and then, pointing to Owen, said, "What about him?"

"My cousin. He was born like that. Can't speak or hear. But Uncle Georgy loves him. I brought him with me. Just a chance it might help," said Dr. Cretu.

The meeting was over. Dr. Malenkov called in a nurse, a stocky middle-aged, battle-weary woman.

"Nina," said Dr. Malenkov, "take Dr. Cretu and his cousin to see Georgy Zhukov," and then ushered them all out of his office.

Before they saw Zhukov, Nurse Nina asked them to put on white gauze masks to protect themselves.

"It's safer if you wear these. It's better here now than it used to be. But you should still protect yourself. A couple of years ago a third of our patients were dying from TB. We buried about one hundred a month. But now the World Health Organization is helping us. We're getting more money and more drugs," she said.

She turned on her heel and plodded ahead of them to the corner of a ward unit where a hollow-cheeked, frail old man sat on the sagging mattress on his metal-framed bed. He was leaning on a walking stick that anchored him to the floor between his two bony knees. The man who sat there was only a shadow of the strong oak-like Zhukov that Owen had found tilling his vegetables in Safonikha.

Nurse Nina said, "Don't stay with him too long. I doubt if he'll know you, anyway. I'm sorry." She then departed and left them there.

There were no other patients in the ward. Georgy Zhukov looked at them. There was no recognition. Of course, there wouldn't be in the case of Dr. Valentin Cretu. They had never met each other before. And the masks didn't help either, Owen decided. The old man was coughing now, a deep racking cough that shook his frail body. Owen stepped out of range of the cough and pulled down his mask.

"Mr. Zhukov. My name is Owen MacDara. Do you remember me? I went to see you in Safonikha in May. We talked about the KGB...about the Congo. I told you that the President of the United States had sent me to see you. I asked you about the death of Dag Hammarskjold in the Congo. The U.N. Secretary-General. Do you remember?" asked Owen, watching Zhukov for a sign of recognition, any sign. But Zhukov said nothing, trying to suppress his coughing, and looking intently at Owen. His eyes were bright, abnormally bright, the eyes of one whose mind seemed to be fired by the wasting of his body.

Dr. Valentin Cretu spoke through his mask.

"Owen, I'm afraid Dr. Malenkov is right. He doesn't remember you. I doubt that he would know his own mother. I'm afraid you'll learn no more here. Whatever you were looking for is going to stay that way. Maybe that's why Zhukov is here. To shut him up. If it is, they've succeeded."

"Oh, I know that's why he's here. This proud old man would never steal. He was framed. I'm afraid there's nothing we can do for him. Except hope that the drugs ease his pain. OK, let's go," said Owen, putting on his mask again and looking at Zhukov for the last time.

But Zhukov had taken his hands from the walking stick and propped it against the bed. He was unbuckling his belt and pulling it through the loops. Owen stopped and watched. Zhukov slid a long chisel-like thumbnail along a section of the belt and the seam came apart. He reached in with his bony fingers and took something out, something that looked like a piece of paper that had been folded and folded until it wasn't much larger than two postage stamps. He reached out and gave it to Owen. He still didn't speak but there was just the faint trace of a smile at the edge of his lips.

In the car on the return journey to Kemerovo, Owen MacDara gingerly unfolded the piece of paper given to him by Georgy Zhukov. The writing was small, neat, and precise – and Russian. He knew enough of the language to get the gist of it. This was the mirror image of the revelations in the Wainwright diary. Confirmation that the orders to kill Hammarskjold had come from Washington and Moscow. This was what Misha Kedrov wanted. This was what he might already know. This was news that would topple the fragile Russian Government. This is exactly what Misha Kedrov wanted. It all became perfectly clear to Owen MacDara. Misha would get his revenge. And profit from it handsomely. His *maffiya* would be the only organization to survive the chaos that would ensue.

A perfect revenge. Kedrov had to be stopped. At any cost.

Sixty-six

The Bunch of Grapes Pub,
Knightsbridge,
London

Conor Brady took the first London taxi he saw at Heathrow Airport and, less than thirty minutes later, he alighted in Knightsbridge. The taxi driver, normally a loquacious Eastender, sensed that his passenger desired silence. So the only words he uttered on the entire trip were "Where to, Guv'?" at Heathrow and "Thanks, Guv" when he dropped his passenger in Knightsbridge – which was just the way Conor Brady wanted it.

He let himself daydream on the ride into London. *I'm not getting a kick out of this any more. Too many assignments. Too many years. Something's happening to me. Something I hadn't experienced before. I'm losing the need to live on the edge, to feel that adrenaline rush that goes with the job. I'm getting too old for this game,* he thought. *Maybe I should retire. That's a good one! Do old revolutionaries and assassins retire or do they just fade away like MacArthur's old soldiers? More like 'blown away'.*

Conor didn't need the money anymore. The ten million he'd stashed away in Zurich would do. He didn't need this deal. But he couldn't turn it down. Misha had made him an offer he couldn't refuse. One million dollars! Half up front and the rest when the job was done. Zurich had already confirmed that first half million was now sitting in his account. Misha wanted this one badly. So Conor had accepted. He owed Misha. But he still thought that he might make this his last. Retire? Where? Maybe I could risk going home, he contemplated. But where is home? Buenos Aires? No! He had wrenched Buenos Aires out of his heart a long time ago. But he did admit one thing to himself. He wanted to see his father again.

"Thanks, Guv'" Conor's reverie now broken, he paid the driver, and got out on the corner of Knightsbridge and Sloane. He walked down Sloane Street towards Sloane Square, took a right on the King's Road, went about ten blocks into Chelsea, took another right into a quiet residential street until he reached number 28, a Kedrov Enterprises property. Misha kept private houses like this in a number of places, well placed for discretion, privacy and the absence of a trail through hotel registers. Once inside, Conor stripped, took a two-minute George Bush shower, dressed casually, and then made himself one of his favorite Spanish omelets. Two cups of coffee later, he locked the front door and strode back towards the Kings Road. He had no time to waste.

Conor's Chelsea base was well chosen. In less than twenty minutes, he had reached Knightsbridge and positioned himself where he could watch the front door of MacDara's house. If Misha's intelligence had been correct, Leslie Scott would be here. And this is where MacDara will go if he makes it out of Russia. He'd been lucky. He'd escaped the hit at the Kempinski and gone to ground. Misha was scouring Moscow for him. *If he makes it out of Russia. Let me correct that*, thought Conor, *when MacDara makes it out of Russia.* Conor had no doubt about that. The man had more than nine lives. In fact Conor had developed a grudging respect for Owen MacDara's abilities. *Yes, he'll come right here. And I'll be here to greet him.* Still, there's no need to approach this assignment with any less rigor than normal. Be thorough. Pay attention to detail. Never assume anything. Conor knew that this made the difference between success and failure. And, in his business, failure could be fatal. So he waited and watched. An hour passed. Then he saw him – another who waited and watched. A fidgety other, incessantly smoking, leaving a circle of cigarette butts at his feet. There could be no doubt. He's watching MacDara's house too. But who? Why? Misha had said nothing about this. That must mean he doesn't know. Who? MI5? No, this watcher's definitely not MI5. In fact he doesn't act like a covert operative of any agency. As Brady teased his brain on the matter, a decision was forced on him. Another joined the fidgety one. Only a nod of acknowledgement passed between them. A replacement. The fidgety one stubbed out his last butt, stuck his hands in his pockets, and walked away. Brady decided to follow him.

The fidgety one stopped outside The Bunch of Grapes, a pub in Knightsbridge, lit another cigarette, and then disappeared through the doors of the pub. The clock over the bar said 5 p.m. *Busy! Must be the early happy hour crowd or the late liquid lunch crowd, maybe a little of both*, thought Conor, as he edged his way to the bar and ordered a pint of Guinness. As he waited for the head to settle on his pint, he scanned the place until he found his quarry, sitting at a corner table in the back, talking to another man. Conor sensed something familiar about the other man; about the way he used his hands as he talked. Just then the man stopped talking to the fidgety one, raised his head and looked directly across at Conor, as though he'd been told to do so. It was instantaneous. They knew. Their minds clicked. The tape rewound. Back, back, all those years. They're standing together again in the North African desert, in that Libyan training camp. A huge smile transformed the man's face. He got up, walked straight to Conor, stood facing him for just one moment, and then grasped him in a bear hug.

"Conor, bejasus! It is you, isn't it, you old blackguard? You haven't aged a damned day!"

"Marty! Marty! Marty!" At a total loss for words, taken by surprise, Conor felt compromised. But his pleasure at seeing Marty O'Neill again drove that feeling away, "You haven't aged much either."

"Don't lie to me, Conor. Come on, come on, join us!" ordered Marty, giving Conor just enough time to grab his pint and follow.

"Billy, move over. Make room for an old friend. Conor, this is Billy Clancy," said Marty, almost as an afterthought. Billy nodded to Conor, made a space at the table, and lit a fresh cigarette with the glowing end of the butt between his lips.

"So, how long's it been? Twenty years?" enthused Marty, touching his glass to Conor's and toasting, "Slainte!"

"Twenty-three years exactly, Marty!" said Conor.

305

"Always exact, Conor. You haven't changed. That's what I remember about you. Exact. You were always exact. You did everything exactly by the book. Remember?" and, without waiting for Conor to answer, he turned to Billy Clancy.

"Billy, Conor and I did our basic training together – in North Africa!"

Billy's eyebrows raised with the surprise of it all and he ventured, "Is Conor with us, then?"

At that, Marty leant back in his chair and almost toppled over laughing. "No, Billy! Conor is what you might call an independent. Isn't that right, Conor?"

"Marty's right, Billy. I have no great cause. Sometimes I envy those who do," said Conor.

Marty, sensing a serious tone in Conor's voice, looked over at Billy. "Billy, we're finished anyway. I want to spend a while with Conor. I'll call you tomorrow."

Billy knew his place. He stood, gulped down the last of his drink, stubbed out his cigarette, said goodbye to Conor and left. Marty looked at his watch. It was 6 p.m.

"Listen, I don't know about you, Conor, but I'm hungry. What're you doin' this evening? No plans. Good. OK, you're having dinner with me. Let's go. I know a good Indian place. Not too far from here. You like Indian, don't you? " Marty rambled on between nods from Conor, who knew that he didn't stand a chance of getting out of it.

A short fifteen-minute walk later, they were ushered to a table for two upstairs at Salloos on Kinnerton Street.

"So what brings you to London, Conor? Or should I know the answer to that question already?" Marty spoke in his low persuasive Kerry brogue, never taking his eyes off Conor's face.

"Come on, Marty. There's no need for you and me to beat around the bush. You know you didn't run into me in that pub by accident."

"OK. You're right. I know why you're here. You're still working for Kedrov, aren't you?"

"You've done your homework, haven't you, Marty?"

"When you died in that plane in Amman, I didn't believe it. We have contacts. I was curious. So I asked some questions."

"Alright, Marty. Let's put our cards on the table. Why are you babysitting Leslie Scott?"

"That's easy. We're doin' a favor for someone."

"Who?"

"Another easy question. The President of the US. He doesn't trust his own people on this one. Besides, he knows we owe him a favor. The way he looks at it, we wouldn't be in negotiations with the Brits if it weren't for him. He has a point. And we may need him again. So we're doin' him a favor. We're taking care of his young lady. You're not goin' to screw that up for us now, Conor, are you?"

"I want no fight with you, Marty. I still remember Libya. The endless talks. Discussions. Arguments. I could never match your passion. And I envied you your *'cause'.*"

"I remember too, Señor Kelly. You're still a Kelly. Your grandfather was proud to be a Young Irelander. I wanted you to join us then. I want you to join us now."

"I didn't join you then, Marty. Why do you think I'd join you now?"

"Ah, Conor, there's been a lot of water under the bridge since then. You've had plenty of time to think. You need to believe in something, Conor. Besides, you can't be sure you'll succeed this time, can you? And we don't take prisoners. Even for old time's sake."

Conor had to admit to himself that Marty made sense. This new approach had caught him at a vulnerable time. Just when he was thinking about *'retiring'*. But, when he stopped *'daydreaming'*, he knew there was no *'getting out'*, no *'retirement'*, no place for him to go. *Maybe Marty is right. Maybe I do need to believe in something. Maybe I need to leave a legacy for the Kellys. For my father.*

"Suppose I were to consider your offer, Marty. What do you propose?"

"Well, I'd like you to meet someone and talk about it. No obligation. Why don't you let me do that before we burn any bridges here?"

"OK. Set it up."

"Good. Meet me at The Bunch of Grapes tomorrow. Twelve noon."

Sixty-seven

Irish Club,
Eaton Square,
London

1:00 p.m.

Big Charlie Magee was under no illusions. Marty O'Neill had been adamant. They did not need this Conor Brady as an enemy. Not now. Not ever. Even though Eduardo Kelly Herrera, or his alter ego Conor Brady, had not become a household name like Carlos the Jackal, Marty considered him even more dangerous. Best to try and recruit him. Get him to defect. Convince him that Ireland needed its diaspora, although *'the cause'* didn't need men like him anymore. *The war is over.* Now we'll talk, convince and cajole our way to a United Ireland. True democracy at work. Deep down Big Charlie had his doubts about that but it was the only game in town.

The darkly lit, wood paneled interior of the bar at the Irish Club on Eaton Square gave no indication of the time of day outside. Big Charlie propped his back against the bar and he had begun to savor his first pint of the day when Marty O'Neill and Conor Brady came through the door. Marty made the introductions and left. Big Charlie sized up the challenge standing facing him: agile, dark complexion, blue eyes, good looking, the kind of countenance found in the people of the west of Ireland, many of whom had more than a drop of Spanish blood.

"Conor, Marty's told me all about you. I've been looking forward to meeting you. They've got a private room for us at the back of the club. We won't be disturbed there. What'll you have?" said Big Charlie.

"The same for me," said Conor, pointing to Big Charlie's pint of Guinness. The bartender told them he'd bring it back when it was ready.

When they were alone Big Charlie wasted no time: "Conor, I know all about you. Your family. Your grandfather. The reason you had to leave Argentina. Marty's filled me in on all of that. So we don't need to waste any time here. Marty invited you to join us. He said you were thinking about it. But I want to hear what you have to say."

"Charlie, I'll be honest with you. I don't believe in anything very much. Sure, when Marty met me in Libya, I was working for the PLO. Not because I wanted a Palestinian State. It was a home of sorts for me – for a while. And I loved the danger, the anarchy of it all."

A knock on the door interrupted them and the bartender entered with Conor's pint of Guinness. He had traced the outline of a shamrock on the surface of the pint's creamy head. Conor picked it up, saying, "Even your drink is conspiring to recruit me."

Big Charlie waited for Conor to savor his first

swallow of the Guinness and then prompted him to continue: "So why does Marty believe that you might be considering joining us?"

"OK. I'll be honest with you. I want to quit and you might be the answer. It's that simple. I know it'd be better if I said I believed in your cause. If I said I wanted to follow in my grandfather's footsteps. But that would be a lie. Oh yes, I envy you your 'cause'. Your belief that there's something worth giving your life for. But not even a drop of my Kelly blood makes me feel that," said Conor.

"Then I'll be straight with you too, Conor," said Big Charlie. "We don't need your expertise in the movement. We hope the Good Friday agreement will work. And we hope the guns, everybody's guns, will rust in the ground. But we're practical people. We don't want you against us on this thing we're doing for the Americans. We don't need that. So we're willing to cut a deal with you. Buy you off, if you want to put it crudely. And maybe my romantic side says we owe one to old Patrick Kelly."

They both said nothing for a while, only sipping their Guinness. Finally, Conor said: "I'll need guarantees. The right to live in Ireland. The protection of the Irish and British governments. An amnesty. Just like your political prisoners. Can you do that?"

"I think I can. But I doubt if you'll see anything in writing. You'll just have to trust me."

"Trust, Charlie? I'm afraid I'll need something else. An understanding. Some evidence."

Big Charlie had already considered all of this. The meeting was going exactly as he had anticipated. He looked directly at Conor. "Conor, I need something in return from you. If I get you your deal, I need to know what we're up against here. I need to know what you came to England to do. That's the

quid pro quo. Do we have a deal?"
"We have a deal," said Conor Brady.

Conor Brady felt good about the deal. Still, it meant that he had to break his contract with Misha Kedrov. And lose a million too! But everything's a trade-off. It's a cheap price to pay for his 'retirement'. And he didn't feel that he was being a traitor. They already knew about Misha and there wasn't much he could add. When he thought about it he realized that he really knew very little about Misha Kedrov's plans. *So I'm simply removing myself from the game. And the Irish and the British are willing to pay well for that.* It gave him a sense of his own worth. *But what about MacDara? He doesn't know any of this. He'll still be gunning for me. It still might be a case of self-preservation.*

Sixty-eight

Moldova

Dr. Valentin Cretu slowed his car to a crawl as they approached the border crossing into Moldova. Looking at his passenger, he said: "Remember, you are my cousin. My retarded cousin. You are deaf and dumb. Keep that look. I'll do the talking for both of us."

Owen MacDara looked the part. He even felt the part. Unshaven for the past week, his eyes red-rimmed and blotchy from lack of sleep, he had adopted a vacant stare, and purposely looked straight ahead as Valentin Cretu spoke. A dribble of saliva appeared at the corner of his mouth and ran down his slack lower lip.

Two guards manned the border. One seemed to be in charge. He did the talking. The other appeared to be just a functionary. Dr. Valentin Cretu got out of the car and approached them. The guard examined their identification documents and pointed towards Owen, who could see Valentin's body movements as he explained the sad condition of his cousin. The functionary walked back to the car and said something to Owen, first in Russian and then in

Moldovan. Owen didn't budge, stared straight ahead vacantly. The guard walked away again, and Owen could see him shake his head as he approached the other guard who was now handing back the documents to Valentin.

The leather folder displaying the doctor's medical credentials helped to impress the guard, especially the five folded US $20 dollar bills inside. He palmed the dollars as he returned the folder. Valentin thanked him, walked back to the car, never looking at Owen, started the engine and moved slowly past the border post.

They drove across the border into Moldova. But they didn't speak for at least a mile. Then Dr. Cretu looked across at Owen MacDara again: "Now you don't have to look like an idiot any more."

"Valentin, I've been playing the part like my life depended on it. And it probably did. So it's hard to give it up. But I'll try," said Owen, now grinning from ear to ear.

"We're not far from Kishinev now. You'll probably see more police before we get there. We have plenty of them in Moldova. But we shouldn't have any trouble. If any of them stop us, this always works," said Valentin, gesturing with his hand and rubbing the thumb and fingers together intimating the passing of a bribe. "Your papers are good. They passed the test so you shouldn't have any problem getting to Bucharest. It's easy going back and forth from Kishinev to Bucharest. We should be able to get you out of here in a couple of days."

Exactly three days later Owen MacDara, traveling under his own passport, boarded a British Airways flight from Bucharest to London.

Sixty-nine

**Kedrov Industries,
Moscow**

I must not fail!   That refrain echoed through
Alexandr Gelman's head as he returned to Kedrov
Industries for his final rehearsal at 8 p.m. on Friday.
No one worked late on Fridays.   They'd have
exclusive use of the audio-visual equipment in the
main conference room for their '*dry run*'. Alexandr
could feel the moisture in the palms of his hands as
he opened the double doors to the conference room.

Misha sat at the end of the table. "Alexandr!
Come in! Come in! Are we ready?"

"Yes, Misha. I set the system up before I left.
I only have to load the software," said Alexandr. It
was always Misha when they were alone, and it was
always Mr. Kedrov when they weren't.

"While you do that, let me run through things
again," said Misha, as he stood up and walked
around the conference room.

"Yeltsin will be sitting here!   And Clinton
here! The rest, Chirac, Blair, Chretien, Kohl will be

here, here and here. Yeltsin has just introduced me
and I have moved up here to commence my keynote
address. That's exactly when you and your three
colleagues enter the room. You will be dressed in
military fatigues, your faces covered in balaclavas,
and you will be armed with Heckler & Koch machine
guns. And you will say?"

"Everyone! Hands on the table! Do not
move!"

"But I will not obey. I will try to rush you."

"Right! I will move quickly and hit you in the
stomach with the butt of my gun. You will double
over in agony. I will then speak to them."

"Tell me again!"

"I will say: 'We are the Russian Liberation
Army. We are fighting to free our country. We are
fighting for democracy. Real democracy. Not the
sham of the G7! Or is it the G8, Comrade Yeltsin.
You have followed in the footsteps of all our great
Kremlin leaders. Right into the arms of the US! A
sham! But we are here to expose your sham. No, we
are not going to kill you. Or take you hostage. We
want you to watch a video that we will broadcast
over the national television networks in each of your
countries. We will broadcast it to your people now.'"

"Great! But don't hit me so hard," jested
Misha.

"Just enough to make it look real. Make them
believe that we're your enemy too!"

"Good! Are you ready? Let's go!"

"Everything is here. On this single DVD. We
will already have installed the system in the G8
conference room to run your keynote presentation.
When I hit the enter key, just like this, we're on!"

Alexandr hit the enter key and Misha dimmed
the lights in the conference room.

The opening page filled the wall-to-wall

screen and it asked:

WHO KILLED HAMMARSKJOLD?

The narration started with the death of UN Secretary-General Dag Hammarskjold in the Congo, and the killing of the Acting UN Secretary-General Alexander Ridge in Moscow, followed by the display of the KGB documents showing that Hammarskjolds' death had been *'arranged'* by Washington and Moscow. It argued that Ridge had found out and had been killed by the White House and the Kremlin in an attempt at a cover-up. Then it showed the evidence: the KGB documents again, an interview with Zhukov that he obviously didn't know was being filmed, the role of Kearns and the CIA and, finally, the stunning climax: a video of a very beaten and tortured Wainwright *'confessing'* the names of those who ordered the assassination of Hammarskjold.

"Excellent! Just excellent!"

"Misha, let's go over the next steps. One more time."

"Alexandr, don't worry! They'll be so shocked they won't be able to see a thing. While you're running your video, I'll get up and make my way to the main bank of light switches. When the video ends, I'll throw the switches and turn the room into total darkness. Your team will make their exit, dispose of the military fatigues and the balaclavas, and escape as planned. You will put your authorized identity badge on and return to the systems workroom. As far as you're concerned, you saw and heard nothing! It's so simple! I love it!"

Pat Mullan

PART EIGHT

The Redemption

Pat Mullan

Seventy

Heathrow Airport,
England

Owen MacDara slung his carryon bag over his left shoulder and strode first off the flight at Heathrow. Minutes later he sat in a taxi on his way into London. Tired and weary, he dozed on the short ride from the airport. Good at catnapping, he could do it anywhere, at any time. His US Army buddies used to make fun of him, saying that he'd sleep through a mortar attack. Since the killing in the Kempinski, he'd slept little. Being on the run and getting a good night's sleep were not compatible. Nearing the city, he shook himself awake and considered the next twenty-four hours. A shower, shave, and a change of clothes. He had a craving for spaghetti bolognese, a baguette, and a good bottle of red. Soul food. Fortification for the battle that was sure to come. But first things first. He had called Big Charlie from Bucharest but Charlie wouldn't talk, insisted instead that Owen meet him as soon as he landed. And that's exactly where he was headed now. The shower and the soul food would have to wait. Leslie too. At least she'd been in good hands. Big Charlie would have taken care of that. Still, MacDara knew that there were no certainties in this life. If Misha Kedrov had tried to *'take him out'* in Moscow, then maybe he had tried to *'take out'* Leslie too. No opposition. Clear the way for G8. Goddamn! *And where's Conor Brady? Where did he go after killing Kasparov in Texas? He's here!* Of that MacDara's certain. *Brady is here! But where? And what will he try to do? Take me out? Of course! He's an assassin. That's what he does best. Kedrov would have contacted him by now. Told him that the Moscow 'hit' had failed. That I am still alive. And on my way here. Yes, Kedrov would know that I am on my way here. That's it. Brady will try and stop me getting to Birmingham. But I have one ace that Brady doesn't know about. Big Charlie Magee. His people will be watching.*

Big Charlie Magee waited in his favorite place, the Irish Club on Eaton Square. The two other men with Charlie surprised Owen. He had expected to meet Big Charlie alone. Charlie introduced them: Marty O'Neill and Major Robin Cooper. He briefed Owen on Conor Brady, the *'deal'* he'd done with him, and why he had to bring the Prime Minister into the picture. Owen lost it. "Goddamn it, Charlie! This was not in your remit! We only asked you to watch out for Leslie Scott. Not start running your own show! And I do not trust Conor Brady."

Charlie kept his cool and waited till Owen finished his tirade. "Brady's safer where we can keep an eye on him. I don't trust him either." Big Charlie explained that he had no choice. "You were in Moscow. There was no way to contact you. If Marty here hadn't recognized Brady, we wouldn't be in this situation. Then again, maybe we'd have been in a much worse situation. Who knows?"

"OK, Charlie. So where are we?"

"That's what we want to ask you. Let's back up a bit. I have an open channel to 10 Downing Street. Have had for years. It doesn't matter if you know his name or not. It's James Metcalf. To the public, James is the PM's Chief of Staff. But, to the PM, James is more like your National Security Advisor, what's his name? Shields, that's it. James Metcalf is the PM's Bart Shields. Anyhow, I couldn't do this deal for you without letting the PM know. I had to tell him about you, about Leslie Scott, and what little I knew about this G8 threat. Of course he was angry – to put it mildly. He called your President – chewed his ass out, I believe. But, after the President explained, he cooled off. He realized that he probably couldn't trust anyone in MI5 or MI6 either. So he asked Metcalf to put a team together. A team we could trust. And to make that team available to you. That's it. We're waiting for you to tell us what to do. In case you're worried Metcalf would trust the Major here with his life. And I would trust Marty O'Neill with mine. I hope I never have to."

Owen looked directly at O'Neill and the Major. "Tell me about your team."

"There are eight of us. That includes the Major and myself. I have three men. Handpicked. The best!" said Marty O'Neill.

"And I have three men I'd trust with my own life too," said Major Cooper.

"Can your people work together? That's the important test," asked Owen.

"We are professionals. So are our men," said the Major. "Our personal feelings don't matter."

"And what about you, Marty? How do you feel about this?" asked Owen.

"I'll be honest. I'm not comfortable. But we'll do the job. You can rely on us. I give you my word on it," said O'Neill.

"Alright, gentlemen. Meet me in two hours' time at my house. Charlie will give you directions. And bring every map, plan, layout or other detail you can find about Weston Manor. I'll brief you then."

Wembley

Owen MacDara met Conor Brady on neutral ground. A *'safe house'* in Wembley, not far from the stadium. A house used by people needing protection from those who intended to kill them. Big Charlie had arranged it through James Metcalfe.

They stood, ten feet apart. Sizing each other up. Owen MacDara saw that Conor Brady was the same height as himself. Conor Brady thought that MacDara's intensity was a good match for his own. Neither spoke. Neither shook hands. They sat down in the kitchen, keeping the table between them.

Owen finally said, "I don't trust you. You must know that."

Conor shrugged his shoulders; "I saved your life once."

Owen stared, unsmiling, "And you expect me to thank you for that. You were playing with me. Some kind of cat and mouse game. I suppose it's boring being a terrorist!"

Conor laughed. "Terrorist! Ha! What do they say, *one man's terrorist is another man's patriot.*"

Owen shouted, "Bullshit! And you know it, Kelly! You dishonor your Irish grandfather! You kill for money, not to free your country. You work for a gangster. You're just a common criminal!"

Conor's eyes blazed, "Keep the Kelly name out of this! The Kellys of Argentina are proud of their grandfather. What do you know about me? About my motives? Don't think you know who I am! You know nothing! Nothing!"

Owen had cooled off. He didn't trust Conor Brady, but Brady was right. Owen did not know him. Brady was an enigma, but the die was cast. For good or bad, Brady had switched sides. Owen would have to go with that. For now.

A minute or two passed while they let the dust settle. Owen broke the silence. "Charlie Magee told me about your 'deal'. I have to accept his judgment. But I'm not happy about it. Everyone on my team needs to be trusted. You have to make me trust you. I need to know that you are not using this deal to sabotage us! How do I know that you are not working for Misha Kedrov?"

Conor answered, "You don't know! So you'll have to, as you Americans say, 'trust your gut.'" He looked indignant and then launched into a monologue, "I don't care about your great USA! Do you want to know what I really think? I think that your great USA is a tyrant, driven by greed and religious fanatics! You talk about democracy. You talk about evil. I'll give you evil! You call your black people 'niggers!' You pretend that your women are equal. But no, you treat them like sex objects. How many women run your country? None! How many black people run your country? Very few!" He stopped, fire burning in his eyes, and pointed his finger at Owen, "And your Ireland? I don't care about your cause. Why should I? What did it ever do for the Kellys? What did my grandfather get out of it? Is his name known in Ireland today? No! Nobody has ever heard of him!" He paused to get his breath and launched into his tirade again, "I cut a 'deal', as you say, with your governments. I'm not naïve. I know why they did it. They do not want me as their enemy. I took advantage of that. I want out. I want to live in a country where I am not a wanted man. One day I want to go back to Argentina. As a free man. See my father again – before he dies. That's my motive! Purely selfish! And you can trust me on that."

He had backed Owen into a corner and Owen knew it. *A complex man, this Conor Brady,* thought Owen, as he said, "We've got work to do. Marty O'Neill is waiting for us."

They had arrived separately. Now they left together.

Heathrow Airport

Alexandr Gelman flew into England as a member of the Russian advance party. They would smooth the way for Boris Yeltsin and the Russian delegation – insure that there were no last minute glitches that might embarrass the Russians, especially in front of the Americans. The Insect was with him. Leslie Scott had the DVD ready and Owen had made arrangements to get it to the Insect at his London hotel.

The computer system, a simple 'plug and play' installation, that Kedrov planned to use for his address to the G8 conference at Weston Park, had been shipped two weeks earlier. A separate telephone switch had been installed for the conference. It contained all the links that Kedrov needed for his broadcast.

It only remained for Alexandr Gelman to assemble his team. His '*Russian Revolutionary Liberators*'. This team of fifteen had already been handpicked by Misha Kedrov months before. Fourteen had entered England during the past three months, six legally and eight illegally. The six legal entrants had acquired student visas to study English. The last team member, already in England, served as a secretary at the Russian embassy in London, a cover for her deeper role in Kedrov's worldwide *maffiya* network.

Weston Park,
Staffordshire

An unholy alliance! That's what it is, Marty O'Neill thought to himself. He'd never have believed he'd see the day where he'd be on an operation with '*the old enemy*'. Yet here he was, planning the deployment of a joint Irish Republican and British SAS force. He wasn't alone in his feelings. SAS Major Robin Cooper thought that it was bizarre to be on the same team with people he had hunted down in South Armagh. Their operational HQ was a large '*tourist*' caravan with German license plates, a common sight in the English countryside at this time of year. A map of Weston Park lay spread out on the table.

The Major spoke: "This perimeter wall. Right here. It's about five miles long and completely encloses Weston Park. There's about 1,000 acres inside this wall. Over here – that's the Hall itself. That's where they're having their summit."

"They sure don't build things like that any more," said O'Neill.

"No. Nobody can afford to own places like this today. Many of them are open to the public just to provide enough income to keep the banks from foreclosing," said the Major.

"The Earl. Doesn't he own a restaurant or something?" asked O'Neill.

"Yes. Porters. In Covent Garden. He's also a gourmet chef. I think he's even President of the Master Chefs of Great Britain," said the Major.

"Now that's the kind of Earl you just might get me to like! I'd sure like to spend an hour or two in his wine cellar!" said O'Neill.

"Wouldn't we all! But I'm afraid this isn't much of a social visit. Let's go over the operation one more time," said Major Cooper.

The Major believed that you couldn't be too prepared. *Something we both have in common,* observed Marty O'Neill. Never assume anything. You'll live to regret it if you do.

International Convention Centre, Birmingham

'*Walkabouts'* scare the Secret Service. Memories of the Kennedy assassination and the more recent attempts on Ford and Reagan were never far from the backs of their minds. And this President's a *'touchy-feely'* one who liked to *'press the flesh'.* A people's President who seems to gain strength from every hand he shakes, every baby he kisses, and every young woman he encounters.

The Secret Service had reason to be nervous. The President was unpredictable. Today was no exception. As they watched him, he broke away and headed towards a nearby pub. Totally unplanned. They scrambled to cover him.

Inside The Black Swan the young proprietor rushed to greet the President. He wasn't the least intimidated by this unexpected visit. In fact he saw it as publicity he couldn't buy. A golden opportunity. "Welcome to Birmingham. And to The Black Swan, Mr. President."

"Thank you," said the President, "I just feel like a beer."

"Well, you've come to the right place. We're proud of our local beers."

"You're the expert. I'll have a pint please."

Two Secret Service men stood on either side of the door behind the President. A third walked directly into The Black Swan, casting an expert eye on every customer. Owen MacDara was sitting at the bar. He slid off the barstool and approached the President. The Secret Service men moved forward. The President gave them a signal with his right hand and they moved back again.

"Owen, this must be brief," said the President.

"Everything's in place, Mr. President. And the '*keynote*' event – exactly as we suspected," said Owen.

"We're in your hands, Owen. The Prime Minister and I are relying on you," said the President, "I'll expect you at Weston Park first thing tomorrow morning."

The brief encounter was over almost as soon as it had begun. The President emerged a minute later on the second floor balcony overlooking the street. Relaxed and smiling, he sat down and finished his beer while the photographers clicked away below. This photograph would make page one of all the evening newspapers.

Seventy-one

Weston Park Manor, Staffordshire

Prime Minister Tony Blair finished his welcoming speech to loud applause from his audience of peers. The TV cameras captured the smiles of the G8 leaders, showing their best faces to the world. They sat in an open-ended rectangle, with the open end housing a speaker's rostrum, floor to ceiling screens, and a loose configuration of computers, telephones, and communication equipment. Guests and support staff sat around the perimeter of the conference room.

After fifteen minutes, the TV networks and journalists were invited to leave. The conference took a short break and then commenced in private. Owen MacDara stood at the back, alert and expectant.

Tony Blair got the summit underway. "I am sure you all join me in welcoming our newest member." He raised his hand and stilled the spontaneous applause, "We feel that it is appropriate

331

to ask President Yeltsin to open our conference." He raised his hand once more to stop any further applause before it commenced.

President Yeltsin glanced around the table at the other leaders and, with just the hint of a smile, said, through his translator: "Thank you, Prime Minister. We are pleased to join you. We know that our economies no longer stand alone. We are dependant on each other. Russia is committed to playing a full part. We have much to offer and we also have much to learn. Today Russia is a new frontier. A frontier of individual energy and achievement. It is an exciting time. Our new entrepreneurs are building our new Russia. I have asked Misha Kedrov, Chairman of Kedrov Industries, to give the opening remarks today. I don't think that I need to introduce him to you. In a few short years he has made his name known in your countries too."

Conor Brady bit his nails. He looked at Marty O'Neill. Marty gave him the 'thumbs up' sign and a confident grip on the shoulder. They stood in the shadows close to the front entrance of Weston Park. The police and security chiefs assigned to protect the conference had been briefed in advance by MI5 so the Cooper/O'Neill team had full access. O'Neill's men were positioned along the main entranceway.

Leslie Scott felt anxious. She had twisted Owen's arm to be there. General Shields did not know. If he did, she reckoned he'd have *killed her* for putting herself in harm's way. But she needed to do this. Sitting on the sidelines had never been an option, and she had a score to settle for the murder of Old Theodore. Too much Washington desk work had given her cabin fever and the time in London, while necessary, had been just like one of the lonely, boring stake-outs she'd been on in her days as a cop in the

NYPD while she attended law school at night. She knew that Major Cooper had placed her close to himself. It was obvious that he felt responsible for her welfare. She did not know that he objected vehemently when Owen MacDara agreed to assign her to the team. The major felt that it was too high a risk.

Leslie crouched near the rear entrance to Weston Park. Major Cooper and the other half of the Cooper/O'Neill team had positioned themselves strategically around the rear of the building.

The major was on his mike to Marty O'Neill. "There's something moving back here. We see them. At least four or five. Moving out from the stables. We're going to engage."

Marty replied, "I'll send half of my team to join you, leave half here."

The major looked at Leslie. "I want you to stay here. Don't move." Then he commanded his team just as O'Neill's reinforcements joined: "They don't expect us. Spread out. Find a target. When I give the signal, shoot to kill!"

G8 Conference

Misha Kedrov rose from the chair directly behind President Yeltsin and walked smartly to the speaker's rostrum. "Thank you, President Yeltsin and Prime Minister Blair. I am very excited to be here and I thank you for the opportunity to address this summit."

He nodded to an unseen technician and the lights dimmed. The rostrum light illuminated his face, making him the focus of all eyes in the room. Exactly what he wanted. No one saw Alexandr

Gelman and his people enter and merge into the dark shapes of the computer configuration that abutted the speaker's rostrum.

Kedrov clicked a button and the large screen to his left lit up. A title appeared: RUSSIA AT THE MILLENNIUM. He moved to the center and addressed the G8 leaders, "In fifteen short years Kedrov Enterprises has grown from a small St. Petersburg business to a truly global enterprise. I am here to tell you that Russia today is poised to grow from an emerging new economy to the dominant economic force in the world by the year 2025. Yes, I predict that the first quarter century of the new millennium will be Russia's! Do not fear that! A strong Russia will be a stronger partner for all. We are not here to dominate. We are here to lead."

It happened exactly as rehearsed. Well, almost exactly. Misha Kedrov continued speaking, his face illuminated by the rostrum light, when a man in military fatigues, his face covered by a balaclava, jumped up and pushed him away from the rostrum. Kedrov fell to the floor. Alexandr Gelman had made his move.

As the lights in the room were turned up, Owen MacDara called Marty O'Neill, "It's going down!"

Gelman shouted in Russian and English, "Everyone! Hands on the table! Do not move!"

The G8 leaders were stunned. Armed figures, all in military fatigues with their heads covered, stood around the conference room. But one person disobeyed. He was a US Secret Service agent, under cover as conference support staff. He pulled a gun, aimed at Gelman, fired, missed, and died in a burst of gunfire.

Gelman yelled again, "We will kill anyone! Anyone! Do not move!"

Misha Kedrov picked himself up from the floor and rushed Gelman, who stepped aside and hit him in the stomach with his gun. Kedrov doubled over and fell to the floor again.

Gelman took the microphone. "We are the Russian Liberation Army! We are fighting to free our country! We are fighting for democracy! For real democracy, not your G8 sham! Comrade Yeltsin, you have taken our country into the arms of America! We are here to expose you! Not to kill you! We are here to end this sham! We are here to tell the world who you really are." He reached inside his fatigue jacket and held a DVD aloft: "We want you to watch a video. This video will be released to the national television networks in each of your countries. We will broadcast it to your people now." He handed the DVD to one of his team who moved to the computer and inserted it in the drive...

When they got Owen's signal that *"It's going down!"* Marty O'Neill and Conor Brady were already on the move. Leslie Scott had defied Major Cooper's orders and moved in from the rear. The three of them converged at the outer doors to the conference room. Marty looked at Leslie, "You shouldn't be here," but knew that his words were meaningless.

RUSSIA AT THE MILLENNIUM faded and the large screen went blank – just for a moment. Then a new title appeared: MISHA KEDROV – *Chairman of Russia's Maffiya!* followed by the face and voice of Tom Brooks, the well known NBC news anchor: "This is a special program, brought to you by the world community. Before you hear from UN

Secretary-General Kofi Annan, I want to show you the face of someone you already know, someone you believe is the face of the New Russia. He name is Misha Kedrov and his face is truly the face of evil..."

Marty O'Neill, Conor Brady, and Leslie Scott entered the room and ran towards the G8 leaders. They reached President Clinton, Prime Minister Blair, and President Yeltsin just as Misha Kedrov saw Conor Brady. He knew now that Brady had betrayed him. He also knew the game was up.

Alexandr Gelman stood transfixed.

Misha Kedrov grabbed a machine gun and yelled at Gelman, "Cover me!"

The three G8 leaders moved, close together, crouching, towards the door, protected by O'Neill, Brady, and Scott.

Kedrov fired at Brady, missed and hit Leslie Scott. Her blood spurted everywhere and she died in the arms of Tony Blair.

Gelman fired just as his head exploded from Marty O'Neill's bullets.

Conor Brady jumped in front of President Clinton. A stray Gelman bullet found his left temple. There was a look of surprise on his face as he crumpled at the President's feet.

Owen took a machine gun from one of the dead and ran after Misha. Owen ran outside, but saw no one. Misha had fled. Then he heard the rumble of an engine, and ran towards the sound. Suddenly a black car shot out from behind the stables and raced toward him. He jumped aside and, as it sped past, he saw Misha Kedrov sitting beside the driver.

Owen raced towards the front entrance where the vehicles were parked. He took the keys to the first one from a young policeman. The wheels spun on the gravel as he plunged the pedal to the floor. He could see Misha's car in the distance. *'Don't lose him, don't lose him,'* were the only thoughts in his head.

Ten miles from Weston Park, Owen was closing on Misha's car when he heard a train's horn somewhere nearby. But he didn't see anything. He dismissed the sound and concentrated on his driving. He could see Kedrov's car rounding a bend in the road up ahead.

The train's horn seemed louder. He rounded the bend and then he saw the level crossing. "Damn! Goddamn!" Owen swore. The train barriers fell. He'd missed it. Kedrov's car sped away on the other side, almost kicking up its wheels in derision. He couldn't crash the barrier. He watched as the train's locomotive crossed the road. It blared its horn in warning. He hoped there were few cars. There were – less than ten. As the last car crossed the road, the barrier rose in the air and he shot across with his foot to the floor.

The delay had cost Owen valuable time. He watched the needle reach 80, then 90, and he held it there, whizzing past vehicles ahead, once barely avoiding a collision with a startled driver in the oncoming lane. He thought to himself: Still *no sign of Kedrov. He could be anywhere. Maybe he's taken one of those side roads. Gone to ground. But, no! That makes no sense! Kedrov is fleeing. But where? To safety? Back to Russia? Definitely! He's got to get out of the country...*

Owen's mind was racing like his car's engine, churning thoughts with every touch of acceleration. He almost missed the sign: MICROLIGHT FLYING – *Enjoy the Fun and Freedom of the Skies!* ... and

the airfield too!   He put on the brakes, hard. Saw
the control tower and the roofs of some hangars. He
turned the steering wheel and the wheels spun under
him. He headed for the entrance to the airfield. His
senses sharpened and his adrenaline flew. *This has
got to be it,* he felt. It was easy to enter. No real
security. Who would need it?

He passed some caravans parked in the grass
and a car with a microlight airplane sitting on its
trailer. Some small planes, Cessnas, sat outside the
first hangar. But nothing larger. The first feelings
of doubt crept in. *Damn it! I was so bloody sure!*
thought Owen. A sign pointed to a café and bar. He
followed. It led him to the second hangar. His heart
jumped. It was there. Sitting on the tarmac. A
Gulfstream jet. Had to be Kedrov. *My gut's right!*
His heart jumped again!

He had to stop them. He put the pedal to the
floor and the jeep jumped from 30 to 80 instantly.
Alarmed people standing near the Cessnas shouted
at him. Holding his right hand on the machine gun
and his left on the steering wheel, Owen headed
straight for the Gulfstream. The door was starting to
close for departure. The jeep bounced under him as
he drove it straight across the grass. *Must cut him
off before he accelerates for take-off,* Owen told
himself. He bounced off the grass onto the runway.
The Gulfstream was right in front of him. He drew
parallel. Someone fired at him. He swerved the jeep.
Suddenly his windscreen shattered. He felt pinpricks
on his face from little shards of glass. He stood on the
accelerator, passed the jet and raced ahead. The jet's
engines roared as it started its take-off. He swung
the steering wheel and turned the jeep, braking to a
hard stop. Holding the machine gun, he jumped out
of the jeep, and fired at the plane's tires. But the
Gulfstream had already accelerated for take-off. He

fired again. *No good! No fucking good!* he yelled. The plane lifted off, barely clearing the roof of his jeep.

Owen rolled over on the ground, tossing the gun away in frustration. He looked up at the departing plane. His heart jumped again! Wisps of smoke clung to the undercarriage. In moments it grew thicker and darker. Flames appeared, brief yellow tongues at first, soon raging fiercely, engulfing the plane. Owen watched, hypnotized. The Gulfstream lost altitude, veered sharply to the right, and headed down. A large cloud of black smoke rose into the air from the ground.

Seventy-two

The White House,
Washington, DC

The President's phone was buzzing. He picked it up and said: "Send him in."

The door opened and Owen MacDara stood there, aware that all eyes were on him. Examining him. Expecting to see some sign of the ravages of recent days. But they were disappointed. MacDara looked like he always did – as though he was arriving to attend just another board meeting of Global Management Associates.

"Sorry, I'm late, Mr. President. The airport. Usual chaos."

"Glad you could make it, Owen. We won't talk about the events of the last week. Not today. We'll keep that for another time. I'd just like to say again that our nation owes you a debt that we'll never be able to repay."

"Thank you, Mr. President," said Owen, feeling that his response was just a formality. He nodded a greeting to General Bartley Shields and

CIA Director Richard Smallwood.

"Dick, I believe you have something for me," said the President.

"Yes, Mr. President," answered Dick Smallwood, getting up, reaching in his inside pocket and handing across Jack Wainwright's notebook. The President browsed it, stopping at pages indexed by their dog-ears.

Finally he got up from his chair and walked over to the shredding machine in the corner of his office. Tearing the pages out of Wainwright's notebook, he fed them to the shredder and watched them turn into confetti. When he had finished he walked back to his desk and faced the three people in front of him. General Shields said, "You did the right thing, Mr. President."

The President said: "There never was any Wainwright secret. Secretary-General Hammarskjold's death in that plane crash in the Congo in 1961 was an accident."

Pat Mullan

Fathers and sons ...

Seventy-three

**Buenos Aires,
Argentina**

Owen MacDara caught the overnight flight from Miami to Buenos Aires and slept most of the way. He woke up half an hour before landing with a feeling of ambivalence about his mission. The box between his feet carried an urn holding the ashes of Eduardo Kelly Herrera. *Why am I doing this? After all, he was a hired gun, an assassin. His ashes should have been tossed in the garbage. No, he saved my life. And the President's too. I want to believe that that was the act of the real Eduardo. That act of redemption. That's why I'm doing this. That and maybe the ghost of old Pat Kelly. My Irish Nationalist soul. Ready to pay a tribute to an old rebel by bringing his grandson home. All rationalization. God damn it!*

The flight landed on schedule and, an hour later, Owen MacDara stood face to face with Carlos Kelly Herrera, a white haired eighty-four year old with an erect aristocratic bearing.

"Mr. MacDara? So good of you to come."

Without waiting for a response, Carlos turned and Owen followed him across the flagstone patio and between the granite columns that guarded the open front door; a tall oak Spanish style door suspended by huge black iron hinges. They entered a large open space, almost Roman atrium-like. The flagstones changed to reddish Italian tiles that bordered a gleaming oak floor. The centerpiece was a circular carpet displaying the Kelly coat of arms: a triple tower supported by two lions on a blue background under a gold crown crest. From the entrance foyer, a wide marble staircase swept gracefully to the upper floor. Carlos climbed and Owen followed till they reached a door at the end of the corridor. Carlos unlocked it and they entered a time capsule, a space that had not been disturbed in a quarter of a century. Carlos spoke again: "This is my son's room. I always hoped he would return."

It seemed to Owen that there would never be a right time to hand the urn containing Eduardo's remains to his father. Yet, oddly enough, this felt like the right time so he walked across and handed the valise containing the urn to the old man. Carlos opened the valise, took out the urn, and moved towards the window, where he placed it on a table that commanded a view of the gardens outside. Turning back he asked, "Do you have a son, Mr. MacDara?"

"Yes, I did. But he died at birth."

"I'm sorry. Eduardo was the last male. The Kellys of Argentina died with him."

"I'm sorry, Señor Kelly."

"It was meant to be. I'm a fatalist. It's my Irish blood. You should know about that, too, I suppose," Carlos said and without pausing continued, "Tell me about my son. I need to know."

Seventy-four

**Blauvelt,
Rockland County,
New York**

The cemetery was seldom used any more. Most of the gravestones dated from the eighteenth and nineteenth century. The Quackenbush graves were among the oldest. Jacob Quackenbush, Ruth Whiteside's earliest ancestor in America, was a Dutch settler who had entered the country when New York was still known as New Amsterdam.

It was a pleasant afternoon, dry with a late spring breeze carrying some of the warmth of an early summer. Birds were singing and chirping in the grove of trees that shielded the cemetery from the main road.

Owen MacDara had come alone.

A new headstone sat incongruously on a freshly maintained grave. It marked the final resting place of Kate and his baby son. Owen leant forward and placed a single red rose in the center of the grave. Raising his eyes, he read the chiseled-out words:

Kate Quackenbush Whiteside
And her infant son,
Henry Whiteside MacDara.

For the first time in months, tears welled up in his eyes and he let himself cry. Ruth had not told him that she had put the baby's name on the headstone; the name he and Kate had decided on if the child had been a boy. Looking at the headstone and reading his own name there, he felt the loss of his son. Not just a baby that didn't have a chance to exist. No, this was his son resting here with Kate. He felt awkward standing there. He wanted to say something, but didn't know what. He knelt, instinctively, at the graveside.

Oh Kate, I loved you so much. I died inside when I lost you. And our son? What would he have been like? Oh, I don't mean what would he have looked like. I mean, what would he have been like inside. In his mind. In his soul. Half of you and half of me. More of you, if he'd been lucky.

But it wasn't to be, Kate. And I must go on. So I came here to say goodbye. I came to let you go. I have to move on. You understand that, don't you?

He stayed on his knees for a long time. Then he got up, turned around, and walked away. He didn't look back.

Author's Notes

Pat Mullan

REUTERS, August 24, 1998.

PLOT TO KILL HAMMARSKJOLD

CAPE TOWN · South Africa's Truth Commission chairman, Archbishop Desmond Tutu, yesterday released documents that, he said, suggested a Western plot was behind the death of the head of the United Nations in 1961. Tutu said the Truth and Reconciliation Commission, which is investigating apartheid-era crimes, decided to release the documents although it could not verify their authenticity. "The commission has discovered...documents discussing the sabotage of the aircraft in which the UN Secretary-General, Dag Hammarskjold, died on the night of September 17 to 18, 1961," he said.

The letters, under the heading the South African Institute for Maritime Research, or SAIMR – said to be a front for the South African military – include reference to the US Central Intelligence Agency and the British MI5 security service. "In a meeting between MI5, special ops executive and the SAIMR, the following emerged," reads one document marked Top Secret, "it is felt that Hammarskjold should be removed." The document said, "I want his removal to be handled more efficiently than was Patrice." The CIA last year opened its files on Cold War assassinations and admitted it ordered the murder of Patrice Lumumba, Congolese independence hero and pro-Soviet prime minister. Another letter headed 'Operation Celeste' details orders to plant in the wheel bay of an aircraft explosives primed to go off as the wheels were retracted on takeoff. Hammarskjold and fifteen others were killed when their aircraft crashed entering what was then Northern Rhodesia, now Zambia, where the UN head was due to meet rebel leader Moise Tshombe to negotiate a truce in the Congolese civil war.

The UN sent a peacekeeping force to the newly liberated Congo in 1960 when the new government asked for help in the face of mutiny in its army, secession in Tshombe's Katanga province, and the intervention of Belgian troops. Newspapers at the time alleged British involvement in a plot to kill Hammarskjold to prevent UN support for Tshombe and his diamond-rich Katanga province.

"We have it on good authority that UNO (the UN Organization) will want to get its greedy paws on the province," reads a letter dated July 12, 1960. The letters came to light as Truth Commission researchers were combing South African security documents in preparation for the commission's final report. Tutu said the commission mandate to investigate such matters expired at the end of July, and the commission therefore decided to publish the documents *with names of individuals deleted* and hand them to Justice Minister Dullah Omar. The archbishop said he hoped releasing the documents would help set an example for more openness in government.

CHE GUEVARA

"The first thing to note is that in my son's veins flowed the blood of the Irish rebels," said Che's father, Ernesto Guevara Lynch, in a 1969 interview, "Che inherited some of the features of our restless ancestors. There was something in his nature which drew him to distant wandering, dangerous adventures and new ideas."

Connacht Tribune, Ireland
Friday, March 15,2002

Che Guevara's daughter, Aleida Guevara, a paediatrician/gynaecologist who works in a hospital in Havana, is coming to Galway to trace her roots back to one of the Tribes of Galway. She is a descendant of the Lynch family and will visit the ruins of the family home in Lydican in Claregalway and one of the famed family's many castles. Che Guevara's grandmother, Ana, was the daughter of Patrick Lynch (from Lydican) who left Galway and married in Buenos Aires in 1749.

Pat Mullan

Pat Mullan was born in Ireland and has lived in England, Canada and the USA. He now lives in Ireland. He has published articles, poetry and short stories in magazines such as *Crannóg,Buffalo Spree, Tales of the Talisman, Writers Post Journal.* His short story, *Galway Girl,* was short-listed for the WOW Awards and was published in the new WOW Magazine in Galway in April 2010.

Recent work has appeared in the anthologies, DUBLIN NOIR (published in the USA by *Akashic Books* and in Ireland and the UK by *Brandon Books)* , *City-Pick DUBLIN* (published by *Oxygen Books* in 2010 to mark Dublin being chosen as UNESCO'S City of Culture for 2010), and *NOIR by NOIR West* (from Arlen House) in 2014.

His first novel, *The Circle of Sodom,* received two nominations, one for Best First Novel and one for Best Suspense Thriller, at the 2005 *Love Is Murder* conference in Chicago. His second novel, *Blood Red Square,* was published in the US in 2005 and a new edition, published in 2011, is now available on-line as a paperback and as an ebook. His latest novels, *Last Days of the Tiger* and *Creatures of Habit* are now available on-line as ebooks on Amazon Kindle, Barnes & Noble's Nook, Kobo, and elsewhere; they are also available in paperback.

He is a member of *International Thriller Writers, Inc.* and *Mystery Writers of America.*

Visit him at: www.patmullan.com

Pat Mullan

www.ingramcontent.com/pod-product-compliance
Lightning Source LLC
Chambersburg PA
CBHW020326180626
46812CB00001B/64